TEST ENVIRONMENT

PIXELATE

BOOK 1

XAVIER P. HUNTER

CONTENTS

GAME REFERENCES

BACK MATTER

CHAPTER 1
REPLACED

"SOMEDAY IT'LL BE you getting replaced by AI!"

"My father-in-law owns the company."

Arnold O'Connor shook a finger as he gritted his teeth and tried to come up with a way to still be right. "Well... how hard can it be screw the boss's daughter?"

Ian blinked and rocked back in his desk chair. "Whoa! OK, tough guy, we were *going* to talk about severance, but now you're just fired."

"Hold on. You just laid me off. You can't—"

A few taps on his laptop, plus one final, smug slamming of an Enter key, and Ian smirked. "Already done. Fired for cause. No severance. No unemployment."

In Arnold's mind, an hourglass filled with dollar signs turned into a toilet and flushed.

"YOU CAN'T FUCKING DO THAT!"

"Already done."

Ian's office door had been open. Outside, amongst the cubicles, the clamor and buzz of everyone still employed by Omicron Logistics ceased. Arnold twisted around, took note of all the heads popping up above the level of shoulder-high walls covered in gray felt, and saw them all hastily duck back down.

He slammed Ian's door shut.

"There are laws! You laid me off. You can't just... just..."

"Fire you for screaming at me in front of the whole company? Thanks for that. Nice to have witnesses for the labor board."

Arnold felt lightheaded. The office swam around him.

He stumbled out in a daze.

When Shane pulled up in his raggedy-ass twenty-year-old F-150, Arnold couldn't remember calling him for a lift. Nor did he remember packing the cardboard box Shane took from him and stowed in the crew cab.

Numb inside, Arnold climbed in and buckled his seatbelt on autopilot.

"You OK, man?" Shane asked as they drove off.

Out the window, Arnold watched trees planted in patches of dry grass whiz past them. They passed a Starbucks, but what did he need caffeine for? They drove by a Chili's, but he had no appetite. A theater was showing like three different movies he'd wanted to see if someone had asked yesterday, but right now, he couldn't care less.

He turned to his friend. "I'll figure out some way to make next month's rent."

Shane chuckled. "Bro, you just got shit-canned. Last thing on my mind is your share of the rent."

Arnold shook his head. He watched bits and pieces of Austin slip past him as Shane piloted them back to the apartment. "Tell that to Bonnie."

Bonnie was Calvin's girlfriend. The two of them shared the largest of the apartment's three bedrooms. The four of them split the rent three-and-a-half ways, using a system Bonnie had concocted. Supposedly, the math was set up to compensate for the couple sharing a room but both putting a drain on the utilities. Privately, Arnold considered it a scam to get out of paying that last half share. But none of them had been willing to confront her over it.

Shane made good money. He could have afforded a place of his own but chose to live with roommates to save for an early retirement or some shit. Calvin worked security at a bank. Stable. Low-risk. He'd reached the limits of his ambition and seemed happy there.

Bonnie was a paralegal. Near as Arnold had it figured, paralegals were to lawyers as paramilitaries were to soldiers. They had a similar set of skills, albeit not as polished and with no government sanction of those skills. And she'd used that knowledge in crafting the apartment's roommate agreement.

Moreover, Bonnie was seven months pregnant. She and Calvin had been making noise about needing more space. They already had a bassinet in their bedroom, ready and waiting, and it wouldn't be long before the kid outgrew that sleeping arrangement.

Whatever Shane said about Arnold not needing to worry about rent, Bonnie would be expecting his share come the first of the month. Otherwise, Arnold was going to bed tonight in what would soon become the baby's future bedroom.

Until now, money had never been an issue. Arnold's job at Omicron Logistics had been rock solid. He kept a suite of spreadsheets up to date, tracking trucks and boats and trains and planes. Theoretically, all over the world, but mostly across Mexico, China, and the southwestern US. Plus, for whatever reason, one client in Ottawa.

He'd been solid.

He'd never missed a rent payment.

But he'd also never gone to college, had a bad back from a summer working for a shady construction company right after high school, and his only major job skill was just shown to be easily replaced by AI.

Shane had to go back to work once he'd dropped Arnold off at the apartment. He'd promised to bring Arnold back when he felt up to driving. That thirteen-year-old Civic sitting in the Omicron Logistics lot was probably good for a month's rent at this point. Maybe. But then how would he get to his next job?

Not that Arnold was working on that just yet. Still in shock, he settled onto the couch with a controller in his hand and racked up a respectable KD ratio wrecking noobs with nothing better to do in the middle of a weekday.

Hours melted.

Arnold's brain went numb.

Beer may have been involved.

Last night's leftover pho disappeared from the fridge.

A work-friendly button-down shirt ended up discarded in the bathroom.

Rather than turn on the AC and get accused of wasting electricity, he took off his pants.

That was how Calvin and Bonnie found Arnold when they arrived home together after work.

"Oh my God. Shane said you got fired," Bonnie stated, hands on hips, looming over him. "He didn't mention you turned feral."

Arnold blinked. When he died in-game, he took in his roommates standing there, judging him. Then he realized that he'd busted down a whole six-pack, his t-shirt was sweat-stained, and he had a takeout carton of fried rice balanced on his boxer shorts.

Calvin stood behind his girlfriend, arms folded, still in uniform. "Sir, I'm going to have to ask you to remove yourself from the couch."

Since his buddy had used his "homeless guy in the bank" voice on him, Arnold cracked a weak smile. "I've had better days."

"Go put some clean clothes on, or I swear to God, I'll Febreze you right there," Bonnie ordered.

That was a threat normally reserved for Shane, and she'd carried through on it more than once when he came home from the garage too tired to shower.

Arnold put up his hands in surrender. "No mas."

When he headed into his room to at least throw on some jeans and a fresh t-shirt, Calvin followed, tapping on his phone. "Hey, man. I was poking around on my break. Think I found something that might interest you."

"If it's one of those sugar mama sites..." Arnold warned.

"Check out the link I just sent you."

It took a minute for Arnold to locate his phone. When he dug it out from under his work shirt, he unlocked it with a fingerprint scan and found the incoming link.

He read the headline aloud: "ANACHRONISM INTERACTIVE Looking for Participants to Train Its Innovative Monster AI. Huh..."

When Arnold looked up, puzzled, Calvin shooed his gaze back toward the screen. "Read the actual article."

Arnold skimmed aloud to prove he was covering everything. "Local participants ... dedicated, hardcore gamers ... non-invasive encephalography ... train a new generation of non-player-character behavior." He chuckled. "C'mon. They can't be serious. They're talking about, like, mind-reading and shit. Just fucking program a better AI."

"Keep. Reading."

With a sigh, Arnold returned his attention to the article. "Lengthy process ... iterative, sequenced learning algorithm ... yadda, yadda, yadda ... Oh."

"You saw it, didn't you?"

Arnold nodded. Dutifully, he read the last bit as well. "Chosen participants will receive a stipend of $1200/wk."

The apartment door opened. Shane strode in.

"Just in time," Calvin called out.

"You showed him?" Shane asked.

"Yeah."

"He gonna do it?"

"Dunno," Calvin replied. He looked to Arnold with a sly smirk. "Whatcha say, bud? Think you can sit around and teach a computer to play video games?"

It had been five years since he'd broken up with Jenna. Since then, all he'd really done with his time was work and game. He could have added sleep to the list, but those two activities also dominated his dreams.

Might as well crash two helicopters with one laser pen.

"Yeah. Why the hell not? If you can't beat AI, join 'em."

CHAPTER 2
INTERVIEWED

THE NEXT MORNING, Arnold showered, threw on an old-school Zelda t-shirt, and headed down to interview for what amounted to a job, no matter how Anachronism Interactive pretended it wasn't. Probably had something to do with benefits, unemployment insurance, or some other cockamamie workaround to employment laws.

The company nestled inconspicuously in an Austin office park. Red brick and black glass. Manicured shrubbery. Ample parking. Shane and Calvin had taken his keys and gone back for his car late last night, so Arnold didn't look like a complete scrub showing up getting a ride from a friend.

Anachronism Interactive had the third floor of the building, just above an oral surgeon's office and below a place that 3-D printed educational toys. If the video game thing didn't pan out, he considered stopping in upstairs to see if those guys were hiring.

For now, he stepped off the elevator and entered through an unassuming frosted glass door. On the other side, a guy with immaculate hair manned the front desk.

"I'm here about the ad?" Arnold left it halfway between a

statement—in case this was the right place—and a question—in case it wasn't.

The receptionist glanced down at Arnold's t-shirt. "You don't say." He reached behind the desk and produced an iPad, handing it across to Arnold. "Fill out this survey. You can use the Copernicus Room, just down there on your right. Bathroom is just past it."

He took the offered tablet. "Wow. Just like that? No prescreening? Not even asking my name?" Arnold asked, barely able to believe it was this easy.

The receptionist leaned across and pointed to the screen. "It's all on there. Name and everything. It's a very advanced form. We do very advanced things here."

Arnold put up his hands, one of which held the offending iPad and its very advanced survey. "Point taken. Do I just bring it back to you when I'm done?"

"Sure thing! And if I'm at lunch, just drop it off on my desk."

Arnold frowned. "At lunch? It's only like 9 a.m. How long is this survey?"

Leaning an elbow on the desk, the receptionist regarded Arnold conspiratorially. "Depends. How good are you at surveys?"

Arnold laughed off the question and followed the directions he'd been given. From the left side of the reception desk, it sounded like the din of a typical office environment. Past the front desk to the right side, Arnold found a quiet corridor lined with doors, each bearing the name of a scientist.

Galileo Room...

Edison Room...

Copernicus Room!

He let himself inside and flicked on a light switch to illuminate a room with no windows. A wobbly round table flanked by a pair of plastic cafeteria chairs supported an ancient-looking conference phone.

"Yeah... Real advanced shit."

Closing the door behind him, Arnold settled in. Then, realizing his chair wobbled too, he switched to the other and found it firmly planted on the floor.

He huffed a sigh.

Alone. Tiny room. One lonely overhead fluorescent panel for light. A rumbling whoosh of the building's AC.

And an iPad.

Arnold turned on the device and was greeted with a sign-in.

NAME:

He tapped in "Arnold O'Connor."

`NO, FULL NAME.`

Arnold blinked. Then he smirked. OK, maybe these guys weren't such amateurs after all.

He tried again from a blank prompt. "Arnold Kyle O'Connor."

That seemed to satisfy the questionnaire. It continued on.

It started out with basic stuff like his birthday, gender, height, and dumb shit that probably didn't mean anything for a job interview. In the back of his mind, Arnold kept a watch for those employment discrimination gotcha questions that places weren't allowed to ask. After all, the promised $1200 a week wasn't chump change, but a discrimination lawsuit could go a long way floating him until he found another job.

Then the fun stuff started.

`WHICH OF THE FOLLOWING GAMES HAVE YOU PLAYED (SELECT ALL THAT APPLY)?`

The screen filled with a huge list with checkboxes beside each. Older games. Some merely retro, others pure classics from the Golden Age of arcade games. Arnold's parents had been into classic gaming, stuff that was before even their time. He'd grown up on this shit.

SUPER MARIO BROTHERS? Hell yeah.

METROID? Of course.

PAC-MAN? Who hadn't?

A warm glow of nostalgia brewed in Arnold's belly as he read off names of games half-forgotten, half-remembered, and lost to the mists of childhood. Rather than linger on that feeling, he skimmed the rest of the list and realized that he knew all these games.

All but Rodek's Revenge.

He checked the rest and moved on.

WHY DIDN'T YOU PLAY RODEK'S REVENGE?

The question came with a blank box that filled the rest of the screen, like they were looking for an essay.

Arnold spoke aloud as he tapped in his answer. "Never heard of it. Maybe it was a Japanese title with limited North American release. I mainly played stuff that went mainstream."

WHICH OF THE FOLLOWING GAMES HAVE YOU BEATEN?

The same list popped up again, minus the probably-made-up Rodek's Revenge.

Arnold took a little longer this time going over his selections. Some were obvious.

LEGEND OF ZELDA? Hell, he'd been there, done that, and was *literally* wearing the t-shirt.

Every Mario game, same deal. Never started one and didn't end it.

He'd gotten the best ending on any of them where there was more than one.

But then there were gotchas.

No one "beats" Pac-Man. Same went for Centipede, Galaga, basically any of the classic arcade cabinet games that just ramped up indefinite difficulty. The same went for SimCity, which you could technically beat scenarios of, but as a sandbox game, its "true" mode was open-ended.

YOU LISTED TETRIS AS A GAME YOU BEAT. EXPLAIN.

Arnold grinned as another essay field appeared for him to justify checking that box.

"I won a tournament. I beat everyone else AT Tetris, so I'm counting that."

It was a local 16-and-under event, so it wasn't like he was world champ or anything, but as far as Travis County was concerned, he was once junior champion.

WHAT IS YOUR MOTHER'S MAIDEN NAME?

That one drew a scowl. This had taken a turn for the personal in a hurry. Was the questionnaire trolling him back for his snarky Tetris answer, or was this whole business just an elaborate phishing scam? If so, they'd gone wrong by aiming their efforts at unemployed gamers.

"Smith."

NAME OF YOUR FIRST PET?

"Spot."

Arnold wasn't fucking around with these people by giving him the answers to any theoretical security questions. If Anachronism Interactive wanted to drain the $42.93 from his bank account, he was going to make them work for it. And good luck if they wanted to take out credit cards in his name.

WHICH OF THE FOLLOWING GAMES HAVE YOU PLAYED (SELECT ALL THAT APPLY)?

A second list with checkboxes named more modern games. And by modern, they seemed to span from polygon graphics up to last month's latest releases. This was a trickier prospect, since his parents hadn't bought him every console.

He'd still managed to have played about half of the listed titles.

WHICH OF THE FOLLOWING GAMES HAVE YOU BEATEN?

When it relisted only the games he'd selected, Arnold was able to truthfully keep most of them checked yet again. He wasn't generally a quitter.

WHAT DID YOU EAT FOR BREAKFAST?

A curveball of a question, but Arnold couldn't imagine the harm in answering. It was neither a potential phishing angle nor anything he could think of the labor department objecting to. Unless he picked something super ethnic or medically prescribed, there was little to work with. Maybe they just wanted to see how he reacted to weird, unexpected shit.

"Breakfast burrito and an iced coffee."

HOW YOU TO TAKE YOUR COFFEE?

Arnold laughed. OK. This *was* reacting to all his answers. If this was a YouTuber pranking him, it was fucking worth it. He'd still demand his $1200, but he'd walk away satisfied.

"Why, you going to bring me a cup?"

NO. JUST MAKING CONVERSATION.

There was another blank field and no follow up question. Arnold waited, then realized it was still looking for an answer about his coffee.

"Iced. I like my coffee iced."

RANK THE FOLLOWING GENRES FROM FAVORITE TO LEAST FAVORITE.

A daunting array of boxes stared at him. While every entry made sense, if asked for a number, he never would have guessed there were this many different genres of video game.

The boxes could be dragged around the screen and snapped to where he left them. Arnold did his best to arrange them in his order of preference.

Survival. A newer genre, this hit a sweet spot of danger and progress.

First-Person Shooters. Classic test of player skill and reflexes.

Puzzle. Admittedly, this was a sitting-on-the-toilet genre, but it was hard to ignore the amount he played it.

Action-Adventure.

Real-time Strategy.

Fighting.

Simulation.

Platformer. These had been a favorite as a kid, but he'd mostly grown out of them.

Stealth. Boring.

Sports. While Arnold could watch football on TV, no force on Earth could get him to care about it in a video game.

Racing. A one-sport genre that didn't even warrant watching on TV.

Casual.

Party. These last two were basically non-games. Casual was pure time-killing. And party games were just an assortment of mini-games that no one would play if the main game was any good.

Then he got to one last genre.

RPG. These were the real deal. Role-playing games were an escape into a totally different world. Become a hero, not just some dude with a bunch of guns and a life counter. Arnold dragged that box right to the top of the list and hit ACCEPT at the bottom of the screen.

Arnold was feeling pretty good about his answers. No lie. If these guys didn't want him for whatever reason, they'd be rejecting him for who he really was, not some guy trying to guess what they wanted to hear.

Then, to his dismay, a new message popped up.

SECTION 2: HOBBIES.

"Ugh. That desk guy wasn't kidding, was he?" This could very well take all morning, depending on how many sections there were.

Then it occurred to him to ask.

He navigated a series of simple selections until he reached an open-ended query.

WHY DO YOU PREFER OUTDOOR ACTIVITIES IN THE NIGHT OVER DAYTIME?

When the prompt came up, instead of answering, he asked, "How long is this questionnaire?"

HOW LONG IS A PIECE OF STRING?

"What kind of question is that?"

THE SAME KIND AS YOURS.

"Can you just say how long this is going to take?" Then, realizing the question he'd asked was no more answerable than his previous attempt, he added, "How long did it take the *last* person to fill you out?"

THREE HOURS, FOURTEEN MINUTES.

"Fuck." Arnold said the latter aloud rather than typing it in.

IN THEORY, BY WASTING TIME, YOU ARE PROLONGING THE DURATION.

"Wait, did you hear me swear?"

I HAVE VOICE RECOGNITION.

"Can I just answer verbally?"

YOU ARE THE FIRST APPLICANT TO SUGGEST IT, BUT I DON'T SEE WHY NOT.

Slouching back in his chair, Arnold gave his tapping finger a rest. "Well, well, well. Let's get this sucker filled out then. Hit me!"

CHAPTER 3
RECRUITED

THROAT RAW FROM hours of chatting with a chatbot, Arnold slumped in his chair when the iPad finally declared.

ALL FINISHED. ISAAC WILL BE HERE SHORTLY TO COLLECT ME.

"Isaac... is that the front desk guy?"

NO.

Rather than press for an answer, footsteps out in the hall culminated in the door opening from outside. The one doing the opening was a skinny, scruffy, round-shouldered guy who had to have been in his mid-to-late fifties. He had round wire-rimmed glasses and a flannel shirt unbuttoned with a Nirvana t-shirt on underneath.

"Hi, Arnold. I'm Isaac," the man greeted him, offering a weak but enthusiastic handshake. "You wouldn't believe the number of applicants that the length of the questionnaire just weeds right out. Congratulations!"

"I think I would. Believe it, that is. And you're congratulating me just for finishing, or...?"

"No. You're in."

"Wait. Just finishing was enough? I went through all that trouble just to—"

"No, no. Of course, not. I've been reading your answers as you went."

Arnold blinked. "Wait. YOU were the guy typing back and forth with me?"

"No. That was Sigmund, our in-house AI. You wouldn't *believe* how much easier it is to program an office assistant chatbot than it is to come up with intelligent monster behavior."

"I think I would, actually."

"Right. Of course, of *course* you would. Otherwise, we'd be hiring guinea pigs for our upcoming office assistant software and letting our applicants get outsmarted by ultra-sophisticated computer games while they waited, rather than the other way around."

Arnold wasn't going to be steamrolled in this conversation, even though Isaac's energy was undeniable. "Did… you just call me a guinea pig?"

Isaac put his hands up and his head down. "Apologies. My bad. My staff keeps telling me not to use that term. Also 'test subjects,' 'scanning targets,' and 'brain donors.'"

"WHAT?"

Isaac grinned. "Don't worry. It's just words. Words don't matter. The technology matters. And the technology is both harmless and *awesome*."

"So. Um. I'm a little unclear on something. Did I or did I *not* just get the job?"

"First off, it's not a job. Think of it like a psychology experiment or a drug trial. Except we're not playing mind games with you or injecting you with stuff. Making you wear a helmet covered in electrodes? Yes. Asking you to play hours and hours of video games? Also yes. Are we building a mind-reading machine? OK. That's a third yes, right there, but that's where it stops. We're not writing anything to the brain. It doesn't change *you* at all. We're just collecting data to make better games. And given your responses on the survey... that sounds like it matters to you."

Arnold paused to consider.

Clearly, games were a huge chunk of his life.

More clearly, he was going to be in some serious financial trouble in a big hurry if he didn't come up with some cash by the beginning of the month.

"You're not like, some front for the Department of Defense or something, and I'm going to be training autonomous drones to murder people with no human intervention, am I?"

Isaac shook his head solemnly. "No. We lost that bid. JUST KIDDING. Wow, you really do play too many video games. BUT THAT'S FINE. Maybe for the first time in your life, that's going to be a major financial windfall for you."

It was hard to call $1200 a week a windfall. Solid work, sure. Better than he was making at Omicron Logistics. If he could find a way to drag out this... whatever it was, maybe he could actually save up some money, maybe invest or some shit. "Any chance this goes on past four weeks?"

Isaac shrugged. "Better odds than of being struck by falling orbital debris. Worse odds than me winning a Nobel Prize."

"Soooooo... you're saying there's a chance?"

The scientist broke out in a grin. "C'mon. You must be hungry. Cafeteria downstairs sucks. All the offices in the building share it. Vegan crap. You're not vegan, are you?"

"I was born here in Texas." Best Arnold could tell, any vegans in the state were imported.

"Nice. Anyway, we've got a Tex/Mex place down the road. Brendan usually takes lunch orders around now. We can order up some tacos, catch you up on what we're trying to do here, and get you started this afternoon." He grinned expectantly, clearly waiting for a response.

Arnold didn't know what to make of this development. He'd expected to come in, fill out some paperwork, maybe talk to a couple people. He didn't expect that he'd spend the whole morning having a weird conversation with a chatbot and start working that afternoon.

"Um. Sounds good."

Menus whirled and a pad and pen came and went. Arnold ordered some carnitas tacos and a bottle of Coke. Isaac went with steak tacos and a Corona Lite.

The scientist caught Arnold blinking in surprise. "What?"

"Nothing," Arnold answered quickly. He was barely on this boat. The last thing he needed to be doing was rocking it.

"It's hardly beer. It's just... Corona."

Brendan turned out to be the name of the guy working reception. He snatched up the lunch pad that had been passed around among a gaggle of strangers Arnold could only assume he'd eventually meet. "Don't fall for it. We don't condone drinking on the job around here. Isaac just doesn't work here."

"Wait. You don't?"

Isaac snickered. "Nope."

"Then...?"

"I own the company. Semantics. This isn't work for me, it's—"

"A passion," Brendan finished with a melodramatic flourish, covering his eyes with a forearm.

A dour little man approached, wearing the kind of suit found on car salesmen and accountants. "Hey. I'm Glen, from accounting." (nailed it!) "I also do HR. And you need to sign an NDA before these numbskulls get all our secrets stolen by Russia."

"Russian spies don't care about NDAs," Isaac told Glen with a clear implication that this was an ongoing debate that had just been reopened. He turned to Arnold. "You should still probably sign it. If nothing else, he won't pay you if you don't. And he stopped reimbursing me when I Venmo money to the guinea—I mean the participants."

While everyone waited for their lunch delivery, Arnold borrowed a spare rolling chair and sat off in a corner to review the document.

Dad had always warned him not to sign anything unless he'd read it. But End User License Agreements had sapped much of his willpower on the matter. At best, his efforts could be categorized as skimming.

Everything his eyes glommed onto seemed boilerplate. Arnold was agreeing not to talk about what he saw or did as a part of... well, he still wasn't a hundred percent sure. But whatever it turned out to be, he couldn't say jack shit about it.

Legalese and jargon warred with bland, standard English words devoid of significant meaning.

Lunch showed up, and Arnold's mouth watered.

"How's that NDA coming?" Isaac asked, peering over his shoulder as Brendan set his meal down on a nearby desk.

Arnold checked. The whole time lunch had been in the works, he'd managed to progress the slider bar maybe 1/10th of the way down the side of the screen. "Umm..."

Isaac nodded "No rush. You can set it aside, grab a bite, get back to it after." He turned to Brendan. "We heard anything from our afternoon applicant?"

Lunches delivered, Brendan was headed back to the front desk with the last remaining meal when he paused. "You still want him coming in? Seems like a waste if we have our last spot filled."

Isaac patted the air with his free hand as he finished chewing a bite of taco. "Just in case. You know..."

The implication was clear. If Arnold decided not to sign the NDA, they had a backup waiting. He wasn't sure he believed them that this was the last spot. But obvious power play or not, the dynamic was clear: he needed them way more than they needed him.

On the little borrowed desk before him, Arnold had his lunch to one side, the iPad on the other. Dollar signs danced in his head. One was maybe $15 worth of Tex/Mex. The other, $4800 for a month's work, if these guys played ball and kept him the full four weeks.

The choice was clear.

Arnold scooped up the iPad, and the instant the screen came on, swiped down to the bottom and scribbled something resembling his signature.

"Super. Finish up your lunch, then we'll get this party started!"

CHAPTER 4
EXAMINED

"TAKE YOUR SHIRT OFF, PLEASE."

For a place that was nominally a video game company, that wasn't a phrase Arnold had been expecting to hear. Maybe, if he'd read his NDA fully, somewhere it would have at least tangentially mentioned a medical exam prior to actually seeing any of the cool technology.

Dr. Ruger was a woman in her middle years. Blonde hair in a bun. Round face obscured behind glasses. A scowl that looked more permanent than directed at either Arnold or his reluctance as he complied with her order.

"Didn't know this job was going to be demanding," he joked.

She checked his heart and lungs, shone a light in his eyes, looked down his throat, all the general annual physical stuff. Since he'd just lost access to health insurance, Arnold figured that he'd take whatever medical care he could get.

He answered all her basic questions, then one struck him a little off-center. "Have you ever worn corrective lenses?"

"Um. No. 20/20 vision all the way." He answered this as she used a gloved hand to hold one of his eyelids up.

"What about contact lenses? Doesn't have to be for

corrective purposes." She moved to the other eye. "Colored lenses just for fashion or maybe as part of a theatrical production or Halloween costume."

"I like Halloween as much as the next guy, but I don't go putting in contacts."

"Go ahead and put your shirt back on," she informed him.

Relieved that this apparently wasn't going any farther into weird territory, Arnold obeyed. While he was wriggling into the sleeves, he heard her rummaging in the cabinets behind him.

The examination table was a versatile piece of furniture. Dr. Ruger pushed and yanked. A clack of a clasp releasing came just ahead of her pulling up half the table into a back rest. "Lean back and relax."

Scooting along the paper protective sheet, Arnold did his best to get comfortable. The doctor held out a small case made from a glossy white plastic. Arnold watched as she popped it open. With gloved fingers, she removed a tiny glass hemisphere.

"These contacts are a key part of Anachronism Interactive's proprietary data gathering system. They are multifunctional; they will read your pulse and blood pressure, track and record eye movements, and offer an augmented reality display."

"Wow," was all Arnold could think to reply as his mind considered the fact that she was clearly planning to jam that thing into his eye. "Um. Could I have a minute to think about this?"

"It's better not to think. Everything is going to be fine. Just breathe normally."

With one hand, the doctor held his upper and lower lids apart. He got a look at a thin ring of circuitry around the outer rim of the lens just before it got so close it became a blur. As soon as the lens touched his eye, he winced, squeezing the eye shut just as the doctor removed her fingers.

Eye watering, Arnold blinked to try to see.

"There. That wasn't so bad. One more. Nothing to worry about."

Knowing that the only thing possibly worse than getting one lens put in was having it be for nothing, Arnold gritted his teeth and leaned back. The second lens brought on a new wave of watering eye.

Dr. Ruger caught him by the wrist as he reached up to rub his eyes. "Don't. If you need drops, say something. The lenses are fragile."

"They could break in my eye!?" Arnold exclaimed.

"No. But you can damage the circuitry. They're not cheap. Now, let's have a look." She whipped out a pen light and checked both of his eyes. "Good. Good... Everything looks normal. Now, don't try to remove the lenses yourself. Every shift, you'll stop by here, and I'll install them. Before you go home at the end of the day, I'll take them out for sanitizing. If you want to go out to lunch, stop here first. Trying to wear them out of the offices here will result in them going opaque."

"Proprietary. Got it."

"Good. Most of the testers order in. Less work for everyone involved. There will always be a proctor on hand. Either in the room with you or on closed-circuit. If you need something, say something—eye drops are a big one, especially for a non-contact-wearer such as yourself. Isaac or one of the other scientists will meet you in Room 6. Any questions?"

"What if the batteries run out or something? Will I be blind?" The idea of getting stuck with non-see-through contacts in his eyes terrified him. Not only wasn't he supposed to try to take them out himself, he wasn't sure he could manage if he tried. The thought of touching his own eyeball grossed him out.

Frankly, if Calvin had told him in advance that cramming stuff in his eyes would be part of the job, he would never have showed up this morning.

Sunk cost fallacy, they called it.

Yet here he was...

"Nothing to worry about. First off, the lenses use next to no energy. They recharge by physical pressure, and routine blinking is enough to keep them charged during wear. If for some reason, you blink less than average—and as someone who doesn't wear contacts, I assure you, you won't—then just shutting your eyes for a few moments will fully recharge them. Second, they're clear lenses. The darkening feature is purely for security."

"But couldn't someone looking to steal them just take them out?" Arnold blurted. The questions just seemed so obvious, so necessary. He had to say *something.*

Dr. Ruger smiled condescendingly. "Do you plan on stealing yours?"

"No," Arnold admitted.

"Then don't worry about what might, theoretically, happen if you tried. OK?" Her smile turned sweet and—if Arnold was any judge—playfully threatening.

He chuckled uneasily. "Right. Room 6, you said? Where's that?"

The doctor took out her cell phone. A couple taps and a swipe in his direction, and suddenly an arrow appeared in mid-air.

Arnold reached out to touch it, but his hands passed right through.

"Good. Spatial awareness. Stereoscopic vision. Excellent. Tell me, what color is the arrow?"

"Green."

She tapped on her phone a few times. "And now?"

"Red."

"Good. There will be a full colorblindness suite mixed into your testing, but good to know you've got the basics of color vision covered. Just follow the arrow. It'll show you where to go."

"OK. Thanks."

As Arnold left the examination room, a reminder flashed in front of him.

`CLOSE DOOR BEHIND YOU.`

He did so with hardly a thought.

Was he going to close it anyway, just to be polite, or had the lenses planted the suggestion so seamlessly that he only thought that? The mere fact that Dr. Ruger could make stuff appear in his eyes from her phone was creeping him out a little.

Maybe more than a little.

Arnold's eyes itched. He resisted the urge to rub them.

Psychosomatic, he told himself. *All in your head.*

He passed briefly through the outskirts of the cubicle area. Curiosity drove him to glance over and see what was going on.

The arrow, which had turned back to green when it started guiding him out of the examination room, turned red.

`WATCH WHERE YOU'RE GOING.`

Arnold stopped in his tracks.

The FUCK?

Once he halted, the arrow returned to its green hue, aimed off to his right, and began pulsating.

OK. Maybe it wasn't a creepy control feature to prevent him from looking around. Maybe it was just a safety feature to keep him from stumbling into shit.

A creepy safety feature.

Rather than linger and test his boundaries on Day 1 of this gig, Arnold headed to Room 6 without further delay.

Instead of Isaac waiting for him, there was a younger

woman—still a few years older than Arnold—in a white lab coat.

She ambushed him at the door, shutting it behind him and taking him by the arm to guide him into a room with stark white walls and a scattering of institutional-grade furniture. It looked like every room from every psych ward in the movies.

"Hi, I'm Kelli, that's Kelli with an I—I have two eyes, and yes you don't need to make the joke—I'll be running you through Orientation Day. Since you're our last applicant for this round and it's after noon already, we're going to try to compress this a bit. Based on your intake form, you should be up to the challenge."

"What will I be doing?"

"First things first, you'll be sitting in this chair." She pulled out a wheelchair and held it for him. As he climbed in, she added, "Buckle the belt. Some scanning subjects get disoriented, and this is our workaround to peeling you off the floor."

Arnold snapped one of those little push-clasps, the kind you'd find on a hiking backpack, and tugged the strap tight around his waist. Using her shoe, Kelli folded down two footrests, and Arnold set his feet on them without needing to be told. She rolled him up to the most basic and boring of desks, basically just a white laminate table with chrome legs, and locked the wheels.

"Now what?"

"Sit tight," she joked. There were two other doors in the room. She opened neither of them, but instead popped open a panel on the wall. From inside, she pulled out a contraption that looked like the thing Doc Brown wore on his head in Back to the Future.

"What's that thing?"

"It's a hat. You're going to be *very* fashionable. This is

where you get to be glad that NDA works both ways. Now, look straight ahead and try to hold still."

Arnold did as instructed. He could watch her working via the reflection in a blank black TV hung on the wall facing them. "In theory, what would happen if I did move?"

"This would take longer. Look, nothing here is actually dangerous. In fact, this is a good time to distract you by going through my personal FAQ for the program. First things first, this helmet contains 96 neural probes, which we'll be calibrating to associate your brain functions to outside stimuli; in layman's terms, that means we'll be seeing what neurons are firing when you solve puzzles, react to in-game dangers, succeed, and fail."

He was feeling like Kelli was pretty chill, so he allowed himself to joke with her. "I'm *pretty good* when it comes to video games. You might not see a lot of failing."

She twisted his head a few degrees. "I said hold still. And don't worry. We'll make *sure* you fail. It's not a reflection on you as a person or even a gamer; we need to know what those neural responses look like."

"Ow! What are you doing up there?"

"Adjusting the probes. The closer I get them to your brain, the better the data."

"Well, I think you went a little too tight there."

"A little too tight is perfect. You'll get used to it, you big baby. A lot too tight starts to crack bone. If I was allowed to drill tiny holes in your skull—I'm joking, I'm joking. Trust me; I've worn that thing plenty. You'll hardly notice you're wearing it by the end of your orientation."

Time and again, Arnold winced as the probes tightened into place. It felt like wearing cleats on his head.

"Anyhoo, to continue my FAQ... Yes, I'm single. No, I don't date scanning subjects. No, I won't change my mind after your scanning is complete. Consider this: I'm going to know more about your brain than any lover or psychiatrist ever will. Trust me; you don't want to date someone holding that kind of information imbalance. The sessions are 4 hours at a stretch, as best we can manage it. One before lunch. One after. There are five other labs like this one, and you're in mine for the four weeks. While it is outside the scope of the program, the proctors *have* been known to help set up scanning subjects with *one another* based on compatibility criteria that those online dating sites could only dream of. So be *extra* good and cooperative. You hear me?"

"Loud and clear," Arnold replied. Listening to her babbling was distracting from the headache building up, probe by probe, in his head.

"Great! Now, as for some details. There is no food or beverages allowed in the lab. The only exception is water, which we provide. The door on the right is the bathroom. The helmet's cord is long enough to reach inside. There's a stop to keep the door from damaging the cord. I will *not* be spying on you. The rest of the workday, I get my fill. I'll usually be here to help, but if I'm not, go ahead on your own; just be careful. You'll be top-heavy and dragging a cord and maybe a little disoriented.

"Now, that should do it. Any questions before we get started?"

Arnold leaned his head side to side, only daring a slight movement. The helmet had to have weighed ten pounds.

"Have there been any accidents or side effects?"

Kelli laughed. "You bring this up *now*? Lucky for you, the answer is basically no. Not anything major, anyway. Side effects include little red dents all over your head that go away within about half an hour of taking the helmet off. Eye strain. Headaches. Weird dreams—"

"Wait. Weird dreams? Like, weird how?"

"You're participating in a science experiment. You've *already* had a weird day. Shit gets sorted out in your sleep. I actually have an understanding of dream neuropsychology at a post-graduate level, but I don't think I have time to teach the course you'd need to understand it all.

"As for accidents? We'll, that tripping on the cord on the way to the bathroom thing happened twice before we started making, like, a point of emphasis about it. We've also had a participant soil himself because, apparently, he got all engrossed and didn't pay attention. Oh, and there's puking."

"Um..."

"Don't worry. You don't strike me as the sort. I bet you go on roller coasters and look don't get vertigo looking down from ten stories up."

Arnold gulped. "Actually, I get motion sick."

"The other door over there? That's where we keep the games and physical puzzles for the testing. Also, cleaning supplies. I have cleaned up enough vomit by now that I'm basically numb to it. If you think it'll be a real problem for you, we've also got smocks. Would... you like a smock?"

Arnold had woken up hung over and stained with his own puke enough times not to want to head back to the apartment that way after what was, on the surface, a workday. He didn't feel good about it, or particularly manly at the moment, but he had to face facts.

"Yeah. I'll take a smock if you don't mind."

CHAPTER 5
DEBRIEFING

AT THE END of the day, Arnold was drained. Despite the temptation, he resisted the urge to call Shane again for a ride home. That was one of those cards to play maybe a couple times a year, tops, not back-to-back.

It was an easy drive, even after dark. Kelli had kept him late, late enough that Dr. Ruger had gone home and she'd had to take the lenses out of his eyes herself. Arnold found himself stopping extra long at every stop sign, every red light, just being doubly sure that what he was seeing was really there.

Amazing what a few hours of not trusting your own eyes could do.

When he walked through the door, an aroma of ginger and soy sauce hit him immediately.

"Hey! He's back! What, tech place doesn't get bars or something?" Shane asked jokingly. "Never mind. Grab whatever. Calvin had a coupon."

Arnold surveyed the spread. There was a little of everything. From that place over on Chestnut. Mouthwatering, but for one small problem.

"I already ate."

"Ooh, la la," Calvin teased. "Eating on the company dime already, huh?"

Arnold yawned. "They had me start today after an interview that lasted pretty much all morning. I was the last to join up, apparently, and they fast-tracked me catching up to the rest."

"What was it like?" Calvin asked as he chewed a mouthful of noodles, carrying the carton and a pair of chopsticks around the apartment with him.

"Can't say," Arnold replied. "Had to sign an NDA. Last thing I need is to get sued." When he'd signed the thing, he'd really been expecting the document to be a non-factor, a cudgel to beat him with if he ever went public with their proprietary shit; Arnold would have never done so, and thus it was a pointless document. But he hadn't anticipated how its mere existence would save him from putting into words one of the most profoundly weird days of his life.

"Ca'monnnn," Shane wheedled. "NDAs don't apply to spouses or roommates. No court would blame you for telling us about the place. It's not like they're doing Top Secret military research or anything." He paused for a beat, blinking, cheek puffed full of rice noodles. "Wait. ARE THEY?"

"If they were, I could tell you even less," Arnold assured his friend. "It's just... it's a game company, and they're certainly on the cutting edge with some stuff. Can't say any more than that."

Maybe it was in the document somewhere, but Arnold had no idea, legally speaking, where that line was drawn. Obviously, he could admit walking in and out of their building. That he'd responded to an ad. That they were paying him to do something for them. He'd done some Googling in the parking lot before driving off, ignoring Shane's texts for lack of knowing what to say.

Dr. Isaac Chandler was a PhD, not an MD, but his degree

was neuromechanics—which was a separate Google, since Arnold had never heard of it—so there was a lot of overlap between him and a medical doctor as far as knowing a human brain. He was also on public record as working for Anachronism Interactive and had done a number of interviews. The only stuff he could find about Dr. Kelli Chang was from years ago, on the Cal Tech website as a TA. She didn't even use social media under her real name, or she hid her profile well.

"If he doesn't want to tell us, don't pester him," Calvin scolded as he went back to fill up a plate with crab rangoon and potstickers. "It was probably boring as hell."

The interview, maybe. The rest... anything but.

"OK. All right. I won't expose Arnold to any legal action. But at least tell me this..."

"What?" Arnold inquired, ready for some kind of trap.

Setting down his carton of noodles, Shane fixed Arnold with his full attention. "Are you looking forward to going back tomorrow?"

That was far more subtle a question than he'd been preparing for. Insider trading tips, whether any of the women working there were hot, even something about the overpowering smell of mouthwash lingering on him—though maybe Arnold was just overly aware of that one—those were the kind of things he expected out of Shane. But without having to tell anything *remotely* covered by any conceivable NDA, he managed to sneak in a question that answered far more than a blow-by-blow recounting of the day's adventures ever could.

"He's hesitating," Calvin declared as self-appointed arbiter of the question. "That means he's not."

Was that true?

Today had been fucked up and then some. Looking at the afternoon's events objectively, Kelli being kind of fun and good natured about how odd everything was, lampshading the mad science going on, and anticipating Arnold's fears and physical distress... well, if she'd been a humorless old dude, it all would have been creepy.

A toilet flushed. The bathroom door swung open. Bonnie marched out and headed straight for the buffet. "You should eat something. We've got too much food, and I don't even think there's room in the fridge for all the leftovers."

"Leave something out. I'm seriously stuffed." As an apology for keeping him late, Kelli had put pizzas on the company credit card. That had been hours ago. Arnold just didn't have an appetite, preoccupied with convincing his brain that everything he saw was there, everything he heard came from real, live people, and that when he fell asleep tonight, those dreams would fade with the coming of morning.

Today's dreams, nonsensical flotsam that didn't belong in his head, clung stubbornly.

"At least take a cookie," Shane told Arnold as one was already arcing through the air toward him.

He caught the cookie, tore open the plastic, and cracked it in half. The fortune was stuck to both sides; he couldn't remember whether that was supposed to be good luck, bad luck, or irrelevant. He further broke up the cookie until the paper came free, shoveling the shard into his mouth as he flipped and smoothed the fortune to see what it said.

`YOU'LL BE BACK TOMORROW.`

He blinked in shock, then looked again.

`AN EXCITING OPPORTUNITY LIES AHEAD.`

That sounded more like it.

But the first, hallucinatory fortune seemed apt as well.

"Today was fine. Lot of new stuff to absorb." That was both generous and true. And he definitely, *definitely* needed the cash. "I'll be going back tomorrow."

CHAPTER 6
GUINEA PIGS

ARNOLD PULLED into a parking space with a pre-dawn chill still in the air. He shut off the engine and headlights. By the parking lot's street lights, he took a count of the vehicles already there ahead of him.

"Early birds. Go figure." Programmers always struck him as night owls, so he supposed that the ones showing up before breakfast were on the science side of things.

Blowing into his hands to warm them, Arnold crossed the lot and found the building unlocked. After a brief elevator ride, he was surprised to discover a cluster of people waiting outside the doors to Anachronism Interactive.

"Oh. Hi."

A woman in a denim jacket with the sides of her head shaved sized him up. "Look. Must be the new guy."

He inclined his head. "I'm Arnold."

A quick round of introductions ensued. The one who'd first addressed him was Jane. Chad was a skinny redhead with a sad, patchy beard. Lucas was a fluffy dude with gaged earlobes. Kenny embodied the very definition of average from his smooth face to his short hair parted to one side. Last was Bella; she was five foot nothing with a nose ring, thick glasses, and a mop of platinum blonde hair that was clearly a wig.

"I don't normally wear these," Bella promised. "But for reasons I think we can all understand, I skipped putting in my contacts this morning."

Heads bobbed on all sides. Yeah. They got it. That last thing Arnold might have wanted to do, assuming he needed them, was to put contact lenses back in right after getting those high-tech ones out.

"Do the ones they give us, like, correct vision, too?" he asked.

Bella shrugged. "Don't know if they *could*, but they don't. Steve had to lead me by the arm to the test room. But they did a calibration thing. Any stuff the lenses make up, I can see just fine."

"Are you that blind without them?" Jane asked.

Bella slid her glasses down her nose and peered over them. Using the hand holding her morning Starbucks, she gestured all around Jane. "You are a very pretty smudge." She pushed the glasses back to their proper perch on the bridge of her nose. "They figure out a way to get those crazy ones to correct what I can see outside, I'm buying a pair. I don't care what they cost; I'll sell blood, kidneys, whatever..."

Arnold chuckled. "Don't know if I'd be willing to wear those anywhere but here."

Bella looked to the others. "Oh. That's right. He's a couple days behind us." She turned a mischievous grin on him. "Just you wait..."

"What's that supposed to mean? What's coming up for me in the next couple days?"

"Can't spoil it," Chad told him.

Lucas nodded. "NDA."

"Yeah, but—" Arnold tried to object.

Jane rested a hand on his shoulder. "We wouldn't want to ruin the surprise."

"What surprise?" Arnold had his fill of surprises yesterday. "What am I in for?"

The others had a laugh at his expense.

"Oh. I get it. Haze the new guy. I'm reporting all of you to HR." He aimed a finger around to make sure every one of them knew they were in for it—and that he was totally joking.

"Yeah. Marvin. OOOOOH, scary." Chad lifted his hands and waggled them like a haunted house actor hamming it up.

"Why are we all here so early, anyway?" Arnold asked.

"Isaac's probably just running late," Lucas suggested.

"No, but I mean *why* did they ask us to show up this early?"

Kenny shrugged. "Who cares? You know what? In a few weeks, this will all be over, and we'll never get a chance like this again. I want to get my money's worth."

"They're paying *us*, dumbass," Lucas pointed out. "Not the other way around."

"Hey, never got to ask you since you weren't here on the first day," Bella said, breaking up what might have turned into a proper argument if left to fester. "What are you studying?"

Arnold smirked. "I think *that's* the other way around. They're studying us."

"No. I mean for school."

His face went slack. He swallowed. "Wait. Lemme guess. Did winter break just start?"

Colleges all over Austin were taking time off for the holidays. Why wouldn't an enterprising startup looking for video-game-savvy volunteers be grabbing for those students cut loose from classes as a cheap source of labor?

"Oops," Jane said.

"Sorry," Kenny cut in. "We all just assumed. You know. Since the rest of us are students."

"So, like, what's your deal, then?" Chad asked. "You work nights or something? On disability?"

"Just got laid off," Arnold answered, careful not to use the F word, since he was still hoping to press a claim for unemployment benefits against Omicron Logistics. Not that he expected any of these guys to snitch on him, but the less he kept the word "fired" around, the less likely he was to spill that in front of a state bureaucrat.

"What'd you do before that?" Bella asked.

Arnold scratched the back of his head. How could he make it sound at least a little interesting? "I, uh, kept freight moving around the world. Mostly it involved spreadsheets and emails."

"Sounds like stuff you could automate pretty easy," Lucas suggested.

Arnold nodded. "That's what *they* thought. I'm still hoping for a global shipping jam, but I think my 0.001 percent of the global economy will get by just fine without me."

The door to Anachronism Interactive rattled as someone unlocked the door from the inside. Brendan opened it and ushered them inside. "Sorry about the wait. Isaac is running behind. His kid threw up, and he's having a thing over it."

"A thing?" Jane echoed. "Wipe it up and come to work."

"Is the kid OK?" Arnold asked.

Brendan chuckled as the testers filed inside. "The baby is six weeks. It's his first, and he's freaked out constantly."

"Should we be worried?" Arnold asked.

From down the hall, Dr. Ruger called out, "Jane?"

Jane headed off, leaving the rest of them behind.

Chad laughed self-consciously. "You don't need to worry. *I'm* the one who's got Isaac for a proctor."

"How long's this usually take?" Arnold pointed after Jane.

"Bella?" Dr. Ruger shouted toward the lobby.

Bella flashed a quick smile. "Not long if you don't need the tutorial or a pep talk."

She disappeared in the same direction as Jane.

Rather than continue to chat, Arnold waited as each of them was called down, one by one, him last of the bunch.

"Morning, doctor," Arnold greeted her.

"Sit. Lean back," she ordered.

There was no fussing around. No explanations. She briskly pried each of his eyes open, inserted a lens, and shooed him out of the office. Eyes watering, he could barely see the walls of the hallway, but the arrow overlay was crystal clear.

"Come on, you," Kelli told him, meeting him halfway as he shuffled along and dragging him the rest of the distance to the lab. "You've got a day ahead of you."

CHAPTER 7
LYING EYES

ARNOLD DONNED his smock and buckled his seatbelt. Kelli affixed the helmet to his head.

Before she started tightening, she made him an offer. "If you want a diaper, there's no shame. It's easy to lose track of bodily functions. About half the testers end up using them by the end of the program."

"Half?" Arnold echoed incredulously. "I'll pass, thanks."

A probe snugged against his skull. "Whatever. I don't do laundry, though. All you get is a pair of loaner sweatpants and a trash bag to take home with you."

Explaining that whole situation to his roommates wouldn't be fun, but it didn't sway him. "Still going with a 'no' on that."

The process of getting the helmet adjusted seemed a lot quicker this time. Before he knew it, Kelli pronounced him done.

"All righty. Today's new twist: an upgraded sound system."

"Upgraded how?"

"Hold still," Kelli instructed from out of view behind him. An earplug jammed into Arnold's right ear with a wet, gooey sensation like it had been dipped in honey.

"Eugh. Yuck."

"Get over it." Without a fuss, Kelli shoved in the earplug's mate. The whole room grew quieter once the squish ended.

She came around in front of him and looked him in the eyes across the table. "Can you hear me?"

"Yeah. I hear you just fine."

She poked at her phone. She mouthed a few words.

"(I didn't that time)," he replied, but to his surprise, he couldn't hear himself, either.

Several more taps, and she clapped her hands, a steady beat, utterly silent. "How about now?"

"I can hear your voice but not the clapping."

"Super. You're not actually hearing anything from out in the room right now. Which is great, since yesterday was crazy boring with no music. But I can't have *you* distracted by my Spotify playlist: Music to Study Brains By."

Arnold snickered.

"Today, I'm going to mostly stay in the background. The screen on the far wall and any audio cues will give you all the instructions you should need. I'll be around but inconspicuous. Any final questions before we get started?"

Nothing came to mind. He was filled with questions, but couldn't come up with anything that wouldn't sound like begging to get a graduate degree in whatever made this place make sense. He opted just to roll with it. "I'm good."

"I'm going to try to catch you up to the others, so if we can squeeze on both sides of lunch and maybe stay late..."

"If you're buying dinner, I'm staying."

"Great. Deep breath. Three... two... one... go!"

GOOD MORNING, ARNOLD.

The screen showed the message in bold red lettering.

MATCH THE MOTIONS.

"Okay..."

What motions, the screen didn't say. Then, before his eyes,

a pair of disembodied gloves appeared, the kind a butler might wear, or an old-timey magician. They started out in a surrender gesture.

The gloves clapped.

Arnold clapped. Rather than the sound of his hands slapping together, a little success *ding* rang. Merry. Digital. He could practically feel the dopamine hit from that little, automated praise.

The gloves made a double thumbs-up.

Arnold mimicked and received another ding.

The gloves laced their fingers together. So did Arnold. Then the two gloves turned palm down and went right over left. Arnold mirrored, left over right. They reversed the gesture, and he followed along.

Ding.

Ding.

Ding.

The gloves turned palms toward one another, and when Arnold matched the gesture, spread far enough apart that he looked like a sci-fi robot, there was no sound.

THIS IS THE STARTING POSITION. AFTER AN ERROR, RETURN TO THE STARTING POSITION.

The gestures repeated. Arnold matched one by one. The gestures grew faster, and he kept up, by rote once he got the cadence down.

Then the order shifted.

BRRRRTTTTT.

Arnold winced at the sound. He reached up to cover his ears, but the sound was coming from the earplugs.

"What the hell!" he shouted. "Turn it off!"

Kelli sounded far off. "The screen has your instructions."

RETURN TO THE STARTING POSITION.

Ignoring the sound was impossible. Fighting through a

deafening din louder than his own thoughts, Arnold stuck out his hands in the starting gesture.

The noise ceased immediately.

A red ring appeared in the air before him, hovering disembodied, just out of reach. It swiped around, disappearing counterclockwise. It took about five seconds to vanish, at which point the whole ring turned green, he received another ding, and the ring vanished.

Arnold breathed a sigh of relief.

The hand motion game resumed. He made other errors, but each time, he returned to the starting position after the briefest of loud buzzers.

`RELAX.`

The screen commanded it, so Arnold tried as best he could. He felt Kelli's hands rubbing sore muscles along his neck and shoulders.

"You could be in better shape," she told him. "But the muscle fatigue is good data, too."

When she stopped, the screen was ready with a new challenge.

`MATCH THE BLOCKS.`

A little arrangement of red and blue blocks appeared floating in the air just beyond the table. Spread out in front of him, without him even seeing how they got there, was a jumble of similar blocks.

Easy enough.

Arnold started like the sample image with a row of red blocks along the bottom. When he tried to pick up one of the blue blocks, his fingers passed right through.

"What that—?"

The blue blocks weren't real. He was seeing them, but they were ghostly and imperceptible to the touch.

"How am I supposed to stack imaginary blocks?"

He looked around for some imaginary tongs or a pair of gloves or something that might let him manipulate the blue blocks.

THAT'S HALF THE TASK.

That was about the point where a timer appeared on the screen. It started at 30 seconds and immediately began counting down.

He felt around, wondering if the tool he needed was invisible, hidden by the lenses that were superseding his vision. He found nothing.

"Little help?"

"You're the one wearing the scanning helmet. I can't do your thinking for you."

The timer ran down.

BRRRRTTTTT.

Unprepared, it took Arnold a couple seconds to return to his starting position. The red circle took a good thirty seconds to wind down this time. When the green circle appeared, the puzzle goal rearranged itself. It was still all red and blue blocks with the red ones on the bottom and blue ones above, but the relative heights of individual columns had shifted.

First things first, Arnold rearranged his red blocks—the easy part. Then, just taking a quick guess, tried pinching a blue block between his fingers. When he lifted, the block came along. Halfway to placing that first block, it fell from his intangible grip, bouncing on the table as if it were real, sound and all.

On his second attempt, he was more careful to keep his fingers apart by the width of the block, then he managed to get it into place.

The timer appeared. 30... 29... 28...

Shit. He wasn't going to make it. Frantically scrambling to hit the timer, he fumbled repeatedly, actually ending up slowing down his pace as he had to repeatedly lift the same illusionary block.

BRRRRTTTTT.

Starting position. A breather.

The puzzle rearranged. This time, knowing going in how he needed to do things, Arnold was able to complete the matching stacks before the timer even popped up to hassle him. He tried to gauge it; it felt like maybe he had two minutes to match his stacks, and the final thirty seconds were shown, the way some old games intentionally changed the music when you were running out of time.

Each time he completed an arrangement of blocks, a new configuration would appear. He got a feel—or a *lack of feel*—for the right grip on the blocks.

Then, as he was about to put the final touch on one of the walls of blocks, he dropped a red block through a stack of blue ones.

WHY DID YOU THINK THAT WOULD WORK?

He'd stopped considering that the blue blocks weren't real. Arnold had a rhythm going, matching his constructions to the ones he was being shown. "I forgot the blue ones aren't real."

His half-stacked tower shattered into individual blocks, startling him.

ARE YOU SURE THE RED ONES ARE REAL?

The reference image hadn't changed. But when Arnold attempted to reconstruct his wall to match, his fingers passed through the red blocks now.

"What the fuck..." He refused to touch any more of the blocks. "Nope. I'm out. The blocks win."

A timer appeared.

Even before his thirty seconds ran out, Arnold put his hands in the starting position.

The hovering stack of blocks vanished.

A plate of food appeared in its place. Just a vending machine sandwich encased in cling wrap and a bag of chips the size you'd grab from a takeout counter. Salt-and-vinegar flavor.

YOUR CURRENT LUNCH.

Arnold sneered at the plate. "Cheap bastards. YOU CAN HEAR ME, RIGHT, KELLI?"

CARE TO UPGRADE?

He blinked, which was weird insomuch as what he saw didn't change in the slightest, not even the brief span when his eyelids shut. "Are you... bribing me?"

INCENTIVIZING.

A platter of barbecue wings appeared.

Arnold's mouth watered.

"How are you making me smell them?" He reached up to see if Kelli had managed to stuff probes up his nose or something while he hadn't been paying attention.

BRRRRTTTTT.

HANDS AWAY FROM YOUR FACE.

Without conscious thought, Arnold returned his hands to the starting position.

Angry with himself more than the screen, he snapped, "Dirty trick. What if I get an itch?"

DON'T.

"You say that like I can control whether I... wait... CAN I control that?"

INTERESTING QUESTION. CARE TO FIND OUT?

Arnold constructed several more stacks of blocks, forcing himself to relearn that red was insubstantial and blue were solid.

"Drink," Kelli ordered when the sequence finally ended. "You're getting more exercise than you're probably used to. Rather than a weird, floating cup or something equally trippy, she stepped in front of him with a sports bottle like some NFL lackey running onto the field between plays.

She stuck the end of the squirt bottle in front of his mouth, and he obliged.

"What is this stuff? Some kind of neuro-something-or-other chemical?" he asked after the first mouthful, trying in vain to identify a flavor.

"Electrolytes. You're probably not familiar with them. You can go around drinking beer and soda all the rest of your day, but while I'm responsible for you, you're hydrating."

"How about those wings? Those too unhealthy to eat on your watch? Or are you not responsible for what that screen promises?"

She smirked as she squirted him another mouthful of what he imagined was Gatorade or something similar. "What screen?"

Arnold stared past her as she leaned across the table to hydrate him.

There was nothing there. That whole wall was blank.

"How much of what I'm seeing is real?"

"That's a question you start asking yourself in freshman philosophy."

"Thought you were a scientist..."

"Science is about finding answers. Philosophy is about coming up with questions. If you want to study ants, stare at a ton of anthills. If you want to study weather, get good with computational analysis. But if you want to study the innermost workings of human consciousness, you need to ask yourself some pretty damned fundamental questions about what the difference is between a brain and a mind."

"So... is that a yes or a no on the wings?"

"It's not even 9 a.m. yet. We've got a shitload more work this morning first. I see from your intake form that you're afraid of heights. Brave to admit that to people about to study your brain. I find about half the answers in the Fears and Phobias section are lies. Mostly, it's morbid curiosity that we even ask. So, since you're up front about it, how afraid of heights *are* you?"

"You're not getting me to voluntarily wear a diaper."

Kelli crossed her arms. "That bad, huh?"

It was a sore subject, and one he didn't want getting outside this room. Maybe he came across a little snippy when he told her, "Yeah. That bad. I get dizzy on tall staircases. I don't go on roller coasters. I've never flown and never hope to. So, yes. I'm terrified of heights."

She brushed aside a pile of bland, off-white blocks that looked 3-D printed, and sat down on the table. Arnold craned his neck back to look her in the eye, wary of the top-heavy helmet practically screwed to his skull.

"How would you like *not* to be?"

CHAPTER 8
DECISION TIME

ARNOLD SHUT off the ignition but didn't get out of the car right away. Instead, he sat in the driveway, collecting himself.

It had been three weeks. Day in. Day out. They took his mind apart and pieced it back together. Mind games galore. Sensory trickery. Puzzles that broke the laws of reality. Simulations so real that his mind filled in the details they didn't provide.

And every day, they took him, wobbly-legged and reeling, to clean up, get his sci-fi contact lenses taken out, and ushered him back out into the real world.

Anachronism Interactive staggered their end times so the participants didn't run into one another on their way out. But a couple times he'd spotted someone in the parking lot. He'd seen Lucas lighting up a joint behind the wheel before driving himself home. He'd caught Jane sobbing and decided to let her process the bizarre experience in peace. Chad had offered to go out for beers with him that very night.

But Arnold declined.

He had processing of his own to do.

The last two days had been dating sims. Hyper-realistic. Uncannily human in conversation. Personal on levels he would have balked at sharing with a licensed therapist. But it was also fascinating.

Just the level of technology blew his mind. Knowing that stuff like Anachronism Interactive was working on existed gave Arnold hope that the future would be flying cars and robot butlers in his lifetime.

If they had sprung the dating sim shit on him week one, Arnold liked to think that he'd have had the self-respect to walk out right then and there. But... well, he'd built up a rapport with Kelli. She tricked him and teased him and scared the ever-loving shit out of him, but it was never mean-spirited. She had reasons and explained them. Even blasting an air horn in his face was to prove to him that the earplugs worked.

Thinking. He always had to be thinking. Generating data. Nothing lazy. Nothing automatic. Anything old or familiar would have an added twist to force him to learn. A car steering wheel had been rigged to turn the opposite direction. A custom language he had to order his lunch with. Changing his heart rate to certain target ranges without resorting to physical activity.

He'd been dropped off a virtual cliff with Kelli aiming a fan at his face to feel the rush of wind.

They'd put him on an omni-treadmill and gotten him to navigate underground caverns.

He'd raced Formula 1 tracks until one ended in a brick wall, nearly giving him a heart-attack.

Kelli had let him use the shower in the employees' gym after today. Arnold could still see the women when he closed his eyes. His brain both knew they weren't real and had convinced other parts of itself that they were.

She'd claimed it would be worth it, that it was data the company struggled to gather. In return for being a good sport about it, she promised that, beyond the anonymity he was already medically entitled to, she'd also use the data to compare with other participants who opted in. Not share. Just compare. True compatibility.

Maybe it was a scam. Maybe it was yet another manipulation. Maybe it was just Christmastime, and he felt like he deserved better than spending the holidays alone.

Everyone was back, of course. They were right there, inside the apartment. Otherwise, Arnold would have already gone inside. Leftover egg nogg and peppermint candies. A gaggle of gadgets still in boxes. Phone cameras full of pictures of nieces and nephews and younger cousins opening presents. An artificial tree they'd stop spraying with pine scent from now until they took it down in a few days.

All Arnold needed was peace, quiet, and relaxation. None of which was waiting for him in the apartment.

Maybe he should have taken Chad up on his offer. In lieu of quiet, he could have at least had someone who understood what he'd been through. Then again, if Chad had been through the dating sims too, maybe he was the *last* one Arnold needed to be around.

With a sigh, and with the realization that the chill from outside was seeping into the car now that the heat was off, Arnold climbed out of the vehicle and headed inside.

"Hey! There he is! C'mon, dig in!" The assorted smells of three separate batches of Christmas leftovers wafted over Arnold the instant he opened the door. Shane pressed a beer into his hand before Arnold even had his jacket off. "And don't gimme that 'already ate' crap. You knew we were doing this."

Yep.

Same as every year.

Calvin waved from the table. "Momma doesn't realize it's only Bonnie eating for two, and she's never met a turkey too big to fry."

Normalcy seeped in, slowly at first, like a dry sponge as water runs over the surface before it turns fully absorbent again. By the time he'd finished eating a plate of leftovers and a slice of pecan pie, Arnold was almost relaxed.

Then, Shane set in on him.

"You know, I realize you're out of a job and all. And I know you gotta be a little tight with the cash. But what I *really* want for Christmas is to hear what they really have you doing at that game place. What do you say? Leak a little info? Won't go further than this table. I swear."

Arnold scowled. Shane was an honest guy. But given the tech at Anachronism Interactive, they had to have money for some nasty lawyers if any leaks got traced back to him.

Calvin held up his oath-swearing hand. "Same. Spill, brother!"

Bonnie rolled her eyes. "Yeah. Who would I even tell?"

Arnold's resolve wavered.

"C'mon, man. You've probably got the best stories you're *dying* to tell us."

There had to be a way to dance the tightrope between boring stonewalling and inviting legal action for violating the terms of the NDA he still hadn't fully read.

"All right. First off, there's this hat..."

From there, Arnold picked and chose what he included. He had to tell them about the AR contact lenses, or none of the rest would make sense. Being able to see things that weren't there, seeing things differently from how they actually were, and getting an overlay of extra data like time, heart rate, and progress toward a quest goal all sounded cool as fuck. Then *not* seeing things that actually were right in front of him still freaked him out, so he omitted that detail.

He explained the puzzle games, the flight simulators, the skydiving, the superhero flying, and how he had yet to test it in the real world, but Kelli had suggested that his acrophobia would at least be reduced now, if not gone outright. Of course, he didn't mention *her* by name, either. The last thing on Earth he ever wanted was Kelli and these three comparing notes about him.

Arnold explained the phantom sensations, touching things that weren't there, smelling things that didn't exist, details his brain inserted for lack of external context.

He never explained about the conditioning. Updating his list of the last things he needed in his life, Shane finding out about how he reacted to the sound of a particular buzzer jumped to the top.

Tales of foam pipe swords swung around at inflatable punching bag dragons blended into mundane encountering of mazes where he had to guide a rat to cheese. He mirrored the gestures of an old woman who taught him how to knit, then had to do it while *only* seeing her hands, which would copy his own movements exactly. A plastic toy hammer forged mighty armor. In utter darkness, he shot at monsters located only by sound.

Arnold left off the fact that he'd shit himself the first time one of those monsters had gotten to him. The roar in his ears and the flash of fangs inches from his face had gotten the better of him.

And, of course, he steered well clear of anything that hinted, even obliquely, at the two days of dating sims that would be haunting him for a good long time.

"How realistic were the flight controls?" asked Shane, who'd never come closer to piloting a jet than driving a lifted pickup.

"Like I've ever been in a real cockpit," Arnold fired back.

"Could you like, feel imaginary wind and stuff?" Bonnie asked, his stories eventually piquing her interest.

"The proctor used a fan. Just one of those dollar-store cheapies. Lemme tell you. It worked."

"Think you actually learned how to fight or shoot or anything?" Calvin asked as he continued to pound down Christmas leftovers.

"Doubt it. No weight to the swords. No recoil on the guns. It's all arcade stuff, but it makes sense, considering what they're making."

"What *are* they making?" Shane asked, and it felt like a question that had been burning in everyone's mind as they leaned in for the answer they'd all been searching for. "I've been digging online since you signed up, and I can't even find evidence of any industry people attached to the company. These guys are seriously dark-mode indie and determined to stay that way."

All Arnold could do was shrug. "Couldn't tell you if I wanted. NDA or not, they haven't told me anything solid." Sensing their disappointment, he edged out closer to the precipice of legal exposure and risked sharing more than he'd intended. "But they *did* tell us the final week coming up was going to blow our minds. They're going to figure out which of us has what it takes to be major story characters, and which of us will be relegated to powering trash mobs. As we were leaving tonight, I saw some guys wheeling in this big omni-directional treadmills."

"Like in RP1?" Calvin asked. He'd only seen the movie.

"Bigger. Like, if I could do a split, I wouldn't fall off it."

Shane snickered. "Oh, man. They're gonna have to peel you off the floor. All those cardio and legs days you skipped..."

There had been, from time to time, stretches where Shane wrangled Arnold out to the gym. Maybe, with honest-to-goodness unemployment looming, he'd actually take it seriously for a while. But it had been months since his last guest-pass visit on Shane's membership, and even that had been like two days before he flaked out.

"All I know is, I've got the weekend off, and I'll be going hard my last week in the program. The money's solid. The puzzles have been weird. But after this is all said and done, what I REALLY WANT is to be the end boss of whatever game they're making."

CHAPTER 9
CHARACTER CREATION

ARNOLD BLINKED AND LOOKED AROUND. He'd have rubbed his eyes if Kelli hadn't hammered it into him that the lenses were worth more than he'd make in a lifetime. He didn't remember arriving at Anachronism Interactive that morning, but he was clearly in the lab.

Except that he wasn't.

He was in a white room. Not painted white, just... white. Ambient light came from nowhere. There wasn't a hint of reflection or texture or... no... that was it. There was no texture. These were blank, monochrome panels.

Arnold had grown so accustomed to the lifelike recreations he saw in the lenses that he'd overlooked the obvious: this was a totally computer-generated environment, but a basic one.

Before his eyes, a swirling blue swipe loading indicator spun. Acting on instinct, Arnold put his hands in the starting position, just in case. When the indicator stopped, a message appeared. Rather than the generic system font that the lenses normally used, this was a full-on artist-rendered masterpiece, designed to impress.

And it worked.

WELCOME TO SPIRE OF FATE:

Below, in a decidedly less fancy treatment, was the subtitle...

TEST ENVIRONMENT

Arnold chuckled. OK. Props for getting someone to design the bit they were likely hoping to use in the release version of the game. And it was nicer to have some idea of what they were making. Spire of Fate was nice and generic, not a giveaway of genre or premise. Fantasy, for sure, but then again, the sword fighting and monsters in the dark had already been giving Arnold fantasy vibes since the second week of testing.

"So, what now?" he asked.

The lettering faded out, and a display populated the periphery of his vision. A circular minimap hovered to his upper right. A backpack icon appeared in the upper left. A blank circle showed the lower left, just a small hoop he could see right through. In the lower right, a hamburger button suggested a menu.

Kelli had trained him on air-touch menus. Eventually, he'd had to use one to select his lunch or request drinks and snacks during testing. He's also been allowed to adjust the temperature in the lab and play music during downtime.

He tried the menu button with a tap of his open hand.

HELP

SYSTEM

OPTIONS

LOGOUT

BEGIN GAME

Ever the tinker when it came to his games, Arnold first tried the OPTIONS menu.

The button blinked red and did nothing else.

He tried SYSTEM, seeing if he could adjust any of the hardware settings. That was enough of a novelty that he couldn't resist trying. But that, too, kicked back an error.

Next, he tried the **HELP** button.

"Hello. I am Kelindra, your guide to Spire of Fate. How may I assist you?"

Arnold laughed. The voice was *clearly* Kelli, and she was no voice actress. She had no kind of fantasy take on the lines she'd read—or, he realized, been sampled from her regular speech. Like real-world Kelli, she was flippant and easygoing.

Unless...

"Hey, are you actually just Kelli messing with me?"

"No. I am Kelindra, your guide to Spire of Fate. How many I assist you?"

OK. As much of a prankster as Kelli might have been, he couldn't picture her both committing this hard to a joke *and* not giving a shit that she didn't sound like some fantasy-game narrator at the same time.

"Fine. Kelindra, what can I do here?"

"You are in the character creation zone for Spire of Fate. Select BEGIN GAME to launch the character creator."

All right. Arnold left aside the mystery of how he'd gotten to the lab this morning and focused on doing his best here. At lunchtime, he'd delve into the mystery of his arrival and intake. Given all the other shit that had happened, it wouldn't surprise him if they'd given him some kind of hallucinogen to make this all seem more real.

Because it DID feel real. A lot more real than ever before.

On impulse, he reached for his chest to find out whether he was wearing one of the harnesses he'd seen attached to the omni-directional treadmills at the end of last week.

BRRRRTTTTT.

Before he knew it, he had his hands in the starting position, and the noise ceased.

"OK. I got it. Don't mess with the equipment. Geez. Warn a guy."

Opening up the menu again, he chose BEGIN GAME.

A mirror appeared. Full length. Arnold looked like himself, albeit a pixelated, low-res version of himself. He reached out and touched the mirror. Not only did he FEEL the mirror, when he touched the face, a sub-menu flew out.

EYES

EARS

NOSE

CHEEKS

HAIR

RESET

Neat! He spent a while just fiddling with the sliders and sub-submenus. Even low-res, there was enough detail to mess around with his appearance for what felt like half an hour. He widened his jaw, narrowed his eyes to slits and changed their color to a vivid blue. For hair, he went with a mohawk that turned into a long braid down his back, and he went red-headed. Not *red* red, just the normal deep orange of a ginger.

From there, he adjusted his height and build. Taller. Brawnier. There was a slider for body fat, and he ballooned to obesity and shrank down to bodybuilding contestant. When he finished, he had the look of a young Arnold Schwarzenegger—the zenith of all Arnolds, in his humble opinion. Except that he looked like a version who got his hair cut by crazy dwarven berserkers, and *this* Arnold was AOK with that.

When he'd arrived in this creation area, prior to hitting that button to start the character building process, he hadn't paid much attention to what he'd been wearing. Some generic white jumpsuit, maybe? Bland enough that he'd hardly registered.

Now, however, he was left standing in front of a mirror, cut like the sculpture of a war god, wearing nothing but a leather loincloth.

Arnold took a gulp.

There was a fine line between being alone in here with no one watching and the damn near certainty that a crew of game developers were either watching live or recording this for posterity.

But he had to check. He just... *had* to.

Peeking under the loincloth, Arnold discovered that he was anatomically correct, even if at a shitty resolution. He let the flap of leather flop back down to guard his meager privacy.

"Um? Next? I don't see a button for advancing past this point."

Arnold waited. And waited.

"Hello? Can anyone hear me?"

He tapped and dismissed the game menu.

Then, beside the menu, a new icon appeared in the shape of a beetle or ladybug—Arnold was no entomologist. He tapped the bug icon.

REPORT BUG

There was no keyboard. He'd practiced typing in the air and had gotten OK at it. Kelli didn't try to make him improve, just noted his struggles and quizzed him about his experience typing.

Oh, hell, did Arnold type. Half his day was email and spreadsheets. He'd told her that if he was struggling, anyone who didn't sit at a keyboard all day was in for some hell. Mainly, the lack of a physical surface to rest either elbows or the heels of his hands on made lining up with the keys tricky.

Maybe they'd taken his feedback to heart.

They were asking for it again.

"Hey, there's no way to advance past the appearance screen in the Character Creator."

THANK YOU FOR YOUR FEEDBACK

Arnold waited some more. He paced the room, explored

other appearance options. But the room was tiny, and he liked the way he'd gotten his character to look.

The bug icon glowed and pulsed a faint blue.

Arnold tapped it.

YOUR FEEDBACK WAS HELPFUL. PLEASE ACCEPT A GIFT.

The gift icon spanned so many games that it needed no guesswork. He tapped it at once.

100 XP.

Laughing, Arnold threw up his hands. "I don't even know what **XP** is for here."

Kelindra explained in her disembodied voice. "XP is the abbreviation for Experience Points. They are the currency of character advancement in Spire of Fate. Once you achieve a certain number of experience points, you will advance to a new level, unlocking new abilities and making your character more durable, powerful, and capable.

"Did this answer your question?"

"Kinda. I don't even see my XP."

"You have not finished the character creation process. Once completed, you will enter the world, and your XP total will be available for viewing using the standard character interface."

"OK. But I can't finish the character creation process. That's half my problem."

"To advance to the next step of character creation, select NEXT from the appearance management mirror."

Arnold rolled his eyes. "Yeah, but see? There's isn't..." He was tapping the mirror to demonstrate the lack of the feature she was directing him toward, and he noticed a new button.

NEXT

"OK. Fine. You win. But it wasn't there a minute ago."

Tapping it caused the mirror to vanish. All around him, small circular platforms appeared, each about three feet across.

Above them hovered an array of costumes. At the base of each, a placard in what, to his spreadsheet-trained eyes, was clearly Calibri font, was the name of a playable class.

ARCHER - A Robin Hood style tunic and feathered cap, leather pants and boots. While he had no particular objections to the archery playstyle in most RPGs, he wasn't really digging this look.

Looks mattered, too, in games like this.

CLERIC - Bland white priestly vestments with red accents. Without knowing anything about religion in this game, he didn't really want to commit to the role.

KNIGHT - A battered suit of what appeared to be medieval armor for a down-on-his-luck sword for hire.

MONK - Basically just ripped off Shaolin robes. If these people were going to make a game with any staying power or worldwide appeal, they would have to come up with something a little more original.

ROGUE - Ah, a classic. Basically a ninja, according to the gear on display, a stealth class implied a lot of skulking, and Arnold was feeling more like cutting loose once the game set him free to roam.

WIZARD - Well, if rogues were a classic, wizards were the prototype. Basically, the wizards were the line of demarcation between fantasy and historical fiction. Hard to go wrong playing a pointy-hat in an RPG, and this getup was purple robes and a hat with stars on it.

But Arnold had somewhat pigeonholed himself upon selecting a huge, brawny avatar. Unless he wanted to go the Jean-Claude Van Damme route with a monk, he was oversized for the other classes.

Of course, nothing anyone had told him—which, frankly, was basically nothing at all—suggested he couldn't be a muscle-bound archer or a bench-pressing wizard, he was on display here. People were watching. He decided to play the aesthetic game and stood in front of the knight.

He kicked the pedestal, hoping the name placard was also a button. A real impact stung his foot.

"Wow. That felt pretty real. I'm impressed," he told the ceiling. "But, uh, how do you select a class?"

Kelindra was ready with an answer. "Step onto the platform corresponding to the class you wish to choose."

Easy enough. The platforms were only six inches high. Once he got onto the one with the armor, he realized that it was all exactly his size. At first, nothing happened. The armor was insubstantial. His hand and body both passed right through.

Once he lined up with the armor, however, the weight of it suddenly settled onto his shoulders. With a metallic clatter, he stumbled for balance before catching himself.

"OK. Now THAT was a hell of a trick. Am I... is there some kind of haptic suit I'm wearing or something?"

This time, Kelindra didn't provide a reply.

A difference voice boomed from above, authoritative in a biblical way. **"STATE THY NAME, HERO, AND THUSLY YE SHALL BE KNOWN THROUGHOUT THE REALM."**

With a smirk, Arnold knew he had this one nailed. He'd been using the same online handle since he'd been old enough to name his own characters. Sometimes he had to add a suffix if someone already grabbed it, but he somehow didn't think that would be a problem on a tiny, pre-development, experimental server.

Drawing himself tall, he obeyed the unseen god's command. "Connor," he told it.

And the world dissolved around him.

CHAPTER 10
STARTING ZONE

INSTANTLY, Connor was overdressed. Clad in clanking plate armor, his sabatoned feet crunched in the sand of an idyllic tropical beach. Nearby, waves lapped the shore. Everything seemed... basic.

The sand was a color and a sound of footsteps. There was no hint of texture to it. Every wave rolled in exactly the same, two feet high with a shallow curl and washed to a slightly darker line of damp sand that never moved.

Inland, a jungle of palm trees loomed like crayon drawings, trunks slightly curved. Fronds vivid green and drooping. Once he thought to check for it, Connor found that all of them were clones too, simply rotated slightly from one another to provide the illusion of variety. Tiki torches marched a path through some procedurally generated underbrush that led toward the island's interior.

"Where is this place?" he asked aloud.

On cue, lettering appeared in the air before him.

`KAWAIIAN ISLANDS`

After a few seconds to let him read the name of the starting zone, the letters flew up and shrank to title his minimap.

Currently, that minimap showed a stretch of shoreline and the foremost edge of a jungle. Fog of war obscured the rest.

Connor chose to follow the path. It wound a short distance through a frankly disappointing span of jungle terrain. Then, a clearing opened up, and Connor found himself in a little village.

Grass-roofed huts, fishing nets, and wooden totems gave a half-assed Polynesian feel to the place. When they spotted him, a gaggle of inhabitants exited the huts to gather around him.

Already a little squeamish, given the look of the place, he was relieved to find that the natives weren't some racist stereotype of an island-dwelling people. Waist-high, pale blue, and cherub-faced, they were at least a purely fantasy creation, even if they did throw off vague Smurf vibes.

One of them stepped forward and spoke. Older-looking (as far as it was possible to tell with these baby-faced creatures), with a hunched back and pure white beard, he looked Connor up and down before raising his hands to the sky.

"We prayed, and a hero has come!" The voice acting was clearly Isaac, and he hammed it up to eleven. "Mighty hero, YOU will save us from the lord of the mountain!"

"Sure," Connor replied, playing along. "I'm your guy. You need a mountain lord dead, I'm on it."

He followed a procession out the far side of the village and back into the jungle on the other side.

To his surprise, and not in keeping with the primitive architecture of the village, their destination was a gray stone ziggurat that the elder climbed without explanation. Connor followed, mincing his steps to navigate the staircase carved for shorter legs than his. Then, realizing that the larger stone blocks to either side matched his stride, he used those instead.

At the top of the ziggurat, the elder continued. "For many years, we have suffered under the mountain lord's tyranny. His armies devour our fish. His monsters threaten our fishers. We are no longer safe on the water, and soon we fear there will be no shelter on land, either."

Connor glanced around. "OK. Which way to the mountain lord?" If this was his starting quest, he could well imagine that the "mountain lord" was some kind of simple monster that these unarmed innocents couldn't fight.

"Oh, you are not ready to face the mountain lord yet, hero," the elder told him. "First, you must prepare yourself for the journey, learning the ways of this new land. Our prayers have summoned you from far, far away, and our world must seem alien to you."

"Sure. Makes sense. But, just out of curiosity, can you show me where to find the mountain lord?" Connor knew that this was all some kind of elaborate tutorial. He'd played enough games in his day to know the basics without having to attend RPG kindergarten all over again. How many times could games burden players with rats or slimes or whatever and tell them: "Press A to attack, X to jump," and shit like that?

The elder pointed. The villagers pointed. All those little blue fingers aimed upward and behind him.

Connor turned.

Far off, grainy and polygonal, loomed a towering mountain, impossibly steep, hazy with distance and so tall that its peak lay hidden by clouds.

"Let me guess," Connor asked sarcastically. "The mountain lord lives at the base of that mountain?"

"No, hero," the elder corrected him in all seriousness. "He rules from a fortress located at the very summit of the Spire of Fate."

"Wonderful. Game's title is exactly on the nose." Cynically, he wondered if that was why Kelli had taken the better part of a week hammering on his acrophobia. He still didn't relish the idea of climbing that mountain, but he comforted himself that, were he to puke, it would be Kelli cleaning up the guy out there in meatspace, not him.

Then, a thought occurred. If this was just an elaborate test setup, maybe they'd made a provision for him to skip to the end. "Hey, you guys got a hang glider or a hot air balloon or anything like that around here? Some way to fly?"

"Oh, no. Nothing like that hero. We wouldn't keep anything that would anger the mountain lord so."

"Course not. Why would you have anything that would make my journey trivially easy?"

Another of the villagers came up to him. This one wore a necklace made of tiny animal skulls. The graphics weren't sophisticated enough for him to be able to guess what animals they might have come from, but a small rodent, if Connor had to guess based solely on size. "Would you like to prepare for your quest?" This one, it seemed, had Brendan's voice, and he could practically hear the paper crinkle as the receptionist read his lines like a book report.

Connor sighed and replied in equally wooden dialog. "Yes. I would like to. Prepare for my quest now. Beep." He added the last to make fun of the robotic delivery.

"My name is not Beep. It is Beedeep."

"Oh. My bad," Connor replied, fighting back a laugh. This tech might have been amazing, but Anachronism Interactive was going to have to open up those wallets of theirs to pay for some proper writers and voice actors, not to mention some actual level designers. He'd seen free-to-play mods that looked better than this island.

He hadn't even noticed, but the minimap had drawn in his trek through the village and to the ziggurat. The title above it had even updated to ZIGGURAT, and as he followed Beedeep back, the village, the title updated to KAWAIIAN VILLAGE.

"Hero, we will need to train you how to fight," Beedeep informed him. "Choose your weapon."

The villager stepped aside to reveal a weapon rack that definitely hadn't been behind him a second ago. While the rack itself looked plenty wide to hold four or five weapons, there was only a single option, which Connor picked up.

"Tough choice."

ACQUIRED: BAMBOO SWORD

A pulsing, glowing paper doll version of his character appeared to the left side of—for lack of anything better to call it —Connor's "screen."

He obligingly tapped it.

EQUIPMENT

WEAPON: BAMBOO SWORD

ARMOR: SQUIRE ARMOR

ACCESSORY: NONE

"This is your equipment manager," Kelindra told him. "To change your equipment, go to your inventory screen and select an item to equip. Select the inventory icon in the upper left and equip a different weapon."

Connor reached up and tapped his inventory.

An inventory overlay on a translucent background reminiscent of a backpack appeared before him, cordoned off into a grid of squares.

"There's nothing here. I have no other weapons."

Kelindra wasn't buying that argument. "Select the inventory icon in the upper left and equip a different weapon."

Connor checked the weapon rack to see if another bamboo sword had respawned in place of the one he'd taken. But the rack was empty.

"Select the inventory icon in the upper left and equip a different weapon."

Connor waited, counting in his head.

"Select the inventory icon in the upper left and equip a different weapon."

Sixty seconds.

"Select the inventory icon in the upper left and equip a different weapon."

Another sixty. Great, it sounded like he was going to be listening to that tutorial message once a minute until he figured out a way to equip a new weapon.

The obvious answer was Beedeep, standing there waiting, oblivious to his troubles with the narrator. "Little help, buddy? I need another weapon."

Before the villager could answer, Kelindra spoke up. "To access your weapons, select the equipment manager."

"I wasn't talking to you," Connor snapped.

"Select the inventory icon in the upper left and equip a different weapon," Kelindra countered as if she had multiple personalities that didn't compare notes.

"Beedeep, can you give me another weapon?"

"Are you ready to practice your fighting moves?"

"No. I would actually like to fix the annoying voice that only I can hear, and giving me a second sword sounds easier here than finding a therapist."

"Select the inventory icon in the upper left and equip a different weapon."

That did it. Connor opened a different menu.

REPORT BUG

"Unable to complete equipment manager tutorial due to the lack of a backup weapon in inventory."

THANK YOU FOR YOUR FEEDBACK

Beedeep smiled at him. "Are you ready to practice your fighting moves?"

"Select the inventory icon in the upper left and equip a different weapon."

Gritting his digital teeth—and probably his real ones back in meatspace, he supposed—Connor nodded. "Yeah. Let's practice my fighting moves."

Beedeep led him behind one of the huts. A ring of carved black stones surrounded a clear patch of dirt, but that wasn't their destination. Off to the side, a chest-high scarecrow of bamboo wore a pig skull for a head. "Swing your sword and hit the dummy."

A literal interpretation of those words would have led to Connor lopping off the villager's head. Instead, he followed the spirit of that advice and hacked at the scarecrow.

2

The number rose up over the dummy's head before fading away.

He swung again.

2

And again.

2

"Well, looks like I have the hang of this." If he knew anything at all about RPGs, he was stuck with a practice weapon that did 1d1 damage, and his class or hidden ability scores probably gave him a +1 bonus, giving him a range from 2 to 2 damage that wasn't going to change without either new equipment or level increase.

Plus, every sixty seconds, he heard, "Select the inventory icon in the upper left and equip a different weapon."

He hacked and swung. He stabbed and slashed. A two-handed grip. Flat of the blade. Striking with the hilt.

2, 2, 2, 2, 2, 2, 2

"Great work! You really have the hang of this," Beedeep told him.

"A lot more than you have the hang of that script, bro."

"Select the inventory icon in the upper left and equip a different weapon."

The bug icon glowed and pulsed a faint blue.

Arnold tapped it.

YOUR FEEDBACK WAS HELPFUL. PLEASE ACCEPT A GIFT.

Connor jumped at the chance to tap it.

100 XP.

Nice. Another little batch of XP. Someday they'd explain that bit to him.

More importantly, Connor raced back to find that the weapon rack now contained a bamboo club, staff, and dagger, as well as a sling and a pile of bullet-sized rocks. Considering it the most useful sidearm, Connor picked up the dagger.

His inventory icon pulsed.

"Select the inventory icon in the upper left and equip a different weapon."

This time, when he opened his backpack, there was the dagger waiting for him. He grabbed it, and the sword vanished, replacing it in his bag.

"Select the equipment manager icon again."

EQUIPMENT

WEAPON: BAMBOO DAGGER

ARMOR: SQUIRE ARMOR

ACCESSORY: NONE

"Excellent. Go ahead and equip your preferred weapon."

Connor went back, opened his bag, and grabbed his sword.

EQUIPMENT

WEAPON: BAMBOO SWORD

ARMOR: SQUIRE ARMOR

ACCESSORY: NONE

Beedeep grinned. "You look ready to venture out and get

some practical experience. Head north past the ziggurat and kill 5 Gobos."

Connor gave his little tutorial pal the stink-eye. Was that supposed to be some derivations of goblin? The way he said it rhymed with Joe Schmoe. If it was spelled the way it sounded, he would have expected it to be more along the lines of Rob Lowe.

Before he jumped off this cliff, he was at least going to make the most basic of RPG efforts. "What can you tell me about Gobos?"

"They are pests who work for the mountain lord, stealing our pigs and robbing from our fish traps. They live north of the ziggurat. Will you go there and kill five of them?"

What the hell? Why not? Let's take sides in a political rivalry after only hearing one side of the story. It's not like games ever made the hero out to be a villain, after all.

"Sure. Let's do this."

CHAPTER 11
FIRST BLOOD

PAST THE ZIGGURAT, the minimap updated yet again.

`KAWAIIAN JUNGLE`

For the first time since arriving, Connor saw wildlife. Parrots flapped overhead with what sounded like a stock sound effect for the wing beats. He couldn't pick the game specifically, but he knew he'd heard it before. When one of them landed on the path in front of him, it looked like a plush toy come to life with over-sized eyes and fuzzy feathers and beak.

A tortoise wandering alongside the path looked similarly like a walking plushie.

"That is really not the aesthetic I expected for this game."

Then again, maybe with a name like Kawaiian Islands, that look was just local.

"Eeeeee, chippa chippa chippaaaaa!" A war cry shattered the peace and calm. From nowhere what Connor could only describe as a Christmas elf on meth leapt into the path. Its red coat and stocking cap contrasted with the menace of its sharpened stick, wielded as a spear.

Combat music rose from the surrounding jungle. Kind of a boppy beat, jazzy, felt like it belonged in a 90s JRPG. Connor felt himself bouncing on the balls of his feet, sword drawn, as he allowed his adversary to make the first move.

The Gobo charged.

Connor batted aside the spear with ease and swung his sword.

2

The Gobo hopped back and lunged again. Once more, Connor brushed the attack wide with his blade and parried.

2

"Come on, little bro. How many hit points you got in that little bod?"

2

The Gobo fell over. Clearly, the answer to Connor's question had been either 5 or 6. Until he discovered a weapon that could deal any other amount of damage, that was the best answer he was going to get.

"Congratulations," Kelindra announced. "You have earned Experience Points, also known as XP."

"Thanks. I'm not new at this."

The narrator continued on, oblivious. "In the upper right, you'll see a partially filled circle. This indicates your progress toward your next level. If you stare at it, the actual numbers will show; otherwise, you can get a quick indication of your progress at a glance. The number at the center is your current level."

Connor focused on the swipe circle, which gave him flashbacks to the lab. It was about a quarter full. No. As he kept his eyes fixed on it, he saw it was *exactly* a quarter full.

XP: 250/1,000

The circle partially surrounded a sad little numeral "1," which was his character level.

A few seconds after the Gobo body hit the ground, it disappeared. In its place, a scattering of coins floated in the air.

Connor's hand passed right through, but when he grabbed for it, the coins disappeared.

GAINED: 4 COINS

"You guys really need a more interesting currency system. Even just calling it 'gold' is better than 'coins.' RPGs need a higher standard than a Mario game." He realized as soon as he said it that there were Mario RGPs but decided against correcting himself aloud.

When he didn't see a new tutorial pop up regarding money, Connor opened up his inventory again, and found a stack of coins—visually representing at least nine based on the icon—with a number 4 on it.

"OK, Kelindra, what can I use these coins for?"

Kelindra was right on the ball for this one. "Coins can be exchanged for goods and services."

"Funny." Maybe he wasn't a fancy college student like the other participants, but he knew basic economics. At least far enough to know what the hell money was for. "OK. New question. Where can I see my quest progress?"

"You can view in-progress quests in your Quest Journal."

"Where do I find that?"

"You can view in-progress quests in your Quest Journal."

"Not helpful."

"If my answers are inaccurate or unclear, please use the bug reporting system."

Connor didn't need to be told twice.

REPORT BUG

"There's no Quest Journal."

THANK YOU FOR YOUR FEEDBACK

Connor waited.

When he realized that maybe he wasn't going to get an instantaneous response, he tracked down another Gobo. Even if he wasn't getting credited for these on his quest, it looked like they were 50 XP a pop, plus a little gold.

He tracked one down off the path when he heard a rustle. That rustle was the first engaging, interactive, non-scripted thing in the game to impress him. It suggested that maybe, *just maybe*, there was going to be more to this game than a whack-a-mole loot dispenser with impressive immersion.

When it heard the giveaway clanking of Connor's armor, the thing whirled and took note of him.

"Eeeeee, chippa chippa chippaaaaa!" it screamed before attacking.

Like its comrade, this Gobo was comically inept at attacking. Realizing he was in little to no danger, Connor tried getting cute.

He batted the spear aside again and again without counterattacking, gauging the timing of its attacks, the reach of each thrust. On the fifth attempt to stab him, Connor made an off-hand grab for the half of the creature's weapon.

His gauntleted fist clamped on.

Connor tugged.

The Gobo, a mere fraction of his size, tugged back to no avail. Yet instead of wrenching the weapon from his opponent's grasp, the Gobo clung tight, yanked around like a puppy with a chew toy.

"You have not learned the Disarm attack," Kelindra informed him.

The thing had a grip like a lobster, and Connor was loath to let it have its weapon back to keep stabbing him—or trying and failing badly with. It was a principle thing. So instead of letting go, he reminded himself that this was decidedly *not* a cute, harmless puppy at play, then swung the stubborn Gobo by the spear into the trunk of the nearest tree.

3

Connor smirked. He knew how easily he could have finished the thing off with another blow like that. However, he had Science to perform. With his offhand rendering the Gobo all but immobile as it refused to surrender its weapon, he struck with his Bamboo Sword.

2

The Gobo collapsed. Sweet, that meant they only had 5 HP.

"50 XP" wafted from the creature's head. Apparently, he needed to get the tutorial before seeing the little animated XP gain.

Still no indication of whether Connor was getting credit toward his quest.

YOUR FEEDBACK WAS RECEIVED

That was different that his previous messages on bugs, but the icon was pulsing again.

Connor tapped it despite seeing another Gobo off in the distance, deeper in the jungle.

FINISH TALKING TO ELDER LOHDOH, NUMBNUTS.

Connor blinked in surprise. OK, clearly this wasn't an automated system, and it wasn't *his* fault the devs couldn't tutorial their way off of Yoshi's Island. How was he supposed to know that this Lohdoh character wasn't done with him? Presumably, that was the old guy's name.

Rather than finish up with his quest—based on conjecture and the fact that he could count the Gobo kills on one hand—he headed back.

ZIGGURAT

VILLAGE

Connor had a look around. All the villagers were fiddling with menial, repetitive tasks that looked like they were making no progress on. Several stood in front of their huts or work stations like royal guards, unmoving, unblinking, just waiting to be interacted with. He assumed these would be quest-givers once he got into the quest system properly. Beedeep was probably getting shitty performance reviews for jumping the gun and sending Connor out before he was in the system.

After a brief search of the not-terribly-large village, Connor found the elder in the largest hut.

"Hey, did you have anything else you needed to say to me?"

"Hero, you are destined for greatness. But you are not there yet. I am ashamed that I must ask you to bear so great a burden on our behalf," Elder Lohdoh told him. "To slay the mountain lord will be no small task, but I have every confidence in you."

"Thanks. I'm assuming if I keep at it long enough, I'll get him. That it?"

"When you are victorious, many tales will be told of your heroism. So that all will know of your deeds, I give you this journal, where you might keep a record of your feats."

Lohdoh produced a leather-bound book and handed it to Connor.

RECEIVED: QUEST JOURNAL

As he attempted to open it, the book vanished from Connor's hands. In his UI, he had a new icon that looked just like it.

He tapped, and a ghostly version of the book opened before him.

QUEST JOURNAL

There were only two entries.

SLAY THE MOUNTAIN LORD FOR ELDER LOHDOH: 0/1

KILL GOBOS FOR BEEDEEP: 2/5

Well, nice to know that they only expected him to kill *one* mountain lord. If they needed him to hunt down a whole British Parliament of mountain lords, Anachronism Interactive was in for a one-man players' revolt.

"Thanks, Elder!"

Connor took his leave as the NPC called after him, "Fare thee well, hero!"

Better news, he'd been getting credit for the Gobos he was killing.

Trying to remember where he'd seen that one in the deeper jungle, Connor used his minimap and retraced the places he'd already explored, carefully avoiding revealing new map from the fog of war state since he *knew* he'd seen the guy already once.

There!

In the underbrush, wandering with a readied spear like he existed for no other reason than combat, was the third Gobo Connor needed for his quest.

This time he charged.

The Gobo charged right back at him. "Eeeeee, chippa chippa chippaaaaa!"

Rather than parry, Connor swung with all his might and his momentum in a reckless overhand chop.

2

The Gobo glanced a strike off his armor.

1

"Ow!" Fuck, that actually hurt!

"You have taken damage," Kelindra informed him. "Damage in Spire of Fate is represented by Hit Points, or HP. Check your health display to monitor your HP. If your HP drops to zero, you die. Not just in the game, but in the real world."

Connor's guts leapt into his throat.

Kelindra continued, but it sounded like Kelli wasn't speaking into the mic anymore while reciting her voice lines. "*I'm keeping it in. Because it's funny, that's why. We're having that Broadway girl re-record all these anyway. Go ahead. Edit it out yourself if you want. Yeah. That's what I thought."*

When the relief settled in and the smirk faded from his face, Connor checked the new display that had appeared. It showed...

`HP: 7/8`

"I'm fragile as fuck."

It was a good thing that this Gobo fought like a kid playing lightsabers. It seemed like just sticking his sword out was enough to parry incoming attacks without hardly paying attention. He'd turned aside six attacks as he diverted his focus to Kelindra's nonsense.

`2`

Parry.

`2`

Dead.

`50 XP`

`KILL GOBOS FOR BEEDEEP: 3/5`

Connor checked, and he was up to 350 XP now.

His search resumed, and this time he focused on exploring the rest of the jungle his map had yet to reveal.

Back and forth he swept, methodically mapping the region like some Age of Sail explorer.

He was also up to `12 Coins`. Maybe someone in the village would turn out to be a shopkeeper once he had enough money.

A fourth Gobo was stuck up a tree. Since they were palm trees, that was quite a trick. After a fruitless attempt to figure out ranged attacks, he tapped an icon that was getting all too much use this early in the game.

`REPORT BUG`

"There's a Gobo stuck up a tree. Doesn't look like he

climbed there, since his feet are moving like he's patrolling but he's not going anywhere."

"Eeeeee, chippa chippa chippaaaaa!"

Connor craned his neck and shouted, "Shut the hell up you buggy bastard! Either get down here and die or chill the fuck out!"

THANK YOU FOR YOUR FEEDBACK

The bug icon glowed and pulsed a faint blue.

Nice. That hadn't taken long at all. Connor tapped the icon.

YOUR FEEDBACK WAS HELPFUL. PLEASE ACCEPT A GIFT.

100 XP.

"Eeeeee, chippa chippa chippaaaaa!"

1

HP: 6/8

"Dammit!"

The Gobo was loose, and it was right behind him.

Connor spun and slammed a follow-up attack wide.

2

2

2

Done.

50 XP, 4 Coins

KILL GOBOS FOR BEEDEEP: 4/5

XP: 500/1000

Not bad. He looked down at the spot where a corpse would have been if they didn't evaporate almost instantly. "You were worth more buggy than dead."

That gave him an idea. He still had one Gobo left to kill. Assuming this game worked like most online RPGs, the monsters would respawn over time.

Connor settled in, sat with his back to a nearby palm tree, and kept a vigil on the one where he'd found the buggy Gobo.

Eventually, he saw one fade into existence.

"Eeeeee, chippa chippa chippaaaaa!"

He grinned up at the little buggy ball of experience points.

REPORT BUG

As he opened his mouth to say the same thing again, he remembered that the bugs were clearly NOT automated, not unless the game was programmed for snark—which, he admitted, wasn't the craziest idea, either. But rather than risk someone getting pissed off for pestering them, he rephrased his objection.

"There's a Gobo spawn point on top of a palm tree. It can't get down."

He waited some more, trying to enjoy the ambient music that someone had picked up for cheap from a stock audio repository. If they were getting Broadway performers to voice the characters, it stood to reason they'd be planning to hire on an actual composer for the soundtrack. Not that either did Connor much good at the moment.

THANK YOU FOR YOUR FEEDBACK

The bug icon glowed and pulsed a faint blue, and Connor tapped it immediately.

YOUR UPDATED FEEDBACK WAS HELPFUL.

Damn, no additional XP.

"Eeeeee, chippa chippa chippaaaaa!"

This time, Connor was ready. With his back to a palm tree, there would be no sneaking up behind him. But he'd also paid attention to where the devs had plunked the last one down when he'd reported it broken.

Mr. Doomed Gobo had popped up right in that same spot.

Even from his backside, he fended off the immediate attack with ease.

2

The Gobo stood no chance as he stood.

2

Hopefully, there were monsters in this game that would prove more of a challenge.

2

50 XP, 4 Coins

KILL GOBOS FOR BEEDEEP: COMPLETE

XP: 550/1000

"You have completed your first quest," Kelindra informed him. "Return to the one who tasked you with your quest to receive a reward."

An indicator arrow lit on his minimap, pointing him back in the direction of the village.

Connor trudged off, retracing his steps to get back to Beedeep with minimal risk of distractions. "Thanks. I think I will."

CHAPTER 12
LEVEL UP

CONNOR HAD no trouble making his way back to first the path, then the village, via the same route past the ziggurat. The gamer in him wondered whether there was some dungeon awaiting him beneath the primitive pyramid. The tester who'd been playing this game for what felt like all morning by now was more curious whether Anachronism Interactive had even tried this game for themselves.

He was betting there wasn't even anything beyond this little island developed yet.

"Thank you, hero!" Beedeep congratulated him upon Connor's return. The villagers hadn't budged since his last time here, and the ones working on handicrafts hadn't made the faintest progress on their chores. He'd hoped that maybe at least advancing in the plot would nudge them along to maybe a new state of thumb-twiddling. But alas, no. "Take this as your reward!"

RECEIVED: XPOT

Connor opened his inventory immediately, even as Kelindra explained his new acquisition.

"XPOTs, or Experience Potions, are rewards offered by some quests. You can choose to either drink one now or save them for later. The experience point values can't be seen by examining the XPOT in your inventory."

Connor didn't know what saving one for later was good for. He wasn't planning to make a career out of this game. Once his week was up, he doubted they'd let him near the thing again until it was released to the public.

Grabbing a bulbous vial of pink glowing liquid caused his inventory backpack to fade from view. Left with the XPOT in hand, Connor popped the cork with his thumb and downed it like a shot.

`750 XP`

A golden swirl surrounded him as a majestic gong rang.

`>>>LEVEL UP!!!<<<`

`YOU GAIN`

`1 ATTACK`

`1 DEFENSE`

`5 HP`

`0 MP`

`1 SKILL CHOICE`

Despite the good news, Connor felt a sad hit him in the gut. He's picked a non-magic class in a game with magic. Maybe Knights got spells at higher levels. He wasn't quite sure yet what exactly Spire of Fate considered a knight, whether it was more fighter, warrior, gladiator, or paladin.

`XP: 300/2000`

"Congratulations. That XPOT gave you just enough to reach `Level 2`."

"It didn't, but I can see how your math wouldn't account for bug reporting bonuses."

"Go to your Character Skills chart and choose your new skill."

Since a Knight-shaped outline was glowing at the perimeter of his view, it didn't take calculus to figure out where to tap.

He had three options.

TWO-HAND FIGHTING

SHIELD SPECIALIST

DISARMING ATTACK

Immediately, Connor ruled out the shield. He wasn't a shield guy. Maybe something to have considered before going Knight, but here he was. Unless they really pigeon-holed this class—and from the Two-Handed Fighting option, it sounded like they hadn't—he was going to avoid going sword and board all game.

Disarming Attack seemed like a trap, too. The Gobos were stupidly easy to kill, even armed. And in any fantasy game, most of the enemies wouldn't be humanoid enough to carry weapons. In a medieval simulation, sure. Everyone needed a weapon to really hurt you, so disarming was a great way to turn a duel one-sided in a hurry.

"Is there any way to see what these skills do before I pick one?"

"To examine a skill, hold your palm out toward it without touching."

Well, that was easy enough. It felt like using the Force, but when Connor aimed an open palm at the skills list, the details of their effects showed up for him to make a more informed decision.

TWO-HANDED FIGHTING - When wielding a two-handed or a versatile one-handed weapon in two hands, your Attack increases equal to your level.

SHIELD SPECIALIST - When carrying a shield, your Defense increases equal to your level.

DISARMING ATTACK - When striking an opponent's weapon with an attack, damage that exceeds the target's Defense will cause them to drop the weapon.

That last one, in addition to sounding like it wouldn't apply to a lot of the enemies in the game, also struck Connor as complicated and clunky.

He tapped TWO-HANDED FIGHTING.

"You can now also check your character stats," Kelindra told him.

The skill selection swooped off into a new screen that stayed open behind the selection of his skills.

CHARACTER STATS:

NAME: Connor **TITLE:** None

CLASS: Knight **LEVEL:** 2

HP: 13 **MP:** 0 **ATK:** 3 **DEF:** 3

"I'm a powerhouse," he commented wryly.

"You are strong now," Beedeep told him, and Connor couldn't tell if the guy was reacting to what he'd just said, or whether this was just scripted and the timing coincidental. "You are now strong enough to go to the Dock. Speak with Debebee. Beware. The way to the Dock is not safe."

"Wow. Really?"

"Yes. Really."

Connor laughed out loud. Clearly, either the game didn't grasp sarcasm, or it had a weird sense of humor about itself.

"All right. Which way to the Dock?" Connor asked, and he could almost *hear* himself capitalizing the word, like it was the name of a city or state.

"Through the jungle, past the Gobo Camp."

"I didn't find any... oh. I was probably supposed to wander around and find those five Gobos rather than camp a buggy respawn point. Fine. I'll find the camp, then keep on going past it. Anyone else I need to speak to before I head out?"

After the debacle with missing vital information from Lohdoh, he didn't want to have to hike all the way back here if he missed talking to the guy trying the same knot in a fishing net for hours or the woman picking the same fruit off a nearby tree over and over.

"You should speak to Debebee at the Dock," Beedeep reiterated. "Beware. The way to the Dock is not safe."

"Yeah, yeah. Got that much. But I'm now a master of Two-Handed Fighting, so I assume it's all going to be fine."

He regretted those words the instant he spoke them aloud.

Maybe karma wasn't real.

Maybe it didn't reach into video games.

Maybe Connor believed either of those statements was true.

Before he got himself into any more trouble, Connor set out.

ZIGGURAT

JUNGLE

GOBO CAMP

Well, hell. He'd been within frisbee distance of the place when he'd turned back. And he hadn't seen it from just out of minimap exploration range because the level designer had actually made a smart choice. The camp, which was primitive to put it mildly, nestled in a shallow gully where a stream trickled through. Mud huts used the sides of the gully as back walls, and palm frond roofs blended in with the surroundings.

There was no sign of any Gobo activity. A stone circle indicative of a campfire contained nothing but blackened twigs.

Poking his head inside the huts, Connor discovered piles of unguarded Coins.

10 COINS

Well, the messages that popped up were more convenient than counting, he supposed, that brought his stash up to 30.

The Gobos had nothing else. Either they lived in squalor, had been given the shaft by whoever designed their camp, or Connor turning in that quest to end their menacing the villagers had also triggered a depopulation of anything worth looting.

He continued onward.

There was, in keeping with starting zone protocols, a pretty well-beaten trail leading out of the Gobo camp.

`JUNGLE`

As he ventured, Connor listened to the repetitive twittering of more plush birds in the trees above. Another plush tortoise crossed his path. Rather than see whether it was killable, Connor knelt down and petted the slow-moving creature, marveling at its softness.

He came upon a rope bridge over a chasm that was all of twelve or fifteen feet deep. Ocean water washed through, connecting two islands that had been riven in twain by ancient forces of narrative coolness.

`ROPE BRIDGE`

This didn't seem like the sort of thing developers of a starting area would trap. He tested his weight, and the bridge wobbled. Whether he could swim in plate armor or would die if he fell in, Connor trusted his luck and strode across. After all, it couldn't have been more than a fifty-foot span.

"Eeeeee, ikki ikki ikkiiiii!" Twin shouts came just as two Gobos in yellow caps sprang from the underbrush on the far side of the bridge. Rather than spears, these little runts wielded curved daggers that looked like animal teeth.

OK. Probably level 2 versions of the red-hatted cannon fodder he'd cleared out of the previous island.

"Bring it on, bitches!"

Sword out, clutched in two hands, he marched along the bridge, ready to bring doom.

Rather than attempt combat, the two Yellow Gobos set to work cutting the ropes with those tooth daggers.

"NO!" Connor shouted as he realized he was in the middle of the span and not quick enough to either reach the far side or double back before the bridge fell out from beneath him.

A moment's panicked freefall quickly gave way to a splash and a hasty confirmation that he could not, in fact, swim in plate armor.

Connor held his breath. The water was pretty clear, but the chasm was shaded. With limited light, he scrambled and scratched, seeking purchase to climb free.

The sides were too steep.

Lungs threatening to burst, he...

Well, apparently, Connor could breathe just fine.

He laughed, and there wasn't even a distortion from the water to alter the sound.

Marching up and down the chasm floor, he found steep drop-offs to the deep ocean on either side, and no way to climb back out. He even managed to move his armor into inventory—it took up two slots—and discovered that he couldn't swim.

Well and truly stuck, he figured he could at least address one major issue.

`REPORT BUG`

"The water is breathable and doesn't sound like underwater."

Connor sat back, relaxed in his loincloth, and watched as the same school of plush tropical fish swam by at regular intervals.

`THANK YOU FOR YOUR FEEDBACK`

Connor grinned.

YOUR FEEDBACK WAS HELPFUL. PLEASE ACCEPT A GIFT.

Before he could think to check what that gift might be, he noticed a bar. It started out fully pale blue, not unlike the skin tone of the villagers, and began rapidly to dwindle.

It was labeled...

BREATH

"Oh, shit!" Connor exclaimed, and bubbles escaped his mouth.

In a frenzy, he renewed his efforts to escape the underwater chasm.

Alas, the bar ran out all too soon.

CHAPTER 13
RESPAWN

WITHOUT WARNING OR EXPLANATION, Connor found himself in a fog, surrounded by a circle of stones that looked familiar. Too large a circle to be the gobo campfire, unless he'd been shrunken. But his location became clear when he checked the minimap.

VILLAGE

"Greetings, hero," Kelindra said to him. "You have died. Not every battle can be won with might alone. Will you pay the price to return to life?"

"Do I have a choice?"

"You can decline to return to life."

Not a major choice. Then again, if he was keeping even marginal track of time, it had to be getting on toward lunchtime. Maybe he could use a break.

"Can I log out for a bit? Come back later? Maybe after lunch."

"You have not discovered a source of food," Kelindra informed him.

Connor blinked. Or at least, he tried. Incorporeal and ghostly, he had no physical sensation, and his sight wasn't interrupted by eyelids. "Excuse me? First off, I was just in a fishing village. If they don't *give* fish to their mountain-lord-slaying hero, they at least ought to sell some. Second, what about the logging out bit?"

Without waiting for an answer, Connor tapped the menu button, one of the few UI elements still available to him as a ghost.

MAIN MENU

HELP

SYSTEM

OPTIONS

LOGOUT

RETURN TO GAME

He tapped the LOGOUT option.

It flashed red but otherwise did nothing.

He tapped HELP.

"Hello. I am Kelindra, your guide to Spire of Fate. How may I assist you?"

"Clearly not."

He tried SYSTEM.

Red flash.

OPTIONS

Another red flash.

REPORT BUG

"Unable to log out."

THANK YOU FOR YOUR FEEDBACK

He waited, yet there was no sign of follow-up.

"Fine. What's the price to return to life?" He might as well poke around the game a little while the devs got this figured out. Or actual lunchtime would roll around and Kelli would yank him out via some kind of manual override.

"The XP you have accumulated since your last level," Kelindra replied.

Connor checked.

XP: 300/2000

That basically accounted for his bug reporting bonuses. East come, easy go, he supposed.

"All right. Return me to life. I'll pay it."

He hoped there was a resurrection option later in the game, since he could foresee that price becoming onerous at higher levels. For now, however, with limited recourse, it seemed like a fair bargain.

The ghostly environment faded, and Connor's UI returned to normal.

XP: 0/2000

VILLAGE

First thing he did was open his inventory and put his armor back on.

Then, he tried talking to every NPC around except Lohdoh and Beedeep. None of them sold a damn thing, least of all fish.

With no word back from the dev team about his bug, he marched himself back into the jungle. In fact, for the first time, he tried jogging.

There was no fatigue, and after learning his lesson on the breath meter, he wasn't about to point out that potential omission.

JUNGLE

ZIGGURAT

GOBO CAMP

ROPE BRIDGE

"Eeeeee, ikki ikki ikkiiiii!"

The same pair who'd murdered him were back. Strangely, so was the rope bridge. Rather than take that as a bug, he presumed it reset as would a puzzle in most games. He had to solve it. But aside from the penalty for dying, he had as many attempts as it took.

However, this time they hadn't waited for him to make it halfway across the span.

"Bring it here, you little weenies! C'mon, if you're tough enough!"

Many RPGs had the concept of threat. Part and parcel to that was the concept of taunting, or forcing an opponent to attack you. Normally, this was done as part of a group, where the sturdiest member would tank hits for the rest by drawing the ire of their foes. In this case, Connor just wanted them to attack rather than remain in their defensive position.

But these Yellow Gobos were smarter than the others. Less mindlessly aggressive.

Connor browsed the ground on his side of the bridge and found some rocks. He tried chucking them across the way, but the Yellow Gobos saw them coming and merely dodged aside.

Realizing that either this was a starting zone with an easy solution to this conundrum or Anachronism Interactive had fucked up and put a brick wall into a level 2 quest, Connor made his choice.

"Maybe this is just to test my knightliness."

Sucking in a deep lungful of digital air—and probably one to match in the lab—he bellowed a battle cry and raced across the bridge with all the speed he could muster.

If he could break their resolve.

If he could make them hesitate...

Or panic...

Or fumble their daggers...

Or fly.

Just before the Yellow Gobo daggers cut through the ropes holding up the bridge, Connor leaped.

He didn't make it within ten feet of the far side.

Water rushed up and splashed around him.

Connor found himself back in that fog, surrounded by a circle of stones.

VILLAGE

"Greetings, hero," Kelindra said to him. "You have died. Not every battle can be won with might alone. Will you pay the price to return to life?"

He scowled.

XP: 0/2000

"Yeah. Do it." After all, what did he have to lose?

XP: 0/2000

But something in what Kelindra said stuck with him this time. After his first death, he'd had a lot on his mind. Dying, for one. The price of coming back to life. Reporting his LOGOUT bug. He'd overlooked how she might have been giving him a clue.

When he returned to life, Connor didn't hesitate. He jogged back to the site of his demise.

JUNGLE

ZIGGURAT

GOBO CAMP

ROPE BRIDGE

"Eeeeee, ikki ikki ikkiiiii!"

"Yeah, ikki ikki yourselves," He muttered. Then, he opened his inventory. It took some finagling, but he separated out two individual Coins. Weapon sheathed at his hip, he stood at his side of the bridge, holding one aloft in either hand. "I pay. You let me cross?"

The two Yellow Gobos looked to one another, then conferred in unintelligible babbling that sounded like someone ran break room chitchat through Google Translate.

Two yellow elf-hats bobbed affirmative.

Still holding up his Coins, Connor made his way across the bridge. At the far side, the two Gobos held out greedy hands.

They snickered as Connor paid them each off.

Now, hands free, Connor drew his sword and hacked.

5

With a shriek of surprise, his victim drew his rope-cutting dagger. The Yellow Gobo's companion did likewise.

5

Connor wasn't going easy on them. Dagger strikes plinked off his armor, dealing 0 damage. Not misses but actual zeroes. And his second strike had brought down the first of the pair.

75 XP

5

0 in return.

5

75 XP

Connor gave a quick flourish of his sword before returning his Bamboo Sword to its sheath.

A dagger and a single gold coin floated where each corpse disappeared.

INVENTORY

30 COINS

2 YELLOW GOBO DAGGER

Given that they only had their weapons, Connor couldn't be certain that these were meant to be loot-bearing creatures. But he'd be damned if he was going to let these two amateur freeway toll collectors get away with extorting him.

The hats had been his clue, though.

The red-hatted Gobos were out for blood. Yellow hats were interested in gold. Maybe he was reading too much into it, but this felt like exactly the kind of hammy, cliched game where uniforms matched personalities. Hopefully, someone would take some constructive criticism after this was over and update their monsters to something a little more subtle and a little less Pokémon.

"Eeeeee, ikki ikki ikkiiiii!"

Connor whirled, but there was no one to be seen.

"Eeeeee, ikki ikki ikkiiiii!"

It was behind him.

"Eeeeee, ikki ikki ikkiiiii!"

Where were those shouts coming from?

The path on the far side of the bridge had overgrown jungle growing right up on both sides.

Rather than linger and search, he pressed onward. If these sneaky little bastards wanted to be XP, he'd take them up on their offer. If they thought they could get him to play a Rambo version of ring-and-run in the jungle, they had another think coming.

JUNGLE

KAWAIIAN ISLANDS

That was interesting. As he emerged from the jungle onto another beach, all he had was the generic zone name to go by.

Cookie-cutter waves, just like the ones on the far side of the starting island, lapped the shore.

A wide stretch of beach lay between him and the lone notable geographic feature, a wooden dock that stretched out into the ocean. At the far end of that dock, a pale blue villager awaited him, too far away for Connor to make out any details.

He had to assume that was...

Unable to recall the name, he checked his Quest Journal.

SPEAK WITH DEBEBEE AT THE DOCK: 0/1

The whole 0/1 bit struck him as dubious. How many Debebees at how many docks did they think he might speak to if he wasn't capped at getting credit for one?

Just as he was about to venture onto the sands, he spotted the reason why Beedeep had warned him of danger on this journey. Given that he'd died twice, it might have been easy to write off the Yellow Gobos as the main threat.

But on those sands were crabs as big as golf carts. And, while they still had the island wildlife's distinctive, fluffy "plush" look, their sheer size gave him pause.

`XP: 150/2000`

There were two ways to look at this. On the one hand, those behemoths were terrifying monstrosities that looked as if they could squeeze him in two with one pincer—and they had two. On the other hand, these things were walking piles of XP and he had kinda not a whole lot to lose at this point.

And then again, maybe they weren't even aggressive. After all, Kelindra hinted that there would be non-combat encounters to think his way around.

Connor stepped one foot onto the sand.

The nearest Plush Crab turned and fixed eyestalks in his direction. It clacked its pincers in anticipation.

"So much for non-aggro crabs."

Was he a Knight without so much as "Sir" for a title, or was he an unemployed logistics clerk?

With a battle cry that he never expected to have any effect on the Plush Crab, Connor charged.

This was why he chose Two-Handed Fighting, after all. No chance of disarming a claw. No baiting attacks so he could counter after blocking with a shield.

Straight into the fray.

His first attack glanced off the Plush Crab's hard shell. Not a good sign.

To his added surprise, the Plush Crab picked him up in one claw and squeezed.

Breath exited Connor's lungs in more of a pained gasp than a scream. God DAMMIT that hurt! This was the missing X factor in his decision-making process, something he'd overlooked in his RPG mathematics. No other game he'd ever played physically HURT to lose—those noob-based losses in a certain MOBA he wasn't about to name came pretty close.

2

HP: 11/13

Luckily, the Plush Crab gripped him around the waist, leaving both his arms free. Down came Connor's Bamboo Sword. He struck a blow to the crab's pincer arm.

5

The squeezing continued without a further need of another attack.

2

HP: 9/13

However, now it was hard for Connor to miss. He just hoped this thing didn't have two and a half times as many hit points as him.

5

2

HP: 7/13

The next blow landed with a crack.

>>10<< CRITICAL HIT

As the Plush Crab died, hinting at a hit point total between 15 and 24, Kelindra decided to chime in. "You have struck a critical blow against a foe. A critical his deals double the damage of a normal strike, though other factors may change the final damage dealt."

100 XP

XP: 250/2000

While he had her attention, Connor figured he'd engage with his absentee narrator. "What factors?"

"Critical strike damage is calculated before reductions due to armor, enemy defensive skills, and environmental effects. Critical strike modifiers may deviate from the standard doubling of damage based on player skills, special attacks, magical effects, equipment, and unique circumstances."

"So, it's double damage, except when it isn't."

"Yes."

"Super."

The Plush Crab had no loot. Its fuzzy, yet weirdly armored carcass simply vanished after a few seconds. The next two nearest Plush Crabs in either direction didn't flinch toward him as Connor darted across the sand on his way to the dock.

If he'd been a little less banged up by the encounter, 100 XP a pop would have made these crabs a good source to farm up level 3, but another 18 of them was asking a lot, especially since he'd yet to find a way to replenish hit points, aside from, you know, *dying*.

Melee was almost always a slog at low levels in RPGs. The good ones made it worthwhile in the end. But right now, he kind of envied anyone who decided to play an Archer or Wizard in Spire of Fate.

DOCK

His footsteps still made sand noises as he crossed the wooden planks, then switched to splashing once the dock extended out over the water.

REPORT BUG

"Dock is inheriting the surface of the terrain underneath it for purposes of footstep sounds."

His logout bug was still in the ether, but there was no point *not* putting one in for this. They were worth as much as fighting one of those Plush Crabs, and the bug reports didn't hurt like murder.

"Hello, I'm Debebee," the villager on the docks greeted him in a voice that sounded vaguely familiar from the Anachronism Interactive cubicles. And he *kinda* remembered hearing about one of their coders being named Debbie. He put two and two together to figure out who'd been wrangled into providing this cheery dialog. "Would you like passage to the mainland?"

Connor looked back and shrugged. It had been hours. He hadn't filled out his minimap yet. There was probably stuff he was missing. That whole starting zone was probably riddled with bugs to report. But by the same token, he itched to expand his horizons. Gazing across the sea, the spire that inspired the game's name rose with dark menace, surrounded by storm clouds, beckoning with the promise of greater adventures beyond.

"Sure. When's the next ship due?"

"For 20 Coins, you can ride my raft."

"That's the worst solicitation I've ever heard," Connor joked, but the crude humor was lost on the NPC.

"It's a good raft."

It was also, coincidentally, the exact amount that killing Beedeep's 5 Gobos provided, and there had been no other way to spend money yet. Even if he hadn't pillaged the Gobo camp, he'd have been able to afford this.

"Yeah. I'll get railroaded onto your raft. Here." He pulled 20 Coins from his inventory and handed them over.

Instantly, a log raft with a primitive sail appeared beside Debebee.

Knowing he couldn't swim in his armor, Connor grabbed hold of the mast as he climbed aboard.

"How do I—?" but his question became moot as the raft whisked away from the Dock.

"Have a safe trip!" Debebee shouted after him, waving enthusiastically.

Salt spray flecked his face as the raft carried Connor away from the Kawaiian Islands.

The map updated with a new location.

`WADDAYA SEA`

CHAPTER 14
WASHED ASHORE

THE RAFT RIDE was swift and uneventful. If this had been an older RPG, he'd have figured this place for a loading screen. It pulled up to a matching dock, but the location was far from the desolate stretch of beach he'd left.

Giant letters appeared as soon as Connor arrived.

`LOOKMANO SANDS`

A small trumpet fanfare accompanied the announcement.

Then, once the raft came to a halt, the minimap updated yet again, this time with less cheesy pomp.

`LOOKMANO DOCK`

The villager waiting for Connor at the end of the voyage looked just like the little blue woman he'd just left. "Hello, I'm Bededee. Welcome to the mainland. If you ever get homesick for the Kawaiian Islands, I can send you back."

"How can I get homesick for a place I basically just learned existed?"

"Would you like to go back?" Bededee asked cheerily.

Connor scrambled off the raft before he accidentally triggered a return trip. There was a good chance he'd be forced to grind Red Gobos to afford to get back here. Actually, now that he was thinking of money...

"How much would a return trip cost?"

Bededee responded with a grin, "Nothing. The journey is free. Anything for a friend of Debebee."

Never hurt to ask. "Aaaand, if I went back to the Kawaiian Islands and wanted to come back *here* again? How much would that cost?"

"Why would Debebee charge you money for a service you've already paid for, silly?" Bededee asked as if it were the craziest idea she'd ever heard.

OK. Sounded like he'd bought a bus pass and not a one-way ticket. Great. No need to explain capitalism to these NPCs. Connor would just be happy knowing he could backtrack if needed.

"So, if I want to come back here, Bededee will take me for free?"

The villager laughed. "I'm Bededee. You mean Debebee."

OK. Fuck this gibberish with the names. Connor wasn't ready to file a bug report about shitty, lazy character design. He was mentally renaming them Debby-B and Betty-D. Still a pain to keep straight, but they weren't mere noises anymore.

"Fine. If I want to come back—no matter how many times—Debby-B will take me for free?"

"Yup!"

"Same goes for you?"

"Yup!"

Breathing a sigh of relief, Connor allowed his thought process to advance. "Got any quests for me?"

"Would you like to go back?"

"No."

Connors footsteps splashed down the wooden planks. Without even breaking stride...

REPORT BUG

"Same inherited noise from the underlying surface on Lookmano Dock."

As expected, once the dock was above sand, his boots crunched and shushed. There was no shift as he stepped onto actual sand at the end.

LOOKMANO SANDS

The waterfront itself was a mirror of the one back on the Kawaiian Islands. Same color sand. Same width of beach. But rather than give way to a stretch of thick jungle, here Connor was hemmed in by imposing cliffs that barred journeying to the mainland's interior. And as he gazed upward to eyeball how high he'd have to climb to make the ascent the hard way, he spotted the Spire of Fate itself stretching into the heavens beyond.

After a brief and fruitless attempt to find purchase to climb the cliff face, Connor had his choice of two options. North or South. The shoreline twisted and curved, preventing him from seeing where either choice led without heading a distance in that direction.

With his minimap all but useless for finding anything but his way back to Lookmano Dock, he chose at random and picked South.

Around the cliff, yet more beach wound its way along the mainland's edge, pestered by an endless series of identical waves.

But there was a villager. This whole pale blue aesthetic just wasn't working for Connor. They were, at best, tropical denizens. They should be adapted to constant sunshine, not look like they'd just been pulled from the freezer case at the grocery store. Unless this world ended up giving them a backstory that explained them as refugees from an arctic region, it just made no sense to him. Especially seeing how the Gobos seemed carefully color coded.

This specimen was standing in the surf, repeatedly throwing a net into the water, then reeling it back in.

"Hi!" Connor called out, in case the NPC got spooked by his sudden appearance on this desolate beach.

"Hello, hero!" the fisherman called back. "Hard to catch Spiny Reef Fish. If you could find me five of them, I'd be very grateful."

Rolling his eyes, Connor checked his `Quest Journal`.

`BRING SPINY REEF FISH TO NEEDEEP: 0/5`

"Happy to help," Connor told the guy dryly.

If he had a pet peeve when it came to RPGs, it was busywork quests. No world he'd played had ever been saved because of fishing. At best, many had been saved in spite of it. In the real world, regular everyday folks would have gone apeshit if they found out that the guy in charge of keeping their planet from being hit by a comet or eaten by an ancient dragon or consumed by endless swarms of undead was off on a fucking fishing trip. And, since they probably couldn't take their Chosen One in a fight, they'd at least be harassing him to get moving, giving him shit in every shop he visited, and probably murdering the asshole who gave him the quest.

Yeah, thanks Eugene. Hero McChosenson's the only one who can wield the Cosmos Blade, but I'm sure his time is best spent trying to catch the fish that ate your wife's wedding ring. I can see why she chucked it in the lake in the first place.

Frankly, the same went for a lot of low-level quests. Delivering letters, picking herbs, anything to do with farming and agriculture, all of it was just wily NPCs recognizing free labor and a near-omnipotent OCD butler who'd do just about anything via the power of suggestion.

Connor scanned the nearby water, but the surface was too... well, he was going to call it murky, but the real answer was that it wasn't programmed to be transparent. He couldn't see anything below the waves, let alone pick out a particular sort of fish.

"Um. Hey. You got a net or anything for me?"

"Sure! Here you go!"

RECEIVED: FISHING NET

Heaving a sigh, Connor equipped the net as a weapon. He threw it into the water like Needeep and pulled it back in by the rope he kept clutched in one hand.

Nothing.

He repeated the process several more times with no better luck. He even tried moving up and down the shoreline with no better success.

"Can you give me any fishing tips?"

Needeep was more than happy to share. "A fishing net will catch fish… if there are any fish to catch."

"Screw this."

Connor re-equipped his Bamboo Sword and headed back North up the beach. If this game was gating a key item behind a stupid fishing quest, he'd deal with that when the time came.

LOOKMANO DOCK

LOOKMANO SANDS

North of the docks, the terrain was similar but not the scenery. First off, there were fish skeletons above the high tide line. Bleached and picked clean, they looked like they'd been there a while. And the spines of the skeletons were—and this sounded stupid even thinking it—spiny. That was to say, long spikes jutted from the creature's backs, strongly hinting that these had once been the Spiny Reef Fish Connor was looking for.

There were only three skeletons, so he didn't hold out a ton of hope that merely collecting these would give quest credit. To his mild annoyance, the game wouldn't even let him try. The skeletons might as well have been welded to the sand. And if they weren't indestructible, they were, at the very least, too sturdy for his Bamboo Sword to damage.

But also along the beach, Connor spotted another character. They came up from behind him, back in the direction of the dock.

Wearing the Shaolin-style robes from the character creation screen, the monk blew past Connor at a dead run, jumping frequently and occasionally doing flips in midair.

"Hi!" Connor shouted, but the monk didn't so much as acknowledge his existence.

Then, the monk dove into the water.

"Brave man. Or dumb." He wondered which of his fellow testers had gone the monk route. He hadn't gotten much of a look at the facial features, and he doubted anyone would recognize *him* after all the customizing he'd done.

Moments later, the monk sprang from the water. Running inland, he face-planted into the cliffside, hands scratching and clawing in a vain attempt to climb.

"I hope I didn't look that dumb," Connor remarked regarding his own efforts to scale the rock.

Another player jogged in from the south. Clad head to toe in black, this player had tinkered with the character creation settings on the extremes. Clearly a female avatar, the only skin exposed by the ninja outfit was a span around the eyes and a cutout at the cleavage. The latter was pure fan service. The outfit had the distinct look of male fashion design. And if forced to guess, it was a guy behind the controls as well. The rogue's chest was swollen to the point of absurdity, and the waist was narrow enough that Connor could have closed a fist around it.

Of course, Connor had tinkered with his own avatar as well, and as a Knight he imagined was quite strong—though the Attack stat left some ambiguity.

Also, the rogue's eyes were a vivid red, and option Connor hadn't stumbled across. At the very least, aside from "comical," he'd have described this rogue as "striking."

Unlike the frenetic, kinetic, athletic monk, this character stopped and waved to Connor.

"Hey, who is this?" he asked as he waved back.

Some twitching beneath the mask suggested that the rogue was talking, but there was no sound.

Connor shook his head. "I can't hear you. Can you hear me?"

The rogue gestured with her hands, but more like for emphasis while speaking than actual sign language. Which gave Connor an idea.

He pointed to himself, then his mouth. "Can you..." He pointed to her, then his own ear. "Hear me?"

The rogue shook her head.

Without warning, two daggers appeared in the rogue's hands. He recognized them as Bamboo Daggers from the starting village.

Connor put up his hands. He wasn't looking for a fight. He realized belatedly that one of his hands was wielding his own Bamboo Sword.

Not waiting for the communications gap to clear up, the rogue struck. Two clean blows to the chest.

There wasn't a damage message. Not even a zero. Connor checked.

`HP: 13/13`

He let her continue attacking. Rather than strike back with his sword, he checked to see whether players could interact at all. He tried to tackle the rogue.

Whether his plan would have worked or not, Connor didn't get a chance to find out. The rogue darted out of the way, leaving him overbalanced and without a body to cushion his fall.

Face down in the sand, Connor rolled to his back, prepared to defend himself MMA style if need be.

But instead of a looming opponent waiting to strike, he found the rogue's shoulders heaving with laughter. He did his best to ignore the jiggling that went along with those amused convulsions, since it seemed like blatant manipulation by the dev team, trying to distract other players.

Once she'd composed herself somewhat, the rogue offered him a hand to get up.

It turned out, players *could* interact.

Down the shore, after being ignored during their interaction, Connor and the rogue both turned when the monk popped out of the water, did a flip, then rushed toward them, frantically waving a Fishing Net overhead.

He pulled up short. Connor studied the face as the mouth moved frantically, but the monk's silence was as complete as the rogue's. Unable to read lips and unsure whether the graphics were even good enough to make an attempt, all he could do was shake his head and shrug. Then, the rogue pointed to the side of her head, where an ear would have been under that concealing mask, and shook her head.

With a theatrical sigh, the monk pointed to his fishing net, then the water, then put the net away, used both hands, and pantomimed a diving motion.

REPORT BUG

"Players unable to hear one another."

Because what this RPG really needed, Connor decided, was players interacting with other players. Though he and the rogue both followed the monk toward the water, it was clear that playing charades for every human interaction was going to get old quick.

CHAPTER 15
WATERY REEF

CONNOR WADED INTO THE SURF, wondering how feasible this quest was going to be. First of all, net fishing was for fishing from the water's surface, not below it. To fish underwater generally required a spear or spear gun. Or at least a different sort of net. More crucially, underwater endeavors of *any* sort required a way to breathe.

Once his head was underwater, rather than a breath meter, Connor got a tutorial update.

"This is your first underwater quest, hero," Kelindra informed him. "To swim, you can paddle with your arms and kick with your feet. Angle your body in the direction you wish to travel."

"Can I swim in armor?" Connor asked. It would be a pain in the ass, but if he could take his armor off and be able to swim around freely, he'd temporarily sacrifice its protection.

"No, you must be in water to swim."

"I..." Connor was objecting before he even realized how stupid an answer that was to his question. "Are you messing with me?"

"I'll let you decide that."

Scowling, he glanced to the side and noticed that the rogue

was also paused just underwater, presumably having a conversation similar to his. He couldn't help but wonder whether they all talked to Kelindra or spoke with narrators who sounded like their own proctors.

"Fine. Let me make my question *crystal* clear. Can I use the swim action you described—to its proper in-game effect—while wearing armor like the armor I'm wearing currently."

"Yes."

"Thank you!"

In the distance, he spotted a coral reef. The monk flitted about just above it, throwing his net.

"I hate to even ask this, but can I breathe underwater?"

"It is possible, with certain magical effects, for a character to breathe underwater."

There had been no indication of Connor noticing any of these. But he wanted to get this quest out of the way more than he wanted another dose of 100 XP for reporting it as a bug.

Reaching out, Connor tried a frog stroke, and found he was able to make good time underwater. He swam off to join the monk as the rogue lagged behind.

`WATERY REEF`

The reef was a wonder of imaginary nature. Huge. Sprawling. Extending in either direction along the coast farther than he could see, it was home to three different kinds of aquatic life.

One was the reef itself. Connor had seen enough National Geographic Channel to know that reefs were alive. Another was a type of glowing seahorse the size of the palm of his hand. Lastly, and crucially, there were fish that looked just like they'd leave skeletons like the ones littering the beach.

Down, down Connor dove. When he got close, he equipped his net and threw one around the docile, oblivious `Spiny Reef Fish`.

His Quest Journal didn't update.

`BRING SPINY REEF FISH TO NEEDEEP: 0/5`

OK. Fair. He wouldn't get credit for his catches until he handed them in. Seemed like a weird way to word it.

Until he realized that the fish didn't end up in his inventory.

He had the damn thing in his net.

This was just going to be tedium.

As he turned to head back to shore, he noticed the rogue floating there not far away. She appeared to be speaking, and it could only have been with her narrator, since no one else around could hear her.

Then, to Connor's horror, a breath meter appeared.

Eyes wide, he realized what she'd been up to. He might have been ignoring the bug, but *she'd* just reported it. And, already knowing the fix for this issue, the devs immediately applied it to this underwater zone.

He wasn't prepared. This was too far out and far too deep.

Connor kicked and paddled for his life.

He wasn't soon enough.

The breath meter petered out.

His last, bubbling word before darkness took was cut off mid-scream.

"FUUUUUUU—"

CHAPTER 16
SQUARE ONE

CONNOR REGAINED consciousness in the circle of stones on the Kawaiian Islands at the edge of the village once he'd accepted Kelindra's bargain.

VILLAGE

"Dammit."

He was back where he was hours ago. Wrong side of the docks. Miles from the site of his death. Now the promise of free transport made more sense. He'd gladly have paid for transit if he could have respawned somewhere over on Lookmano Sands.

Fortunately, among the things that *didn't* get reset back to zero on his death were his quests and inventory. He checked both just to be certain.

QUEST JOURNAL

SLAY THE MOUNTAIN LORD FOR ELDER LOHDOH: 0/1

BRING SPINY REEF FISH TO NEEDEEP: 0/5

INVENTORY

10 COINS

2 YELLOW GOBO DAGGER

FISHING NET

He realized that the rogue had been using Bamboo

Daggers. Maybe those were better than the ones the Gobos used. But he suspected that rather than slaughter the Gobos on the far side of the bridge, the rogue had either bargained with them or snuck past somehow.

Well, waiting around and licking his wounded pride weren't going to get him back to that fishing quest.

He jogged through a route he was beginning to know too well for his liking.

ZIGGURAT

JUNGLE

GOBO CAMP

JUNGLE

ROPE BRIDGE

KAWAIIAN ISLANDS

DOCK

"Hello, I'm Debebee," Debby-B informed him as if they'd never met. "Would you like passage to the mainland?"

"Is it free? Have I already paid you once?"

"Yes, and yes."

"Then let's go!"

He hopped aboard the raft, and off it whisked him. The Spire of Fate glowered down at him the whole way, impossibly high, impossibly far off, promising challenges that made his quest to collect fish from a placid reef look pathetically easy.

LOOKMANO DOCK

Betty-D was waiting for him. "Hello, I'm Bededee. Welcome to the mainland. If you ever get homesick for the Kawaiian Islands, I can send you back."

He pointed a finger her way. "I will keep that in mind."

Hustling down the sand, he heard Betty-D repeat her greeting. "Hello, I'm Bededee. Welcome to the mainland. If you ever get homesick for the Kawaiian Islands, I can send you back."

Connor stopped and turned.

It was the rogue. She'd arrived right behind him. Had she suffered the same fate? If so, why hadn't he seen her on the other end of the raft ride?

The simplistic answer was that she was a rogue. NOT seeing one was hardly newsworthy, let alone a mystery. But then why could he spot her so easily now? Connor suspected that there were multiple instances of the same starting zone, and it was exclusive to each player. Made sense. Wouldn't do to have your noobs getting in the way of one another's tutorials.

On a whim, and realizing that if this game was multiplayer, it might also be cooperative, he waited for her at the end of the dock. She pulled up short of him, clasped her hands in front of her, and bowed.

Role-playing, it seemed. He inclined his head in acknowledgment of her apology.

"Hello, I'm Bededee. Welcome to the mainland. If you ever get homesick for the Kawaiian Islands, I can send you back."

The monk came pelting down the dock. When he got to them, he planted a foot and performed an acrobatic leap over Connor and the rogue, then kept right on going, tearing up the beach, arms extended like an airplane, swerving playfully as he shrank into the distance.

Beside him, the rogue chuckled silently.

"Hello, I'm Bededee. Welcome to the mainland. If you ever get homesick for the Kawaiian Islands, I can send you back."

Connor blinked. Who else was there?

A Friar Tuck-looking dude, portly and bald, wearing the Cleric outfit from the selection screen, ambled up to them. He nodded to each with a hand over his heart, then squeezed past. He headed south, in the direction of Needeep's fishing fiasco.

"Hello, I'm Bededee. Welcome to the mainland. If you ever get homesick for the Kawaiian Islands, I can send you back."

A woman in the Archer uniform stormed up, drew an arrow, stared the rogue down, and drew the sharpened tip along her own throat in a clear gesture indicating a threat. But anyone who'd shoulder their way past rather than engage must have already discovered that there was no player-versus-player damage enabled in this game.

Given that there were six of them waiting outside the doors to Anachronism Interactive every morning, Connor finally caught on, and his surprise was minimal when, yet again, he heard the now-familiar, "Hello, I'm Bededee. Welcome to the mainland. If you ever get homesick for the Kawaiian Islands, I can send you back."

The wizard's outfit in *his* version of the character creator had looked nothing like the low-cut, slinky evening gown being displayed on the exaggerated mannequin of an avatar. Tall, blonde, and with breasts that must have accounted for a third of her body mass, Connor decided emphatically that both this wizard and the rogue were dudes out in meatspace.

In fact, he put in his guess that he was practically the *only* one playing his gender here. He was putting that bet in right now. The archer, he suspected, really was one of the women. He couldn't tell yet whether the monk or the cleric was the other.

Had Anachronism Interactive railroaded them into each picking a different class somehow? Had he merely gotten into the creator first, and therefore had the most options? If he'd dawdled, would he have seen classes gray out, one by one, as unavailable? Or had their methods been more subtle?

After all, these people had spent weeks already peering into six brains. Anachronism Interactive probably knew the participants in their study better than they knew themselves.

Whatever the case, there were now six of them on the mainland.

Actually, now that he thought of it, Connor realized what happened.

He laughed out loud, and when the rogue shot him a dirty look, he explained as best he could.

"You..." He pointed to her. "Killed..." Connor stuck out his tongue and grabbed his throat in both hands. "Me..." He pointed to himself, then to her. "...and you." He pointed four more times, not specifically anywhere but generally off in the directions the others had scattered. "And all of them too." Then he grinned.

The rogue nodded along, then chuckled silently and gave a shrug.

Connor gestured with a jerk of his head, then ventured over to the place where they'd last entered the water.

The rogue came along, amiable, with no sign of ulterior motives.

...just like a rogue *would*, he supposed.

Steeling himself for a challenge, Connor equipped his Fishing Net and waded into the water. When it got too deep, he began to swim, staying at the surface where he could breathe. Rather than do his traveling underwater like a SCUBA diver, he made his way to a spot above the reef's location before venturing downward.

WATERY REEF

The water felt more dangerous than before, the wonders more exotic for their lack of open welcome. This was a hidden world, and he was an intruder here. As he angled downward, Connor glanced back to see the rogue right behind him.

Whether the fish would be there for both of them or whether they'd be competing, he just wanted to check the viability of this strategy. The reef was uneven, irregular, following the erratic terrain of the ocean floor. The place he'd gone down wasn't the shallowest part of the reef.

The breath meter wasn't demarcated at all. There was no clear-cut warning signal at the 50 percent mark. Once it got to what Connor eyeballed at about 60 percent, he turned around, reef just out of reach and Spiny Reef Fish tantalizingly close to netting range.

He tried to grab the rogue on his way up to warn her not to continue. But she was agile as ever and easily evaded his grasp.

Connor broke the surface with a fraction of breath remaining.

The rogue didn't come back up.

He swam ashore and watched the docks.

LOOKMANO SANDS.

Though he'd been fully submerged, Connor exited the water bone dry. Rather than a bug, he considered that a perk. And despite finding his armor neither too hot beneath the tropical sun nor prone to trapping sand against his skin, he placed the Battered Armor into his inventory and lay back in the sand to wait.

In the distance, he spotted a tiny figure sprinting down the dock.

The rogue returned, walking up to him on the beach and standing over him, arms crossed.

Connor put up his hands in an exaggerated shrug. Not like he didn't try to warn her.

She put up one finger. An idea?

She pointed first to him, then to the water.

Yeah. They could try again. There were probably a few spots where the reef was close enough to the surface to make the round trip.

Into the water they both headed.

She led the way. Connor followed; after all, she'd gotten a better look than him, and at the cost of her life. When they dove, the rogue took him by the hand. Kicking and a little help from their free hands kept them descending at a rate that felt the same as before.

Partway down, and with plenty of breath left in his meter, the rogue tugged him to an underwater halt.

Still not wearing his armor, she pulled him against her. Her lips found his.

THIS wasn't on his list of expectations at all.

Realizing that this was neither the time nor the place for romance, he kept kissing her all the while trying to break free of her wrestling hold.

Breath meters dwindled.

With his superior strength, Connor was able pull away despite a disadvantageous leverage situation. But the damage was done.

His breath meter was a shambles.

As the pair parted, the rogue clenched her fists and shook them in frustration. He managed to catch a quick glimpse of her beautiful, digitally rendered features before she pulled up the mask, flipped him off with both hands, and the two of them drowned together.

`VILLAGE`

Connor accepted his deal. With nothing to lose, and no real option to refuse, it was getting to be a reflex, like clicking Accept on an End User License Agreement he'd never so much as skimmed.

`ZIGGURAT`

`JUNGLE`

`GOBO CAMP`

`JUNGLE`

`ROPE BRIDGE`

`KAWAIIAN ISLANDS`

`DOCK`

"Hello, I'm Debebee. Would—"

"Yes, bring me to the mainland," Connor cut in impatiently.

LOOKMANO DOCK

"Hello, I'm Bededee. Welcome to the mainland. If you ever get homesick—"

"Nope. I'm good. Thanks."

LOOKMANO SANDS

From behind him, he heard, "Hello, I'm Bededee. Welcome to the mainland. If you ever get homesick for the Kawaiian Islands, I can send you back." The rogue was back and sprinting to catch up to him.

Connor put up his hands. No harm, no foul. Everyone here was new at this. Then, hoping he wasn't out of line here, and that whoever was behind this avatar didn't recognize him either, he smirked seductively at her.

She slapped him.

There was no damage, but the message was clear, if confusing.

Pulling down her mask, the rogue pantomimed exaggerated breathing. She pointed from her open mouth to him. Then she breathed out, pointed to him again, then pointed into her mouth and breathed in.

What was she getting at?

Oh.

Buddy breathing.

Connor nodded his understanding, and the rogue threw up her hands in sarcastic exultation.

It was worth a try.

The developers had forgotten to make holding your breath a thing. He didn't like the odds of them having inserted a mechanic for refilling someone else's breath meter underwater, but he could also think of less fun theories to test.

The pair made their way out into the water, roughly to the

same spot as last time. Diving in tandem, they got their breath meters about a quarter of the way down before the rogue embraced him again.

Lips locked, he waited for her to breathe extra air into his lungs. If he'd understood the charades properly, she'd been offering to give air, not asking him for his.

The breath meter continued its steady decline. Connor shook his head, breaking their joining.

They raced back to the surface. Down the beach, a pair of the other players sat in the sand. A third beckoned to them before joining the sitting two. Curious and a little frustrated, Connor swam back to find out what was going on, rogue close on his kicking heels.

On the shore, the cleric, archer, and wizard were sitting cross-legged, arms folded, backs to the water.

The archer pointed to a spot at the end of the line.

Connor shrugged.

Scowling, the archer pointed again, more emphatically.

When Connor decided he wasn't going along with whatever nonsense these three were up to and turned to head back to the water, the archer leaped up and grabbed him by the wrist. She pointed out to the water, then wagged a scolding finger, then pointed to the line in the sand once again before retaking her seat.

The rogue caught on about the same time as he did.

They were holding a protest.

Players, as employees of this game, were taking a labor action against this bullshit quest.

Connor could get on board with that. He sat next to them and crossed both his legs and his arms.

The monk, the lone missing member of the testing team, zoomed past, evading the archer's attempt to convey their mission before even getting a chance to hear it.

Many minutes later, the monk showed up again from the direction of the dock. Laughing, he vaulted over the line of protesting players and jetted out to sea.

The next time the monk appeared, he cast the group a puzzled look before heading into the water yet again. However, this time, triumphant, the monk emerged from the water with a fish and sprinted off in the direction of Needeep.

Connor's resolve faltered.

This quest *was* possible, even if maybe it was a pain in the ass. As players, wasn't it *their* job to solve the puzzles, not demand they be made easier?

When the monk returned, the smug look in his face said it all. The five of them on the beach watched over their shoulders as the monk disappeared beneath the waves.

Several minutes later, he once more returned via the dock. This time, the monk joined their sit-in.

With no access to clocks and the sun unmoving in the sky, it was impossible to do more than guess at the time that passed. An hour, maybe?

But if time was wasting, it was Anachronism Interactive that needed to bend. They were the ones wasting valuable testing time. They'd allotted a week, and this day had to be winding down. Connor expected to find either that he was starving from skipping lunch or that Kelli had force-fed him without interrupting his gaming.

One thing was clear. These players were done being played with.

Without explanation or preamble, six potion vials appeared, one in front of each of them.

Connor snatched his up immediately. The competitor in him prodded him to take as many as he could get his hands on, but after this show of unity, he couldn't break the implied trust that had formed.

He brought the vial to his lips but didn't drink.

The monk downed his.

So did the cleric.

Neither looked any worse for wear.

Connor chugged his in one go; it tasted like nothing. Actually, it tasted like a fresh breeze, a smell more than a flavor.

But he also saw a little notification.

`WATER BREATHING: 60m`

Good enough. There was no way gathering 5 fish could take *that* long. He joined the others in a headlong race to the reef.

CHAPTER 17
UNDER THE SEA

CONNOR GOT his breath meter back. Before, it slipped away perilously, second by second, like sand through an hourglass representing how long until a watery death. Now, he remained full as he paddled out into the deeper ocean.

WATERY REEF

The others fanned out. Each had their own net. Spiny Reef Fish abounded, but if he had to make a quick guess, there weren't thirty around here. Even before he got to the reef itself, the monk and archer were headed back the other way, nets laden with their initial catches.

Or, in the monk's case, at least his second.

Connor scanned the waters just above the reef. He actually noticed as one of the Spiny Reef Fish spawned. Ready on the proverbial trigger, he launched his net immediately.

The fish remained in the net as he towed it back to shore.

LOOKMANO SANDS

As soon as his feet could reach the sand, Connor bounded and splashed through the surf, his breath meter vanished as he sucked in honest-to-goodness artificial air. He raced past the docks without making the detour. He also noted that he didn't seem slowed at all by running in sand. That felt like an oversight.

REPORT BUG

"Sand doesn't slow down movement. Go to any beach. You'll see what I mean."

While he hadn't hung out with the devs, he'd interacted with enough of them in passing that he granted the possibility that none had ever been outdoors recreationally.

When Connor made it back to Needeep, the fisherman grinned. "Thank you, hero. This will help feed my family."

Connor gave a glance up the beach beyond the fisherman, where the cliffs ran into the sea, blocking overland travel, and back toward the docks. There was no sign of any actual place to live around here.

But his Spiny Reef Fish vanished, and Connor checked his progress.

BRING SPINY REEF FISH TO NEEDEEP: 1/5

Hell, yes! Finally. Back on the RPG noob train.

Jogging the whole way, Connor made it back to his entry point to the water, then dove in once more.

WATERY REEF

The other players had spread out, both in terms of geography as well as pace. Focused on his own fishing and running, he lost track of who might have gone back while he was away. Now that he considered it, neither the monk nor the archer had passed him by on the way here. With a head start, they should have both reached Needeep before him. But he hadn't crossed paths with either of them headed back for a second round.

Was there something he was missing?

Even underwater, Connor slapped himself in the forehead. Yes. Yes, he was. There was perfectly serviceable ocean right where Needeep was standing. The reef stretched beyond sight into the undersea gloom in both directions. It stood to reason that the incompetent fisherman was a clue, not just a net dispenser and quest giver.

Connor stuck around to snare one more Spiny Reef Fish, then headed back.

LOOKMANO SANDS

He watched both directions, spotting the rogue emerging from the water behind him. She was carrying four Spiny Reef Fish, each in their own net.

Where had she gotten extra nets?

Connor hadn't considered asking for more. Maybe he had a shitload of them and either sold them or could be pickpocketed.

Whatever the case, Connor figured out in a hurry that he was behind the game playing this the slow and steady way.

When Connor made it back to Needeep, the fisherman grinned, same as before. "Thank you, hero. This will help feed my family."

BRING SPINY REEF FISH TO NEEDEEP: 2/5

"I want more nets."

"If you lose your net, I can give you a replacement."

Connor didn't have time for this crap. Whether it had been stated explicitly or not, there was a race going on, and while winning might have been off the table, he was determined not to come in last place.

He drew his sword.

"Give me two more nets or I gut you like a fish, Needeep."

RECEIVED: FISHING NET (2X)

The rogue jogged up behind him, noticed Connor with his sword drawn, and rolled her eyes. The fish all disappeared from her nets. Then, she cast all of her nets onto the sand. When she held out a hand, Needeep smiled and nodded.

"Of course, here you go."

A net appeared in the rogue's hand. She threw that one on the ground and held her hand out once more.

"Of course, here you go."

A net appeared in the rogue's hand. She tossed that one aside as well.

"Of course, here you go."

A net appeared in the rogue's hand.

She patted Connor on the cheek, then ran and dove into the water.

Had... had she miscounted or something? He assumed that after bringing back one, she'd figured out how to garner additional nets, then went back for four more. Just as he'd done on his second trip, only needing two more nets to take three fish at once.

There was only one way to find out what she was up to.

Wading back out to sea, Connor sought out his remaining three Spiny Reef Fish right in front of Needeep's fishing spot.

WATERY REEF

There was one!

He snagged it with a disheartening lack of competition. Switching nets, two more came just as easily.

LOOKMANO SANDS

Connor arrived back at the fisherman just as the cleric was toddling up from the northern end of the beach, carrying a single fish. He waited, letting the friar go first. "Thank you, hero. This will help feed my family."

When the cleric turned around and headed back down the beach, Connor grabbed him.

He pointed to the water right beside them.

The cleric blinked a few times. Then he held still. Then his shoulders slumped.

"Yeah, buddy. Took me a bit, too."

The cleric marched off into the ocean.

Shaking his head at the poor guy, Connor turned in a Spiny Reef Fish.

"Thank you, hero. This will help feed my family."

BRING SPINY REEF FISH TO NEEDEEP: 3/5

He produced another, which Needeep took without fuss.

"Thank you, hero. This will help feed my family."

BRING SPINY REEF FISH TO NEEDEEP: 4/5

Connor handed over his final fish.

"Thank you, hero. This will help feed my family."

BRING SPINY REEF FISH TO NEEDEEP: COMPLETE

"What now, Needeep old pal? Sorry about the sword, earlier."

RECEIVED: XPOT

"Sweet." Just as he was about to drink it, Connor questioned why that was his reaction.

Any XP he gained now was just going on the chopping block for the next time he died. The potion bottle had no indication of denomination to suggest how much XP he'd get, and the odds that it was a full level on its own seemed remote. In fact, a new strategy began to form in Connor's mind.

This wasn't a race in terms of distance or speed.

If anything, it would be a race to victory.

Victory came through power, strategy, and gear.

XP was power.

If he had to bet, he'd wager that the others were all going to drink their XPOTs the moment they received them. But why not give XP for quests rather than this clunky intermediary step?

Control.

Connor would control when he got his XP. Right now, his life was cheap. He could take risks, sacrifice himself to scout dangerous areas, rush headlong into battle to take out a key objective, or brave ferocious traps for treasures he might only survive to hold for mere moments before death.

But his inventory was a safe place, at least thus far. Until he had reason to believe otherwise, he'd assume that his inventory was a vault where his shit—including any XPOTs that wouldn't level him up—would remain safe.

"Where do I go next, Needeep? Any advice?"

"I won't go in the water anymore. Not after the cave I found down there. Out beyond the reef, you'll find the entrance. Here, take this. You'll need it."

RECEIVED: WATER BREATHING POTION

On a whim, Connor placed his potion on the ground. "I lost my water breathing potion. Can I have another?"

"Of course, here you go."

RECEIVED: WATER BREATHING POTION

Cackling like a mad scientist, Connor could only hope there was a vendor somewhere later in the game where he could resell these.

As he went into the water to check out the cave, Connor quaffed one of the potions to reset the duration of his water breathing, then checked his Quest Journal and Inventory.

QUEST JOURNAL

SLAY THE MOUNTAIN LORD FOR ELDER LOHDOH: 0/1

EXPLORE THE UNDERSEA CAVE: 0/1

INVENTORY

10 COINS

2 YELLOW GOBO DAGGER

FISHING NET (5X)

XPOT

WATER BREATHING POTION (98X)

CHAPTER 18
UNDERSEA CAVE

CONNOR SWAM OUT with utter confidence. He regretted that confidence the moment he identified it. Paranoia was what kept an adventurer safe, not certitude. Right then and there, he made himself a promise.

He was always going to pay attention to his surroundings. He was always going to assume enemies had a trick or a trap waiting to spoil an easy-looking fight. He was never going to trust that his fellow players had his best interests at heart.

OK, maybe that was three promises, and maybe that wasn't a long enough list. But the in-game swimming was still a little weird and unfamiliar, and it took a moderate amount of his concentration, especially since Needeep hadn't been too specific in his directions.

As it turned out, Needeep hadn't needed to be.

Beyond the reef, the continental shelf dropped off. A yawning abyss opened up, too deep by far to fathom. The 98 water breathing potions in his inventory might not be enough to travel to the bottom.

Or the bottom could have been just out of view, a hard stop rendered invisible by lighting trickery.

Nevertheless, once Connor was over that abyss, a cavern

gaped in the undersea cliff face that it exposed. Down he went, then reversed his angle and headed inland, albeit from what he estimated was sixty or eighty feet below sea level.

With no light source, there was still enough ambient illumination—from what source, who could tell?—to make out the circular tunnel's natural rock walls.

Correction: the digital simulation of natural cavern walls. Everything was still just a little too uniform, too patterned, too stock image for his liking. But unlike some other parts of the game so far, at least there was *some* texture applied.

Inward and under, Connor swam.

He noted a gradual upward angling to the tunnel but couldn't judge the distance traveled to wonder where it might come up.

Because UP was clearly where this was headed.

Connor broke the surface of an underground pond. Instinctively, he shook his head to get water and wet hair out of his eyes. But, of course, there was neither. His plate helmet hadn't hindered his swimming at all, and any part of him out of the water was perfectly dry.

The pond took up maybe a tenth of an enormous cavern. As he swam to the steep edge and climbed out, he noticed that four of his fellow players were already present, loitering not far from the pond. All but the cleric had reached this point ahead of him.

Given the general gung-ho attitude getting to this point, he suspected they had reasons beyond wanting to stick together to be waiting for him.

UNDERSEA CAVE

As soon as he had both feet solidly on the cavern floor, his quest journal prompted an in-your-face update.

EXPLORE THE UNDERSEA CAVE: COMPLETE

RECEIVED: XPOT

Another quest jumped right in behind it.

SLAY THE SEA FROG: 0/1

Sea Frog? Connor had never heard of one. With a 0/1, he assumed it had to be a badass critter, not something to farm in droves. If four other players were lingering here awaiting backup, he updated that assessment to *major* badass.

It would take a while getting back here, but it wasn't the worst trip in the world. With a fresh batch of XPOTs in his inventory and no XP so far this level (that he hadn't already lost), Connor could afford to explore.

Most of the cavern was cast in gloom. They could see to the far side, but the terrain was so shadowy and cluttered with stalagmites that ambushes were almost a given.

Connor sized up his capricious companions, clustered together like the nerdy kids invited to a party by accident.

He realized that most of them had probably already chugged down not only their XPOT from Needeep, but the one for exploring this cave, too.

Connor stood before them, saluted, then drew his Bamboo Sword and headed off to see what this Sea Frog at least looked like.

RIIIIIBBBBBBBBBBIIIIIITTTTT!!!!!

The cavern shook. Connor felt the vibrations through his feet and up into his chest.

Instinct and his new rules told him to beat a hasty retreat. But he literally had nothing to lose except the time it would take to trek back here, plus a water breathing potion he could replace any time from Needeep.

Connor crept closer.

Stealth would never be his forte. Plate armor made its own noise no matter how slowly and carefully he moved around inside it.

In the shadows of a muddy depression at the cavern's far

side, Connor got his first glimpse of the Sea Frog. It had to have been twenty feet tall and roughly the same in all directions. Bulbous eyes jutted from its head. Webbed feet supported its bulk. The wide mouth was surely large enough to swallow a human whole.

But the scattered fish bones all around its lair suggested that the Sea Frog preferred smaller fare.

Rather than gawk at the monster, Connor scanned the area around it. Two elements stuck out. One was a stereotypical treasure chest on the far side of it. And right beside that chest, a crevice sized for transit by adventurers.

The way out.

The reward for defeating it.

This was Dungeon Design 101, except they skipped right to a boss encounter.

Huffing and puffing heralded the arrival of the cleric. He ignored the frantic entreaties of the cowardly four and ambled ahead, not to join Connor but to bludgeon this creature to death with his mace.

RIIIIIBBBBBBBBBBIIIIITTTTT!!!!!

Combat music floated into the air, the kind you'd expect from a cheap mobile game and possibly downloaded the same place overseas shovelware developers got theirs. But, the peppy, brassy soundtrack got Connor's blood pumping just a little before the fight ended.

A tongue shot out. The cleric couldn't avoid it. Limbs flailing and issuing a silent scream, he was pulled through the air and into the creature's mouth.

He didn't come back out.

Well, so much for ideas of a frontal assault. The only way *that* tactic might work was if the frog could die from overeating.

There had to be a trick to this thing.

A hidden weak spot...

A strange substance or item it was vulnerable to...

Some kind of cinematic cut scene with a deus ex machina...

The last one had the kernel of a plan nestled into it. Not that Connor expected Needeep to swoop in at the last second with an enormous net to capture the beast. But something dramatic, something over the top.

The cleric emerged from the pond once again. Connor hadn't been paying attention to how long his musings had lasted, but it had been long enough for him to run and swim all the way back from the Kawaiian Islands.

Rather than rush back in—which Connor would have considered both good data *and* good comedy—this time the cleric hung back with the others.

Wait. Not ALL the others.

Where was the rogue?

Four players lingered near the pond, carrying on a bizarre conversation in pantomime. Actually, more like a heated argument.

Connor couldn't concentrate on figuring out what they were trying to hash out back there. He needed to figure out what that rogue was up to. She'd played ball when it came to figuring out the fishing puzzle. She'd even shared her item duplication hack. But this was a clear chance for an enterprising stealth class to take an insurmountable lead.

It might take hours to solve how to kill this Sea Frog.

It might take next to no effort at all to sneak past it, were one to be naturally inclined toward stealth.

Connor crept closer, aware that he was a scarecrow made of toasters when it came to keeping quiet.

The Sea Frog perked up. Those bulging eyes swiveled in his direction.

Connor took cover behind one of the stalagmites, and the ginormous tongue of the Sea Frog slammed into the rock.

He spared a glance back, looking to see if he had backup here. When he noted that his fellow players were about to use him as a distraction to circle around the Sea Frog and make it to both the treasure chest and the exit, he did the only thing he could think of.

Without so much as drawing his blade, Connor broke into a sprint to head off his companions.

RIIIIIBBBBBBBBBBBIIIIITTTTTT!!!!!

The Sea Frog was no dumb combatant. Whatever Isaac and Kelli and the rest of them were cooking up, they'd managed to teach this frog the field-covering skills of an NFL safety. It leaped into the air and landed atop both the archer and monk.

A tongue darted from its huge mouth, and the next thing Connor knew, he was airborne and about to be swallowed.

Mercifully, the familiar gray of the Kawaiian Islands village graveyard greeted him before he got the full experience of being frog food.

"Greetings, hero," Kelindra said to him. "You have died. Not every battle can be won with might alone. Will you pay the price to—?"

"Yes."

He had no time for chitchat.

VILLAGE

JUNGLE

ZIGGURAT

GOBO CAMP

ROPE BRIDGE

JUNGLE

KAWAIIAN ISLANDS

DOCK

"Would you like passage to the mainland?"

"Yes."

"Have a safe trip!"

WADDAYA SEA

LOOKMANO SANDS

LOOKMANO DOCK

"Hello, I'm Bededee. Welcome to the mainland. If you ever get homesick for the Kawaiian Islands, I can send you back."

"Nah, I'm good."

Connor slurped down a water breathing potion. Realizing that heading all the way down to the sands was a waste of energy, he dove right off the side of the dock and into the water.

WATERY REEF

UNDERSEA CAVE

He arrived back to find the rogue waiting with her ninja mask pulled down and an amused smirk on her face. She gave him two thumbs up.

When the rest of the players filtered back, the fingers they lifted in his direction were less approving. He flipped them off right back. HE wasn't going to be anyone's bait. This wasn't a team sport, best anyone had told him. Any plan that left him behind was a plan he'd do anything in his power to thwart.

A new planning session ensued once tempers cooled.

Their rogue hadn't been hiding to sneak past the Sea Frog. She'd been scouting. And unlike Connor, she'd done it without getting eaten.

She pointed out a stalactite that looked unstable. Using her dagger as a prop, she proposed a plan. Someone would have to lure the Sea Frog to a spot beneath the deadly stalactite. Then they'd have to get it to shake the ground while everyone used every ranged attack at their disposal, combined with the cavern-shaking jump, to knock the stony spear loose.

As the pointing and gesturing debate turned to the subject of who would be their bullfrog-fighter, minus the red cape, all eyes turned toward Connor.

The rogue pantomimed throwing her daggers. The wizard

conjured sparkles from her fingers. The cleric demonstrated a glow of his hand and pointed to indicate he had a ranged attack as well. The archer didn't need to demonstrate that she had ranged attacks.

Connor, for his part, pointed an accusing finger at the monk, who mirrored the gesture.

No one was taking his side.

Fine. If he couldn't convince someone else to die for this ill-fated mission, he could at least propose an alternative.

He threw his Fishing Net down in front of everyone.

Now all the predatory glares in Connor's direction turned quizzical.

This wasn't rocket science. If that Sea Frog ate Spiny Reef Fish—and judging by the piles of bones, it loved the damn things—then it stood to reason that was the way to lure it anywhere. Plus, it fit thematically with the quest they'd just finished.

How many fish would it take to grab the Sea Frog's attention? There was only one way to find out.

The six of them swam back down the tunnel and out into the open sea.

WATERY REEF

Connor had five nets, including the one snagged back from the cave floor and the ones the rogue had discarded to demonstrate the item duping exploit she'd discovered.

Catching Spiny Reef Fish was pretty damn easy by now.

Before long, they were all swimming back up the tunnel, laden with frog chow.

UNDERSEA CAVE

Connor peeked above the water's surface, hoping the frog either wasn't smart enough or wasn't programmed to lie in wait for them.

It wasn't.

He climbed out of the water, beckoning for the others to follow him.

They all tossed their catch down beneath the precarious spear of stone.

When Connor tried to join the others in retreating to the dubious safety of the pond's vicinity, the archer gave him a shove back in the other direction.

"Fine," he told her, even though he knew none of the others could understand, or even hear, him. He stood behind the offering to the god of croaking, cupped his hands to his mouth, and bellowed, "HEY, SEA FROG! COME GRAB A DELICIOUS DINNER, ON US!"

RIIIIIBBBBBBBBBBBIIIIITTTTT!!!!!

The cavern shook, but Connor held his ground. After all, he needed the Sea Frog in a particular spot, and drawing the thing's attention *away* from that spot by fleeing wasn't going to help the plan.

The Sea Frog leaped.

It landed right where it was supposed to. The earthquake from its impact caused a fine mist of gravel to rain down on Connor.

From the safety of the shadows around the pond, the other players opened fire.

He couldn't see damage numbers for whatever they were doing. But the stalactite cracked.

The Sea Frog, smarter by far than its terrestrial brethren, realized something was amiss.

RIIIIIBBBBBBBBBBBIIIIITTTTT!!!!!

It lashed out with its tongue, blaming Connor for the commotion.

OK. It wasn't a LOT smarter than regular frogs.

The stalactite crashed down, push-pinning the Sea Frog to the cavern floor.

Seconds later, the corpse disappeared.

1200 XP

Hell yeah!

He checked, and the response was expected.

XP: 1200/2000

Given the value of the first XPOT, Connor risked it.

He quaffed another.

600 XP

And another.

800 XP

OK. Maybe those would be mysteries until consumed. Maybe it was random. Maybe the game decided when a player picked it up. Without further testing, he'd have to expect a little unpredictability.

XP: 600/4000

A golden swirl surrounded him as a majestic gong rang.

>>>LEVEL UP!!!<<<

YOU GAIN

2 ATTACK

3 DEFENSE

8 HP

0 MP

1 SKILL CHOICE

Before he made his selection, Connor tried to check his character stats, but the skill selection blocked his access.

He had four options.

SHIELD SPECIALIST

DISARMING ATTACK

OK, two reruns there, but there were also...

CHARGE

PARRY

He examined the latter two.

CHARGE - Close the distance to a target in the blink of an eye. Can be combined with additional skills to deal increased damage.

PARRY - Temporarily gain Defense equal to your Attack. Can be combined with additional skills to unlock counterattacks.

Unlike his first batch of skills, this was less of a clear-cut choice, given his play style. Charging was kind of his zug-zug playstyle, great for unthinkingly bashing stuff into paste. That kind of setup worked best in games where gear and character builds could overpower game mechanics.

On the other hand, Parry sounded like a great way to combine a high-attack build with some survivability. He was torn between the two, but since he was seeing Shield Specialist and Disarming Attack again, he took it on faith that he'd get another crack at whatever he didn't pick.

Charge might have been vague about its actual implementation, but he couldn't resist.

The skill highlighted in green, and another prompt came up.

SELECT A SKILL TO FLOAT TO YOUR NEXT SELECTION. OTHER CHOICES WILL NOT BE OFFERED AGAIN.

This was definitely the easier choice. He tapped Parry, then hurriedly checked on his new overall stats.

CHARACTER STATS:

NAME: Connor TITLE: None

CLASS: Knight LEVEL: 3

HP: 21 MP: 0 ATK: 5 DEF: 6

Sweet. Just as he dismissed that view, he realized he was alone in the cavern.

Shit. He'd been so freaking proud of himself for stockpiling those XPOTS, and being the only one to level, that he hadn't even noticed the other players moving on without him.

Not that he blamed them. Ditching a friend was such a Level 2 move.

Jogging to the treasure chest triggered another message.

SLAY THE SEA FROG: COMPLETE

CHOOSE YOUR REWARD

When he opened the chest, two options floated up, ephemeral and insubstantial.

One was a silvery suit of armor. The other, a similar-looking sword.

"I'm offense. Defense will catch up later."

He reached out and took hold of a sword that turned solid and hefty in his grasp.

RECEIVED: STEEL SWORD

He checked again, and his ATK stat had gone up to 7.

Ready to kick ass, he headed into the crevice to catch up with his low-level minions.

CHAPTER 19
MYSTERY PUN

THE CREVICE WAS narrow enough that Connor had to shuffle along sideways. He did so with his new Steel Sword leading. The passage also twisted and turned, never allowing him to see more than a few feet in front of him. Anything could have lurked ahead, just out of view, silent, deadly, already having devoured the others. He refused to creep and tiptoe. His overflowing XP from reaching 3rd level was at risk, but that was all.

That, and an increasingly long run back to this point.

TWISTING PASSAGE

A gentle upward slope suggested that he was returning to the surface, since he didn't feel like he'd traveled far enough laterally to be underneath the Spire of Fate just yet.

Connor was proved right when he exited a cave into a primitive forest.

And by primitive, he didn't mean that there were village huts or pre-industrial societies. The trees all resembled Christmas trees drawn by grade schoolers. Conical evergreens with straight brown trunks, they varied only in size. Clearly, this zone hadn't been a priority for the design team. When an elaborately rendered name popped up, he was even *more* convinced that it had been neglected across the board at Anachronism Interactive.

(FOREST PUN)

Not Forest of Puns, though that would have been campy and lame. Not even just Forest Pun like it was a name. They'd actually left the zone name as a parenthetical reference, plainly marking it for naming later in the process. Imagine a company that purported to design entire worlds failing at coming up with even a temporary name for a forest.

If this place lasted to release unchanged, it would crawl beneath the already low-low bar of "Somehow, Palpatine returned" for sheer studio laziness.

Connor could have come up with decent, workable names right now, off the top of his head.

In fact, this was so egregious an offense that this HAD to qualify.

REPORT BUG

"This zone didn't get a name. If you're looking for some decent placeholders what about... FOREST FORTY-TREES, GREEN WOOD, or, if you're looking to mix a classic Star Trek and in-house personnel jokes, what about FOREST D'KELLI? Seriously, buy me dinner tonight, and I'll help you name whatever shit you've got left over."

Rant over, he set about discovering what was new and dangerous about (Forest Pun).

First off, he noticed the wide-open space. Trees towered over him, trunks as wide as his shoulders, but there was no underbrush, and giant trees meant commensurately giant spaces between trunks. There wasn't even grass. The ground beneath Connor's feet was just green, like someone had spray-painted dirt. Nice, uniform coat if they had, with no signs of drips or gaps, no variation in color or texture.

Reminding himself to remain paranoid at all times, Connor

reasoned that tree trunks as wide as him could easily hide someone his size. He didn't approach any of them, taking the wide spaces between as he explored on foot, sword at the ready, eager to try out his new Charge skill at the first opportunity.

In the distance, he heard the twang of a bow string. No whoosh of an arrow followed, and he kind of remembered the archer's arrows making a whoosh when she loosed them. That either meant she was shooting in some other direction or that there was a ranged enemy around with a half-assed soundboard of combat effects. Given that he was wandering through (Forest Pun), Connor actually weighed the latter more heavily.

However, when the ambush came, it was spears, not arrows that flew his way.

One of the spears glanced off his armor.

0

Another struck him square in the chest.

1

Rather than stick into him or even drop to the green floor of the forest, the thrown spear merely vanished.

He was still fine. He had to assume both that the spear damage was variable *and* that his DEF was right around their ATK to be intermittently canceling it all out.

A quick scan of his surroundings located the throwers.

Two Green Gobos poked their heads out from behind the cover of a single tree, one to the left side, the other to the right.

Connor timed it, waiting for the next throw.

Unsure how to specifically activate the talent, he broke into a sprint and bellowed a wordless war cry.

"Aaaaaaaaah!"

The game world became a blur. It was like jumping to hyperspace as everything stretched and snapped past him. A fraction of a second later, he was standing in front of one of the

Green Gobos, sword still upraised for a strike he hadn't been expecting to become an option so quickly.

Down came his Steel Sword.

10

The Green Gobo reeled.

Then, it fell over.

50 XP

Connor noticed the dagger stuck in the creature's back.

Its companion used its own spear as a melee weapon. Connor had enough practice by now that he deflected the blow easily. It might not have carried any special game effects that the Parry skill might have afforded, but he could at least duel the thing to a standstill. This one was more adept than its Red Gobo cousins, but this was no longer the Connor that had fought Red Gobos.

In fact, whether it was his level, his new sword, or just putting in some reps, the combat was feeling more fluid and responsive.

He struck a blow right into the Green Gobo's chest.

10

After a slight delay, that one fell over, too.

Again, with a dagger in its back.

50 XP

XP: 700/4000

Farther into the game, the enemies ought to be giving out more XP, not less. The Sea Frog, sure, that was a boss. Couldn't expect fire-hose XP from everything after it. But these weren't worth as much as the Plush Crabs.

Not to him, at least.

Whoever was putting daggers into them was getting a share, he suspected, and that didn't sit well with Connor. Clearly, they were no threat to him. He could bash fragile Green Gobos to pieces all day unless they showed a new trick.

But someone, likely someone who took more damage from them in melee combat, wasn't so keen on earning their own XP. They were leeching off Connor's.

And he had a good idea of who.

The daggers were disappearing, too, which suggested that he couldn't just collect them until the rogue ran out. Either she had an unlimited supply magically, they were returning to her inventory as she used them, or—and Connor credited this one as a long shot—she actually *was* running out of them, and thrown daggers were like bullets: one use only.

Connor surprised the next Green Gobo, hidden behind another tree.

`10`

His swing caught it in the back. The Green Gobo gave a startled yelp and tried to bat a thrown dagger out of the air before being struck in the chest and falling over.

`50 XP`

Quickly, Connor leaned left and right, angling to catch sight of the rogue, to see where she might be hiding. He had a decent idea based on the direction of the incoming dagger, but he failed to spot her.

He'd yet to be offered any perception skills of any sort, and he reckoned that she had some kind of game bonus to stealth.

Connor wandered (Forest Pun). He heard signs of the others now and then, growing more distant. Nothing here suggested a quest. No signs of any creatures other than Green Gobos. Given the name, in particular, this zone felt rushed and unfinished, like they needed a filler between the Undersea Cave and whatever came next and hadn't given it much thought beyond that.

His meandering exploration, just tracing back and forth to fill in his minimap, brought Connor to a cliff. Glancing down, he could see LOOKMANO SANDS and LOOKMANO

DOCK. This was the cliff he couldn't scale from the beach. A wicked smirk crossed his face, and Connor quickly hid it.

He sat down, feet dangling over the edge.

He waited.

And waited.

Eventually, either boredom or curiosity prompted the rogue to join him.

She pulled down her ninja mask, allowing him to witness a placid smile of contentment.

The rogue sidled a little closer, rubbing up against him.

They shared a low-res, digital gaze. She pressed closer against him, feeling more real than she looked.

She tilted her head back and closed her eyes.

Connor put an arm around her...

...and tossed her off the cliff.

Flailing arms and legs quickly gave way to a cat-like crouch and superhero landing on the sand below.

A pair of daggers sailed up at him, both striking true. But they didn't even register as attacks.

Connor stood, gave a duelist's salute with his blade, and set off to find the far end of this no-man's zone.

And for a little while, and for the foreseeable few combats, it would be a no-rogue's zone, too.

Heading in the direction of unexplored minimap, Connor crossed paths with three more Green Gobos, each with a plump 100 XP.

`XP: 1050/4000`

He also discovered that the terrain was turning hill. Not, like, slowly rolling terrain, but like a mogul course on steroids. Each of these hills had a distinct, hard edge where the domed shape gave way to flat forest floor. Trees intersected the hills without being planted atop them, trunks foreshortened and undifferentiated branches looming ominously low.

A growl let him know a new encounter was coming before he saw the foe.

Were four wolves enough to qualify as a pack?

If so, Connor had stumbled into a pack of Snarl Wolves. He knew this by holding out a hand toward them to examine them, just as he had with the class skills. The examine function told him little else, however. So either these creatures were basic bitches (statistically, half of them, anyway), or the examine function wasn't meant to convey useful combat info.

Running from wolves was notoriously a horrible idea. Connor didn't live within a thousand miles of a wolf, and he knew that much. These trees didn't look too climbable to a guy in a suit of armor, either.

That left one clear option.

With 1050 XP on the line, Connor Charged.

"Aaaaaaaaah!"

The forest blurred. He swung his sword.

He missed the timing, chopping a swath of air in front of the Snarl Wolf.

All of them attacked in a coordinated assault.

1

2

2

1

OK. This wasn't the time to be fucking around. With the one nick he'd taken from a Gobo earlier, he was already down to 14/21 HP.

The utility of something like that Parry skill was starting to sound pretty good. Maybe these Anachronism Interactive guys couldn't name shit, but they at least had balanced the class skills with the monsters' abilities.

Next level, he promised himself.

However, now that the world was moving at normal speed,

Connor's growing battle reflexes kicked in. The Snarl Wolves wore no armor, and they were tentative combatants, snarling and nipping, trying to circle around behind him rather than pile on and bury him in fur and fangs.

10

The stricken Snarl Wolf yipped and sprang away, using itself as bait to allow the others to surround him rather than be finished off with another strike or two.

Rather than pursue, Connor whirled and struck that one that came at his blind side.

10

That Snarl Wolf, too, then retreated, leaving Connor to face off against two of the creatures while the other two hung back, lurking, waiting for a weakness to rejoin the fight.

10

They weren't even trying now. A lone, unharmed Snarl Wolf ... well, snarled at him as it backed away.

The forest blurred as Connor charged in. This time, his mid-charge swing struck true when the world slowed back down.

10

Now, all wounded, the pack chose guile over valor and fled.

Nope! Not today!

Again and again the forest blurred. Again and again, Connor struck down Snarl Wolves as they attempted to escape him.

10

150 XP

10

150 XP

10

150 XP

10

150 XP

Just like that, it was over.

XP: 1650/4000

The Snarl Wolves dropped no loot, but the XP was good enough for Connor right now. And so much for that Parry skill. Maybe he'd still grab that next level, but he was *plenty* happy with his choice of charge. He still needed to test its limitations, but for now, it was God Mode as far as he was concerned. Just a shame that his added momentum didn't seem to grant any damage bonuses along with it.

As he continued his sweep of the minimap, Connor didn't find any more monsters to fight. Probably, for lack of anything else to do, the other players had managed an efficient job of wiping out the local ecology.

(Forest Pun) just wasn't interesting enough to bum around waiting for respawns either.

He found a wrought-iron fence, ten feet tall and in a state of disrepair that showed off more artistic effort than the whole rest of the zone. The wizard and archer waited by the lone, arched gate, staring into the foothills beyond.

When he tried to walk past, the archer caught his arm. The wizard shook her head.

Moments later, the rogue joined them. Soon after, the monk and cleric both jogged up to fill out their party.

Connor felt a knot in his guts when he realized why. Out there, among the foothills, shambling humanoid forms teemed. The cleric and monk, it seemed, had learned that the hard way.

As the group's obvious choice as tank, Connor took point. Maybe *this* wasn't the place to be Charging off ahead—or alone.

CHAPTER 20
THE HILLS ARE UNALIVE

A FOG GATHERED AS SOON as Connor crossed through the wrought-iron gate.

UNALIVE HILLS

The name was better than the stupid (Forest Pun) back behind him, but not by a lot. The atmosphere, however, was a huge upgrade.

That fog reduced visibility to just a few yards. Things appeared clearer and at greater distances from outside the zone. That didn't seem right.

REPORT BUG

"Fog in the Unalive Hills doesn't affect visibility from the forest zone."

Checking to see that his companions were keeping up, he spotted the archer, rogue, and cleric each making similar gestures to access their own version of the bug reporter.

Connor smirked when, mere steps later, he got a response.

YOUR FEEDBACK WAS HELPFUL. PLEASE ACCEPT A GIFT.

He tapped the gift icon that appeared.

200 XP.

Nice. Either the payout was tied to character level, zone

level, or number of bugs reported. Otherwise, he supposed, killing monsters would be too much easier than mentioning bugs to use the system.

Groans and rattling bones gave the fog a horror flick menace. His growing stockpile of XP made Connor wary of *its* safety more than his own, but the mortal dread of lurking zombies or skeletons or whatever affected him, nonetheless.

`XP: 1850/4000`

Gotta protect that stash. Another 2150 XP and he could go back to being Mr. Brave. Until then, and especially with a rogue who owed him a little payback, he had to play Mr. Smart for now.

A pair of zombies lurched into view, arms extended, gait shambling, wordless utterances of eternal hunger echoing up from rotted lungs.

He had to imagine most of those details, since these fuckers made Minecraft look like an E3 trailer.

Rather than charge, Connor held up his Steel Sword and waited for the zombies, briefly extending a hand to examine them. All he learned was that their proper name was Rotting Shamblers, and they were undead.

Undead. Nice. Connor had been worried there a minute that *these* zombies were still alive and just a little under the weather. Since none of his abilities had anything to do with undead one way or another, all he knew was he didn't want them hitting him.

A bowstring twanged.

One of the zombies toppled with an arrow in its chest.

He glanced over incredulously at the archer. Either these things were wimpy as hell, or she was packing a cannon.

`10 XP`

Immediately, Connor updated his assessment to the former.

Deciding he could take a risk, he lifted his sword and took a mighty, two-handed hack that split the other zombie down the middle. This was one time he was glad of grainy graphics and half-baked coding. He was spared a gory slurry of zombie guts between striking the thing down and its corpse vanishing.

10 XP

How had the cleric and monk died in this area? Connor's thoughts immediately went to his footing. Were there traps? Cliffs? Magic runes?

The zombies kept coming.

Fast as they came in, the six players struck them down.

10 XP here. 10 XP there. It started adding up to real numbers.

It also started explaining how the two careless players had gotten themselves sent back to the Kawaiian Village.

The zombies were endless.

They came faster than Connor could swing a sword, faster than the archer could fire her bow, faster than the wizard could hurl golf-ball-sized gouts of flame.

Connor took a hit. One of the zombies lunged for his face with gangrenous, yellowed fingernails.

3

Three seemed like a shitload, if not for him, then for the other, less armored players. And they were getting hit here and there, as well.

+3

Connor felt a tingle all through his body as warmth seeped in and restored lost hit points. The cleric, it seemed, was willing to do more than just swing his little mace around.

HP: 14/21

Having not entered the zone at full HP, he beckoned for the cleric to keep the heals coming.

+3

3

3

+3

The cleric kept up but couldn't make headway as the zombies kept coming, harder, faster, thicker, the deeper they ventured into the Unalive Hills.

But all the while, the XP trickled in as Connor and the others blazed a trail through the swarm.

Up and down hillsides they roamed, keeping a general heading straight away from the gates.

If this were the kind of game to hide little Easter eggs around, the outskirts of this zone would be perfect. No one was going to wade through a sea of hungry corpses to look for bonuses.

XP: 2110/4000

XP: 2470/4000

XP: 2800/4000

There was no end in sight. They took a break atop a hill, where the high ground gave them enough of an advantage for the cleric to catch up and top off all their HP totals. Or at least, Connor assumed as much. He put up a hand when he'd been maxed out, letting the cleric know he was good for now. Others took up his signal and used it themselves.

Thus far, they hadn't lost anyone.

Once everyone had reported in that they were full, Connor took the lead. He veered them off course on a hunch. Firmer resistance met them the closer they got to the base of the mountain. And from their hilltop break room, risen above the fog, he could see they were only about halfway there. He needed to get to Level 4 before things got too hairy.

Then he'd feel a lot better about making his way to the mountain.

A gong and a swirl of gold surrounded the wizard. The

rogue clapped silently. Connor gave a sword salute but didn't dare take his eyes off the incoming zombies for longer than that.

For a moment, there were not little balls of fire joining their outgoing damage barrage. The zombies made headway.

3

3

+3

4

Four? Shit. The zombies were getting higher level around this part of the zone. He watched his own XP, wondering if he was going to make it.

XP: 3140/4000

XP: 3300/4000

When he saw a pair of fiery puffballs shoot out, followed shortly thereafter by another pair, he realized that the wizard had been picking skills, and she'd finally settled on one that gave her a double-attack.

HP: 11/21

+3

HP: 14/21

4

HP: 10/21

This was still going to be dicey. They needed a refuge. A building, a narrow passage, anything where they could at least funnel the advance of mindless monsters, if not stop it completely.

The six of them were being overrun.

Connor could only imagine his muscles in the real world. Unless they were reading nerve impulses and intercepting them, his arms would be dead useless. He was going to have to call a roommate for a ride home.

4

He couldn't afford distractions.

HP: 6/21

+3

HP: 9/21

XP: 3760/4000

Just a little longer...

He could do this.

XP: 3890/4000

XP: 3980/4000

Two more zombies fell.

This time, the golden swirl surrounded Connor, and the gong rang for him.

>>>LEVEL UP!!!<<<

YOU GAIN

2 ATTACK

3 DEFENSE

10 HP

0 MP

1 SKILL CHOICE

He was heartened to note that his HP refilled.

HP: 31/31

Connor wasted no time, instantly tapping the skill selector.

PARRY

THROW WEAPON

CHARGING STAB

He selected Parry without so much as checking the others.

SELECT A SKILL TO FLOAT TO YOUR NEXT SELECTION. OTHER CHOICES WILL NOT BE OFFERED AGAIN.

Shit. He didn't have time to be reading options. But he couldn't get the selection screen out of his way without picking something. And he wasn't sure he'd be able to Parry if he didn't finish the selection process.

Hesitating, he chose Charging Stab to see again next time. Throwing stuff wasn't his preference, even if it probably covered a glaring weakness in his melee fighting style.

The screen disappeared, and Connor switched to defense.

So long as he didn't attempt to hit them, he was able to hold off four zombies at once, deftly turning aside grasping, claw-like fingers and ravenous, distended jaws with ease.

After a few minutes of this, with zombies piling up on his side, but the party relatively healthy, he realized something.

He took a swing.

13

The zombie fell neatly in half.

Two more got hits in on him.

0

1

Yeah. His DEF had gone up. These things could barely scratch him now. If he managed to gain ONE more level out here, he might be able to ditch the others and forge ahead solo. If his goal was to reach the top of that mountain first, forcing them to repeat this slog of a journey across Unalive Hills would be a huge way to go about that.

A yellow ping glowed on Connor's minimap. He waved a hand for the others to follow and shifted course. If any of them were paying attention to their maps, they would be seeing the same thing as him.

What the ping represented, he couldn't say. But Connor was determined to find out.

Several minutes of zombie mowing later, he discovered the refuge he'd been hoping for, albeit not the one he'd have asked for.

RESPAWN POINT UPDATED

SECLUDED CEMETERY

A small, private graveyard, fenced in along with an adjacent, ramshackle house, somehow remained free of zombie incursions. As all six of them ventured inside, the zombies ignored them, didn't pursue inside, and seemed to forget they even existed.

Both the archer and the wizard attempted ranged attacks from within the confines, but the arrows and balls of fire had no effect. They gained no XP. Connor was stuck at...

XP: 760/8000

This zone might be miserable, but it was a gold mine of XP.

And Connor updated his assessment from miserable to "creepy as hell" when he noticed the tombstones in the private graveyard.

There were six in total, arranged in a three by two grid, piled with fresh turned earth.

One of them bore the name: Connor.

"I don't like this place. I didn't like it before. I like it less now. I don't go in for horror games, and this RPG has just stumbled way too far down the horror route for my liking. I think I'll call it a day here. Come back fresh tomorrow after a shower and a few beers."

If Kelli or anyone on the dev team was listening, they gave no indication.

The others seemed equally fascinated by the grave markers. He used the inscriptions to learn the names of his fellow players.

Their cleric went by the in-game handle "Meatball." Nice to see everyone took their characters seriously.

Limboing under the seriousness bar was their monk, "Slapguy."

The archer, "Calamity," wasn't half bad. Name-wise, at least. It was almost, ALMOST enough to convince Connor that every last one of his fellow players wasn't gender swapping their avatars.

But Connor was sure that their wizard, "Whorelock," was a dude back in meatspace.

Their rogue, "Dizzy," was a whimsical yet inoffensive choice.

The house was a decorative element. Empty and devoid of both furniture and purpose, it was quick to search and just as quick to dismiss.

After a time spent milling around, and several of them tapping the air in vain attempts at UI interactions, Dizzy stood at the gate and pointed out.

Connor sighed.

Yeah. Not much else to be done here.

He took one last try anyway.

REPORT BUG

"Still can't log out. Kinda been a while. Getting worried."

To his surprise, a reply came quickly.

DON'T WORRY. TIME IS SPED UP FOR YOU IN THERE. JUST FOCUS ON THE GAME.

The latter, with no voice or emoji to lend emotional context, came across as vaguely threatening.

For now, at least, it felt like doing what he was told and venturing back out to face the zombie hordes.

CHAPTER 21
CONNOR'S CROSSING

WHEN NEXT THEY SET OUT, Connor felt differently about his companions. They were no longer nameless competitors and adversaries for one simple reason:

He had names for all of them now.

It was harder to maintain a grudge with Dizzy than it was with "the rogue." And it was harder to be low-key attracted to a wizard when he knew one of three possible dudes had named her Whorelock.

If he had to make a guess, the others were all Level 3 now. The fights coming out of the respawn cemetery were still challenging, but they weren't getting chipped down like it had felt last time.

Again, Connor took point, this time heading straight for the mountain.

The zombies grew stiffer in challenge the closer they drew to the towering Spire of Fate, but they never yielded more than 10 XP apiece.

By the time they reached a roadblock, Connor was up to...

XP: 1160/8000

But then they reached an obstacle with no clear way to traverse.

BONE MOAT

OK. That name tracked. It was appropriately creepy for the area, decently fantasy-esque, and accurately described the ravine encircling the mountain's base, chock full of skeletons instead of water.

Connor looked to his fellow adventurers for anyone who had ideas. Dizzy caught him glancing in her direction and backed away, putting up both hands in warning.

Connor mirrored her gesture with less panic. No harm. No foul. He wasn't going to push her in if she wasn't going back to leeching off his kills. Through this whole zone they'd been working together...

Plus, corpses disappeared too soon to consider building a land bridge out of them.

Rather than attempt to descend and fight their way down, the six of them skirted the moat's edge, looking for ways either over or under it. The zombies avoided this area for whatever reason. In-game, it made no sense. From a strictly "what's really going on here" perspective, they weren't programmed to.

What mattered was that they had a break from constant attacks.

They also had a puzzle with no clear solution.

The moat was a good fifty feet across. No skill HE'D come across would allow him to leap that.

Or... could it?

There was nothing on the far side as far as monsters, so he was pretty sure there was no chance of him Charging across. Maybe one of the others had something?

Connor pantomimed a rainbow motion with one hand, an arcing up and over, hopefully clear to the others that he meant crossing the moat.

He pointed to the wizard. She shook her head.

Slapguy? Monks were pulling stuff like that in anime and kung fu movies. But Slapguy bowed and shook his head.

Dizzy, Meatball, and Calamity all shook their heads negative.

Onward they went, painting in the minimap along the way.

They traced a curving path, seeing new bits of terrain as their angle shifted around the mountain's base.

Then, Slapguy tugged on his shoulder, grabbed the wizard's sleeve, shook the archer by the arm. He pointed. On the far side, in the distance, was a drawbridge. It was a good hike to get there, but they headed out as a group immediately.

By the time they got to a point directly across from the drawbridge, they could see that it was a simple structure. On the near side, stonework provided a landing spot for a long wooden bridge. That bridge, in turn, was raised and lowered from the far side via a mechanism of chains and winches. Those mechanisms were guarded by...

Connor reached out a hand toward it.

Bridge Troll.

No other information became available with his inspection. It was a dull reddish color, scraggly, and looked annoyed.

"Let us across!" Connor bellowed.

"No!" the Bridge Troll shouted back.

"Fine! How much to we owe to cross?"

"Bugger up! Don't all yammer at once!" That was when Connor noticed, to his own consternation, that everyone else was attempting a similar negotiation.

He patted the air with his hands, trying to reign in the group, maybe appoint a designated negotiator. Wasn't one of the other testers—maybe Lucas?—a poli-sci major? Brokering peace deals sounded like his sort of thing—whichever of them was Lucas.

But no amount of deescalating could quench the RPG players' drive to be the face of the party.

Connor stopped trying to bargain with the Bridge Troll. Instead, he started doing thumbnail math.

He tried to remember how far he'd been able to Charge, and he'd yet to try it at this kind of range.

What he *had*, however, was a river stone to cross this moat.

Leaving the others to their squabbles, he picked out a skeleton from the Moat of Bones below, bellowed his war cry, and...

"Aaaaaaaaah!"

For form's sake, he took a swing as he arrived, still practicing the timing. He was late this time, but he landed amid the skeletons unharmed.

The skeletons didn't seem inclined to allow him to remain that way.

`3`

`4`

`4`

`4`

`3`

`HP: 13/31`

Shit. These things were hitting for a ton, relatively speaking. Knowing he had little choice but to continue with his plan, he re-aimed himself at an upward angle.

"Aaaaaaaaah!"

Connor rocketed through the air, right up into the face of the Bridge Troll.

This time, he had the swing timed perfectly. BEYOND perfectly, even.

`>>26<< CRITICAL HIT`

The Bridge Troll went down.

`250 XP`

Right about then, Connor realized he'd fucked up.

There was no ground beneath his feet.

He fell back into the Bone Moat, striking the rocky bottom with a painful thud.

6

HP: 7/31

Backing against the moat wall, Connor Parried for all his digital life was worth. Up on the far side, the five other players pointed and laughed at his plight. He couldn't blame them. While it had been a nice enough plan, some key elements of the execution had been lacking. Maybe if he'd charged the Bridge Troll from an angle, he'd have had enough footing to remain atop the troll's side of the moat.

Right now, without a rescue coming down to retrieve him, Connor's best plan seemed to be reversing his maneuver to the players' side of the moat.

"Aaaaaaaaah!"

Nothing happened. He must have been too far away to charge Meatball from here, the one who seemed most like he had a Connor's worth of space between the edge and himself.

While he was trying to Charge, one of the skeletons struck a blow.

4

HP: 3/31

This was it. His last chance. One more hit and he was done for.

Connor just needed to get far enough across the moat to get in range to Charge one of his companions.

He Parried again, but as he bulldozed his way toward the middle of the Bone Moat, he discovered a weakness of his Parrying defense.

It didn't protect him from behind.

3

SECLUDED CEMETERY

"You have died, but your journey is not yet ended," Kelindra informed him. "Rise once more, hero, and press onward."

There was no more choice offered, no explanation of his XP loss. Just on the off chance the rules had changed at this particular respawn point, Connor took a quick look.

XP: 0/8000

Even expecting it, he cringed. Could have been worse, of course. He was still level 4, after all.

UNALIVE HILLS

With the Parry skill and moving fast enough to keep the zombies from closing in behind him, Connor was able to race through the fog without taking any hits—or killing anything, but that was of secondary concern.

What he really needed to avoid was the party figuring out a way across and ditching him.

BONE MOAT

He needn't have worried. A tiny object floated where the Bridge Troll had died, but there was no sign of him respawning yet.

Dizzy led a silent, sardonic round of applause upon his return that caught on among the players.

Unable to offer any defense of his actions, Connor simply took a bow. At least he'd been entertaining in death.

But that still left the problem of getting across.

There had to be a trick. Or a plot device. Somewhere, the game designer had left an intended path to clear this obstacle.

The two possibilities—assuming the design team just hadn't forgotten to include one—were that they either already had what they needed and didn't know it, or that they needed to find their MacGuffin somewhere in the parts of the game they already had access to.

As a debate on the subject ensued via hand waving and angry expressions, the Bridge Troll respawned.

Connor quietly backed out of the argument before anyone else took note of the Bridge Troll's return. *He* had been watching and waiting for it.

"How do we get across?"

"Not my problem!" the Bridge Troll retorted.

The game was up. Everyone could hear the NPC response. Connor now had an audience, at least for half his conversation. "I killed you once. I can do it again."

"Ain't no skin off'n my nose." The creature scratched its nose for emphasis.

This was the most interaction he'd gotten out of anyone so far. Maybe it was a coincidence that they'd scripted some snarky taunts and comebacks for the guardian of this bridge.

"You don't have anything I wants," the Bridge Troll announced. It seemed non sequitur until he realized the thing was answering someone else's comment.

That was it. That was the clue. Somewhere, maybe farther down the Bone Moat, maybe hidden and overlooked in the sparse and seemingly empty house by the Secluded Cemetery, maybe another location nestled in the fog amid a sea of zombies, there was something this thing wanted.

Fuck all those options.

Fighting off waves of zombies was shit work. They'd gone over every inch of that ramshackle house. And who knew how far this moat went... maybe the entire way around the mountain.

No. Connor was going to find a way past this guy and his bridge.

Patting Calamity on the shoulder, he mimed shooting an arrow. She shook her head. When he insisted, she relented.

Fwip! Fwip! Fwip!

Three arrows raced toward, not the Bridge Troll but the handle to lower the bridge. The first missed its mark, but the second and third plinked harmlessly off. Calamity swept a hand that said, "*see?*" without saying a word, suggesting that maybe they'd tried this while he was dead.

After he'd failed to get to the other side using Charge.

Except...

He hadn't failed to get across. He'd failed to *stay* across. He'd killed his anchor to Charge back up. A failing of footing. And yes, falling into the Moat of Bones had hurt. Getting mauled by skeletons had hurt. Getting laughed at by his companions had hurt even more.

Connor determined that *he* was going to cheese out this mini-boss encounter.

His way.

Drawing his Steel Sword, he stepped to the edge of the Bone Moat and studied the skeletons below. He plotted out his vectors. He realized that he hadn't taken a math or physics class since high school and didn't remember the first thing about how vectors worked.

Connor eyeballed it.

"Aaaaaaaaah!"

This time, upon reaching his target, the blur ended in a ferocious Parry. Skeletons pressed in all around. The ones behind him had a free shot at his back.

4

3

But Connor wasn't hanging around.

"Aaaaaaaaah!"

Right up the far side, and to the Bridge Troll he zoomed.

This time he didn't lop the thing's head off. He didn't even Parry. Smaller than him, but surprisingly sturdy, Connor grabbed hold of the Bridge Troll and held on.

"Hey! Get off me, ya git!"

Monster and human stumbled around the Bone Moat's edge until the Bridge Troll managed to break free.

Connor had solid ground beneath his feet. All he needed now was to finish off this prick and be on his way. He spared a glance across at his fellow players.

So long, suckers, he bid them silently. He could have said it aloud for all the difference it made. But just Connor's luck, the devs would have picked that exact moment to get the player voice bug fixed.

2

The Bridge Troll wasn't especially ferocious. He just talked a good game and controlled one side of a crucial moat crossing.

HP: 22/31

Connor was fine. Wielding his Steel Sword in both hands, he took a nice safe swipe, center of mass. The Bridge Troll had no hope of avoiding it.

13

He knew from the previous kill that it had 26 HP or fewer. He could play it safe.

The creature's next attack caught him off guard. It spat in his face.

2

Connor instantly swiped at the gob of nasty goo that clung to him like a softball-sized booger. It stung and burned and...

1

Shit. A damage-over-time effect? It hadn't hit him again, but the goo hurt once more.

Connor hastily swiped one-handed at the creature as he attempted to wipe his face clean of the toxic spittle.

10

That was enough. The Bridge Troll fell.

250 XP

XP: 250/8000

1

HP: 18/31

Sheathing his sword, Connor devoted all his efforts to cleaning off the toxin. But gauntlets didn't make the best wet wipes. The goo smeared as it continued to burn.

HP: 17/31

HP: 16/31

HP: 15/31

This was a countdown to an embarrassing death in full view of his competitors.

He glanced across, looking for advice, for help, for any hints of sympathy.

Frantic gestures meant nothing to him as the goo burned relentlessly.

HP: 14/31

HP: 13/31

HP: 12/31

This was a race he was losing.

He checked his Inventory.

10 COINS

2 YELLOW GOBO DAGGER

FISHING NET (5X)

WATER BREATHING POTION (97X)

He pulled out a Water Breathing Potion, yanked out the stopper, and poured it over his face.

No help.

HP: 12/31

HP: 10/31

HP: 9/31

He was screwed. This Bridge Troll was a death sentence, even in an easy victory. Knowing he didn't have long, Connor remembered that he could at least keep inventory items with him.

Right in front of him, a key floated.

RECEIVED: BRIDGE KEY

HP: 8/31

HP: 7/31

HP: 6/31

This key wasn't going to do him any good on the far side. He needed to get the bridge down so that when he respawned, he'd be able to cross again.

Stumbling half blind to the handle that would lower the bridge, he found that it was held in place by a chain and padlock.

The padlock yielded at once to the key.

HP: 5/31

HP: 4/31

HP: 3/31

Connor grabbed the handle and yanked.

HP: 2/31

HP: 1/31

The bridge descended in a series of jerky clanks, whether through sloppy animation or an attempt to portray the bridge mechanism as rickety, who could say?

Then, the toxin finished him off with the bridge still two thirds of the way up.

SECLUDED CEMETERY

XP: 0/8000

"You have died, but your journey is not yet ended. Rise once more, hero, and press onward."

Connor did just that

UNALIVE HILLS

He drove through the hordes of zombies, sword leading, Parrying a path through with no time for them to attack from behind.

`BONE MOAT`

Connor arrived back to find the bridge perfectly passable. No one was there waiting for him. He'd expected as much. Not only had he died a humiliating death—again—murdered by Nickelodeon slime from a phlegmy radish with an attitude problem, but he'd opened a path for the rest of the players to gain a head start on him.

The bridge sounded like a proper wooden surface beneath his feet as Connor crossed, so he couldn't even report that as a bug. Then again, all the bug reporting system really represented was a text message to the dev team anyway, right?

`REPORT BUG`

"Hey, not so much a bug as a suggestion. In the full version of the game, can you name this bridge Connor's Crossing or something? You guys seem like you can use the help with names."

When he reached the far side, he was startled by a kiss on his cheek.

Whirling, sword in hand, Connor discovered Dizzy, hidden in Stealth and waiting for him. She gave a shy little wave and a jerk of her head to follow her.

Why not? One ally and four adversaries sounded like a better deal than five opponents out to best him.

The two headed for a cavern entrance viewable from the Bridge Troll's side of Connor's Crossing. Together.

CHAPTER 22
INTO THE MOUNTAIN

THE CAVERN LASTED ONLY a few steps before giving way to proper stonework of ancient and timeless construction. For once, the poor lighting and cookie-cutter artwork combined to enhance the ambiance rather than detract from it. Infrequent torches gave just enough light to make out the low, wide, irregular stairs that came often enough that the general idea of going UP the inside of the mountain was unmistakable.

BLACK CATACOMBS

OK. There was a name that fit the game. Maybe the forest was an afterthought of a zone, but it had left a lingering bad taste in Connor's mouth that he was still trying to get rid of.

Dizzy stuck to the shadows as she led the way, avoiding the light of torches as if they were lasers in a spy movie.

Connor followed as best he could, wondering whether she was actively avoiding using her Stealth skill—whose very existence he only inferred, and whose workings in this game remained pure conjecture—or if he had somehow been made to be able to see her despite it.

At the top of an intermittent and interminable flight of stairs, wide enough for four people to fight abreast on, came a landing with a four-way intersection, including the way they'd just come from.

According to the minimap, they'd arrived from the west. To the north and south, dots of torchlight marked a parade route into the gloom. To the east, directly across from them, a similar stairway continued upward.

Dizzy jerked her head toward the north, beckoning him to follow.

Connor didn't *like* following, but he also wasn't the stealthy one taking point. His dungeoneering instincts suggested that the upward slope would bring them closer to their ultimate destination. After all, nothing was more UP a mountain than the peak. Somewhere at the top of this crazy mountain, a Mountain Lord needed some slaying.

From the south, a distant voice called out, "Heeeeelp! Is someone out there? Can you hear me?"

By the process of bug reporting, Connor knew better than to think it was one of their fellow players in trouble.

"Can you hear me?" he asked Dizzy, looking right at her. The shake of her head and a thumbs up indicated that she was thinking the same thing. So long as they couldn't hear one another, that was no player seeking their help.

She headed north. Connor grabbed her by the wrist. In the face of her annoyed scowl, he gestured emphatically south. He was no bleeding heart. He knew this digital nobody wasn't in *real* trouble. But this was a game, and accepting the premise of that game meant engaging with quests—like the one telling them to go kill a Mountain Lord in the first place. Plus, quests meant loot.

Loot meant power.

And given that, rather than scour the zombie zone for MacGuffins to cross the bridge the right way, they'd banded together, fought against monsters too high level for any of them to solo, and cheesed out the bridge, they were probably too low level to be this far in the first place.

"HeEeEeEeEeeeeeeelp!" the voice wailed.

Connor let go and crossed his arms.

Dizzy paused, considering.

Connor pointed to himself, to her, then flexed his muscles.

With a sigh and a nod, Dizzy relented. They needed to get stronger. Some XPOTs. Maybe some new gear. What were they wandering these catacombs for, if not to power up on the way to the end boss? What were they hoping to find if not quest-givers like the one hopefully summoning them for aid?

Rotting wooden doors lined the south passage. Connor kicked them in one by one, lest monsters—or loot—be left at their backs. Only broken coffins and illegible memorial plaques lay beyond.

"HeEeEeEeEeeeeeeelp!" the voice wailed occasionally.

Upon kicking in the third door, an undead humanoid with leathery skin and claws like ice picks leaped at him.

7

HP: 24/31

Jesus! That thing hit like a truck!

Connor instantly switched to Parry, fending off the creature's next attack.

Dizzy has disappeared on him, but by the undead's occasional twitches and flinches, she was hitting it as he kept its attention.

Lucky for him, the Parry skill seemed to make it easier for him to anticipate and react to his adversary's attacks. Unfortunately, it also left him unable to mount an offense. If not for Dizzy, he'd have been forced to either battle the creature to a standstill or hack one another to pieces and see who was left standing.

150 XP

The creature collapsed, snarling in its undeath throes.

Connor had just enough time to extend a palm and examine it before it disappeared.

Razor Ghoul. Undead.

More undead. Good to know. No clues could have led him to that conclusion without in-game assistance.

RECEIVED: 5 COINS

While Connor was distracted, Dizzy had looted. Nice to know the game split the take the same way it split their XP.

Dizzy got his attention with a hand waved in his face. She pointed to the shoulder where the Razor Ghoul had initially struck him. There was no visible wound or anything, but he knew what she meant. She gave a thumbs up, then cocked her head as a question mark.

What could he say? That he was at like three-quarters of his HP total? He gave a nod that he was good to press onward.

XP: 150/8000

It wasn't much to build on, but it was a start.

Connor kicked down two more doors with nothing beyond before discovering the one with the yelling voice behind it. "HeEeEeEeEeeeeeelp!"

"Stand back," Connor ordered.

He smashed in the door with another mighty kick.

Except, instead of breaking, the door held firm. It was Connor who jolted backward by the force of his own blow. He stumbled until the far wall slammed into his armored back and propped him up. He was getting ready to wind up for a two-handed blow from his sword, intent on hacking through the wood, when Dizzy interposed herself.

She crouched at the lock. Connor couldn't tell what she was up to, but it was easy enough to guess.

Clack.

The door popped open with a gentle push from her.

Inside, a blue-skinned villager cowered. "Please don't hurt me!"

"Why would we break into your cell to hurt you?" Connor asked.

"I'm Gulgoo," he said, addressing Dizzy. "The Mountain Lord imprisoned me for trying to map this place."

The two players shared a look. "Can we have a look at your map?" Connor asked.

"Burned it, he did. The Mountain Lord won't allow anyone to document his mountain."

"You're lucky he didn't kill you," Connor joked.

"He *was* killing me. A slow death in this cell, that was in store for me. Becoming one of his monsters, that was his plan. My imprisonment was no mercy. He needed me ravenous in death."

"Wow." This game was a little brutal once you got past the plush wildlife on the Kawaiian Islands. "Any chance you *remember* your way around?"

"Of course I'd be willing to help you," he said to Dizzy, who was clearly carrying on a similar but not identical conversation with Gulgoo. He tapped his skull. "Got it all up here. You lead me out of this place, and I'll make it worth your while."

Connor's Quest Journal pulsed.

SLAY THE MOUNTAIN LORD FOR ELDER LOHDOH: 0/1

PROTECT GULGOO'S ESCAPE FROM THE BLACK CATACOMBS: 0/1

He extended a hand. Connor shook it. Dizzy did likewise.

"All righty then, let's go."

Gulgoo led the way, and Connor realized that they'd started that most dreaded of RPG trials...

An escort quest.

Gulgoo was unarmed. Small. Looked like he didn't exactly have a full rest's worth of HP himself. In combat, he'd be nothing but a liability. Rather than return to the intersection, Gulgoo led them deeper down the cell block.

"Is there any treasure down here?" Connor asked.

"Oh. Loads. But you'll never survive finding it. Better off taking the quick way out with me."

Dizzy shot him a quizzical look. Connor shrugged and pointed ahead. Short of intersections, there wasn't any point of waiting for Gulgoo to take the lead. Better to spot enemies in advance, rather than have to fend off surprise attacks that could fail their escort mission instantly.

After all, the quest goal wasn't to get out of the Black Catacombs, it was to protect Gulgoo in getting there. Connor and Dizzy making it out the far side was a bonus, not a requirement. If they died on the cusp of escape, but Gulgoo made it out, that would be a win.

Assuming, of course, that they could keep whatever reward Gulgoo had in store for them.

Dizzy ventured ahead, returning whenever there was a decision to be made about their path.

Gulgoo led them out the far side of the dungeon area and into a burial ground, a museum of sarcophagi, lit by torch-bearing statues.

One of the statues moved as they drew near.

"RUN!" Gulgoo shouted.

Connor already had his Parry readied. He turned aside a stony strike with a fist the size of his head.

By torchlight, Dizzy beckoned frantically for Connor to follow. Gulgoo was pelting headlong into the darkness, and whatever XP this statue might be worth wouldn't get them a quest reward if Gulgoo got himself killed running into further trouble.

Connor Parried again, backing away. Even one-handed, he got a healthy bonus to his DEF from the maneuver, and he used the hand he freed up to shoo Dizzy off to look after the little coward.

Once they had a head start, and after Parrying a further two attacks, Connor timed his retreat. As soon as his blade turned aside a ponderous swinging fist, he turned on his heel and bolted.

Up ahead, he could still see Dizzy, darting down the halls after Gulgoo, who Connor could no longer make out.

Taking a chance, he tried something he'd been meaning to figure out.

"Aaaaaaaaah!"

He Charged Dizzy. Torches flared into streaks. Connor didn't attempt any sort of attack, but joined her headlong pursuit of their guide.

She looked surprised to see him suddenly appear at her side, but she didn't break stride. Gulgoo was just ahead of them, keeping out front either by careful design or simply being allowed to run just as fast as them no matter what.

"Stop! Slow down!" Connor shouted after the little blue maniac. His minimap was the only thing keeping up with the headlong flight through the torch-lit darkness.

"EEEEK!" Gulgoo screamed as he took a sudden, veering turn.

A Razor Ghoul had appeared in front of him, and Connor wasn't taking any chances.

"Aaaaaaaaah!" Launching a scream of his own, he Charged the undead creature.

13

It swiped at him, but even without the Parry skill active, Connor managed to dodge the strike on skill alone.

A dagger whistled past Connor's right ear. Then another past his left.

`150 XP`

At least the village idiot wasn't getting a share of the XP his protectors were earning.

Without pausing to loot, Dizzy made the turn to keep Gulgoo in sight.

After a moment's hesitation, Connor raked in the Coins that floated above the disappeared corpse.

`RECEIVED: 5 COINS`

"Aaaaaaaaah!"

In one light-speed moment, he caught back up with Dizzy. Then, realizing that just because he *couldn't* attack Dizzy didn't mean he *had* to attack anyone at the end of a Charge.

"Aaaaaaaaah!"

Just like that, he was caught up to Gulgoo. Done with this headlong rush into unknown dangers, Connor grabbed the little guy by the back of the shirt and lifted him from the ground.

"Let me go! They'll get us!"

"They're going to get us because you're racing ahead without any caution or plan. The statue's long gone. You'd hear it if it wasn't. We killed the Razor Ghoul you almost fed yourself too. How about you ride piggy-back and just *point* the way to go?"

"I... uh... OK."

Dizzy caught up just as Gulgoo was climbing atop Connor's shoulders. "Do *not* try to steer me. We don't do Ratatouille here. Just point. I'll go.

Dizzy gave him a thumbs up.

They fought two more Razor Ghouls along the way as

Gulgoo first backtracked them to the intersection he'd veered away from, then along a new course, finding hidden stairwells and passageways that weren't immediately obvious, and triggering one secret door that Connor wouldn't even have thought to look for in a game this half-ready.

With Connor Parrying all incoming attacks and Dizzy vanishing to deal damage via unknown means from undisclosed locations, they were in good shape against any single opponent.

Then, around one bend...

"Daylight! Sun be praised!"

Just like that, Gulgoo scrambled down from Connor's shoulders. Before either of them could stop him, the villager broke away and raced out the arched opening leading to a mountain trail beyond the Black Catacombs.

`PROTECT GULGOO'S ESCAPE FROM THE BLACK CATACOMBS: COMPLETE`

"Thank you! Thank you so much! Please. Take this. As a token of my appreciation!"

`RECEIVED: MAP-MAKER'S WAYSTONE`

For the first time in a while, Kelindra chose to chime in. "You're received your first ACCESSORY. It is a piece of equipment, like weapons or armor. UN-like weapons or armor, accessories are versatile and varied; many can be worn in multiple ways or multiple locations with no change in their magical effects. However, only one may ever be equipped at once. Equipping a new Accessory will return your currently equipped Accessory to Inventory."

In Connor's inventory, the Map-Maker's Waystone appeared as a faceted red gem. He held out a palm to examine it.

`MAP-MAKER'S WAYSTONE - See the location of hidden doors on your minimap.`

Cool. Explained how Gulgoo knew where to find that shortcut.

Connor took another step out of the catacombs, curious what Gulgoo was up to, fiddling in the bushes beside the mountain trail.

`HARD PASS`

The map-maker extracted a bundle of wooden rods and cloth. As Connor watched in perplexity, their former protectee twisted and pulled, stretched and tied. In short order, the chaotic contraption arrayed itself into a fairly sturdy-looking hang glider, albeit sized for someone of Gulgoo's stature.

They were higher up the mountain than Connor had imagined. Even knowing this was all digital, he felt a wave of vertigo as he stumbled back from the sheer cliffside. One look into the Bone Moat, at least ten stories down, was enough.

"Farewell, friends!" Gulgoo bid them. "Oh. One final gift, for staying to see me off."

`RECEIVED: XPOT`

"Thanks! Good luck getting home!" Connor shouted after the map-maker as he drifted off the pass and into open space. The little glider soared on an updraft. Gulgoo banked and disappeared around the spire.

Dizzy was waving as well. She had her red gem worn as a choker over her ninja mask. With her chin down, it would have been all but invisible. But bidding farewell to their guide, she had her head lifted to the skies.

Connor took his and slipped it onto a finger. For him, it became a ring.

Dizzy pulled out her XPOT. She pulled the stopper.

Connor put up both hands, waggling them furiously. This place was dangerous as hell. One false step, and they'd be in the Bone Moat the hard way. He even tried to grab her wrist to stop her potentially wasting the potion.

She pulled away and warned him off with a scowl and threateningly pointed finger from her other hand as she drank.

A golden swirl and a gong told him that she knew what she was doing.

Connor, chastened, applauded her level up.

CHAPTER 23
THE HARD WAY

HARD PASS WASN'T AS HARD as the name made it sound. The two of them walked abreast with room to spare, Dizzy on the cliffward side. Ironically, *he* was the one who got dizzy looking down over that edge. But so long as he had her along, Connor didn't panic. Even without conversation, the journey was companionable.

Then, they came to the first rope bridge.

The Spire of Fate, it seemed, was riven in two, unevenly, with a second, smaller peak just across the Bone Moat from them rose into view as Hard Pass curved around the main spire. And their trail would lead them to cross the hundred-foot span between on a bridge that swayed in the wind.

"I'm ready to log out now."

REPORT BUG

"I can't log out and there's a rope bridge I don't want to cross, and a cute girl who's probably a guy who's going to make fun of me either way if I refuse to budge."

Even as he reported it, Connor knew he was making excuses. This WAS just a game. He'd already died multiple times. A couple of those were even pretty horrible. He'd drowned, been eaten alive, been hacked apart by skeletons. How much worse would a little splat be?

Quicker than the skeletons, that much seemed certain.

Keep telling yourself that, buddy, his brain told him.

Dizzy was tapping her foot from ten feet onto the bridge, watching him as he hesitated.

Connor gave a nod, fixed his eyes on her backside, and followed Dizzy onto the bridge.

Weapon stowed, he held onto the ropes with both hands. For her part, Dizzy only grabbed the safety ropes when the middle of the span blew a good five feet sideways in the wind.

She got ahead of him. Connor kept up a slow, steady pace behind her.

This is horrible role-playing, he scolded himself. You're a Knight. Cowardly knights attack guys with their backs turned and kill downed foes. They weren't afraid of a bridge that's probably hard CODED not to fall.

Dizzy reached the far side. Once there was enough room behind her, Connor made his play.

"Aaaaaaaaah!"

He zipped the rest of the way, slumping in relief right behind her.

Dizzy gave him a hug.

When she set off, taking point on a narrower path on the smaller spire, Connor was left wondering.

That didn't *seem* like a dude thing to do. Maybe his guess about Dizzy was wrong. Or maybe either Kenny, Lucas, or Chad had been more sensitive than he gave them credit for.

"Eeeeee, hoosha hoosha hooshaaaaa!"

The shout came from above. Two White Gobos waved staves overhead in a swirling motion.

A gust of wind assaulted Connor, and he flung himself

against the cliff wall beside him. Dizzy fell prone and spread out to avoid being blown off the trail.

Connor wasn't going to let them keep trying.

"Aaaaaaaaah!"

He zoomed upward to the higher trail the White Gobos were using for their ambush. There wasn't enough ground to stand on where his charge ended, but White Gobos weighed hardly anything and weren't terribly strong.

Connor grabbed one easily. He turned and flung it into open space.

"Eeeeee, hoosha hoosha hooshaaaaa-a-a-a-a-a-a-a!" it screamed as it sailed down the mountain.

Connor fell back to the trail beside Dizzy.

4

HP: 20/31

He needed to find some healing soon. Even a level up would do.

It was several seconds before a notification popped up. Despite Dizzy not hitting it, the XP split was the same.

200 XP

Even the thought of how long it fell before dying made Connor's knees weak.

Dizzy rose to a crouch and flicked daggers up at the remaining White Gobo. One appeared to strike the mark, but he couldn't see what she was doing in terms of damage.

When the White Gobo swirled its staff again, the resulting breeze was hardly threatening.

"Aaaaaaaaah!"

Up Connor went again. This time, he didn't release the White Gobo, let alone throw it. Instead, he used it as a cushion to break his fall.

2

Fine. Half damage.

Even with his weight atop it, Connor didn't kill the White Gobo by body slamming it to the rocky trail.

Dizzy came in with her daggers and ended it manually.

`200 XP`

Coins appeared over the corpse. Both reached for them at the same time. Not that it mattered.

`RECEIVED: 10 COINS`

Their hands touched. His gauntlet. Her black leather gloves. Instantly, they glared at one another. Eyes met. There was nuance there, blurred by the limitations of the graphics. Most of the time, Connor's eyes had gotten used to the discrepancy and started filling in details for themselves. But times like this highlighted some of the subtleties lacking.

Dizzy was more than happy to clarify matters for him.

She made a loose fist with one hand, and jabbed a finger from the other in and out of it repeatedly. Then, she drew that same finger across her throat. She cocked her head.

Connor gulped and nodded. Loud and clear, he got it.

The pair continued onward and upward. On both sides of the spire, the trail switched back repeatedly to keep going upward without spiraling around the entire mountain. They came to another swaying rope bridge back to the main spire.

Dizzy prodded him forward. It was his turn to venture across first, it seemed. She was determined not to coddle him.

Connor edged his way forward, slower than before. Shuffling even. He put one foot forward, not watching his step, feeling for the boards, testing his weight before hastily readjusting his grip and repeating the process.

As he neared the middle of the span, after what felt like hours, a sound ran his blood cold.

"Eeeeee, hoosha hoosha hooshaaaaa!"

"Eeeeee, hoosha hoosha hooshaaaaa!"

Shit! Another ambush, this one from both sides. Dizzy

shoved him from behind, clearly lodging her vote.

Two White Gobos to either side of the bridge twirled their staves. The ones behind them were up one level of switchback. On the far side, their enemies met them right at the cliff's edge.

Connor held on for dear life as the bridge swayed in the hurricane wind the White Gobos summoned. His body went horizontal even with his feet planted on the boards. The bridge swung back down as the gale died out, swinging a few times before coming to a rest.

These monsters were still new to them. Connor had no idea how long it might be before they could repeat that spell. What he needed was to get within Charging distance ASAP.

Hand over hand on the rope, he shuffled closer. Dizzy, done with his shit, ducked and squirmed past him, racing on foot for foes that might be too much for her to handle head on.

What kind of Knight was Connor going to be? Connor the Low? Connor the Terrestrial? Connor, Knight of Beaches and Hills That Weren't Too Tall? He released the rope, drew his Steel Sword, and ran after her.

He had a pretty good eyeball by now for the range on his Charge. Just before he got close enough, the Gobos began their spell again.

Connor skidded in an attempt to halt himself. He let go of his sword with one hand and lunged for the rope as the winds took the bridge out from under him.

Or vice versa. And who really cared? The important thing was that the bridge and he weren't in the same place anymore, and gravity had noticed.

"AaAaAaAaAaAaAaAah!" he screamed all the way to the Bone Moat.

The absolute most insulting thing was landing square atop one of the skeletons, and just before things went black, seeing...

`100 XP`

CHAPTER 24
ONCE MORE, WITH FEELING

SECLUDED CEMETERY

XP: 0/8000

"You have died, but your journey is not yet ended. Rise once more, hero, and press onward."

Connor didn't really have another option.

But to his surprise, upon awakening to life once more, he discovered he wasn't alone. And it wasn't just Dizzy popping in a few seconds after him, clearly no match for the White Gobos, gravity, or both.

Everyone was here.

Meatball, Calamity, Slapguy, and the wizard all loitered by the gate.

A mock cheer went up when Connor and Dizzy joined them.

Slapguy beckoned frantically, then swept a hand for Connor to go first.

Connor burst out laughing when he realized what was going on.

They couldn't get back to the Bone Moat alone! Or even as a group. Connor had been leaning on his Parry skill to make it through the gauntlet. It must have been that nobody else had an equivalent to get them through unscathed. How they each ended up back here remained a mystery. Presumably it was a mystery whose suspects consisted of Razor Ghouls, White Gobos, angry statues, and Sir Isaac Newton himself. That was the gravity guy, not to be confused with the Isaac who probably programmed those physical laws into his computer game.

After his time adventuring with Dizzy, Connor was warming up to the idea of cooperation. After her kill stealing, XP leeching antics and his tossing her two zones back in retribution, neither of them had screwed the other over, and they'd both had one another's backs ever since.

Connor was willing to tank.

But he had a better idea than simply escorting everyone back to the Bone Moat straight off.

UNALIVE HILLS

The Unalive Hills seemed to be an endless supply of zombies. Not that he wanted to spend all day here, even if time was going faster here than in meatspace. Sooner or later, everyone was getting some lunch together and comparing notes. Screw this no in-game chat. The six of them were going to hash some shit out over kung pao chicken and Coke, if not over XPOTs and Water Breathing Potions.

Connor intended to paint the map. By charades, he communicated this plan over a painstaking amount of time, with Meatball being particularly dense and needing multiple presentations of the idea before he claimed to get it.

There was still some chance he'd just given up, decided to go with the flow, and do what everyone else had agreed on already.

With Connor cutting a swath and Meatball replenishing lost hit points, they became an automated lawnmower, blasting down anything that both moved and wasn't them. Connor guided them, trusting his minimap as the canonical party map.

If anyone had missed out on something, they were either going to need a fresh round of charades to raise an objection, or they were going to have to live with an incomplete map.

The XP rolled in.

Well, trickled. But it was a constant trickle. Stuff up in the Black Catacombs and Hard Pass was better XP, but scarce and more dangerous. Right now, for as long as they were still getting XP for these mindless undead automatons, Connor was going to up all their levels.

Meatball dinged.

So did Slapguy.

Same went for the wizard.

Connor had just passed the halfway point, himself.

`XP: 4010/8000`

He was pretty sure that the ones who'd just leveled had been at zero, so that meant they'd just arrived at Level 4.

More and more zombies died. Connor's HP fluctuated less as Meatball's heals started doing +4 instead of +3 per application.

Slapguy was doing more kicks than Connor had noticed before. The wizard was now zapping things with a lightning spell.

By the same logic, Connor reasoned that Dizzy and Calamity, like him, had been Level 4 before they left the Secluded Cemetery.

A ping on Connor's minimap suggested a secret entrance here somewhere. It was well off the direct path from (Forest Pun) to the Bone Moat, so anyone making a beeline for the mountain would have missed it.

He and Dizzy shared a glance. Surely *she'd* seen it as well. They had the same magic item equipped, after all.

She gave the faintest of head shakes. Even with the mask on, he could tell she was smirking at him conspiratorially. This was *their* secret. If anyone was getting in wherever that secret led, it would be them, and them alone.

Connor kept watch on his XP total.

XP: 4740/8000

XP: 6030/8000

XP: 7770/8000

They were coming in for a landing. Short of stumbling into a mini-boss or a trap or something—which Connor SWORE he wouldn't let catch him off guard—he was going to make it.

A golden swirl surrounded Connor as his favorite gong rang.

>>>LEVEL UP!!!<<<

YOU GAIN

2 ATTACK

3 DEFENSE

12 HP

0 MP

1 SKILL CHOICE

He wanted to check in on his overall stats again, but the skill selection was blocking his character details.

But funny enough, when he stopped defending himself as an experiment, the zombies could no longer damage him. The chippy little hits that, through sheer volume, once posed a terrifying threat, were now raindrops beating against his armor. He wondered now, having chosen the Steel Sword, whether he'd have already been this invulnerable had he gone with the Steel Armor instead.

Untouchable, he felt calm enough to take some time reviewing his skill options, even in combat.

Once again, he had three options.

CHARGING STAB

CLEAVING STRIKE

RIPOSTE

He examined them one by one.

CHARGING STAB - At the end of a Charge, stab an opponent with a pointy weapon. Deals double damage.

CLEAVING STRIKE - A killing blow with a swinging weapon can continue onward to strike another opponent.

RIPOSTE - After a successful Parry, quickly attack back for half damage.

Wow. Those all sounded awesome. Frankly, Connor was impressed. It was the sign of a good game where all the options sounded good, yet you still had to choose just one. He could foresee a day when YouTubers and Twitch streamers reduced Spire of Fate to exact numbers and mathematical "best" builds. But for now, this wasn't just the Wild West of character building, it was the untamed jungle.

Half the skills in this game might be broken, buggy, or wildly imbalanced. Connor would be amazed to see Charge remain unchanged in a retail release of this game.

He'd been a Charging madman ever since gaining the skill. Getting double damage hits skewering people with his Steel Sword sounded perfectly in line with his style.

But so did Riposte. Parry was so overpowered. Any regular monsters he'd met so far had been unable to get through his Parry. All he needed was a *little* bit of offense to potentially be able to solo most of this game.

Cleaving Strike... man, that was tempting too. But of the three, he felt like it had less synergy. Maybe a later pick. If he went with high damage output as his role, that would help mow down crowds of foes.

Still, splattering stuff hadn't been his problem yet. Riposte addressed an immediate need. Connor selected it, set Cleaving Strike aside for maybe later, and hoped he didn't spend the rest of the game wishing he could kebab people after a Charge but never getting the chance.

Connor went back to Parrying everything in sight as he reviewed his overall build.

CHARACTER STATS:

NAME: Connor TITLE: None

CLASS: Knight LEVEL: 5

HP: 43 MP: 0 ATK: 11 DEF: 12

SKILLS:

TWO-HANDED FIGHTING

CHARGE

PARRY

RIPOSTE

Dizzy and Calamity dinged too, and there was a general feeling of maybe they'd done enough for now. Maybe these players weren't so hardcore back in meatspace. Connor would have been willing to stay long enough to find out one of two things:

What was the max level in this game?

Or, when would these zombies stop giving XP?

But he granted that this was kind of mindlessly boring and dull. He navigated them back toward their eventual destination.

BONE MOAT

The place was a lot less sinister and imposing with the bridge down and waiting for them. He caught a couple of the others casting wary glances down, perhaps reliving recent deaths of their own down there.

BLACK CATACOMBS

This was where things started getting a little dicey. He knew the way through. Dizzy knew the way through. But the rest of them had either stumbled through via luck to die out in Hard Pass or been devoured while wandering the catacombs blindly. He'd have bet money that no one else had encountered Gulgoo to get guided through. He and Dizzy had interacted with the guy simultaneously, and it didn't feel like there had been long enough for him to respawn for the others.

Rather than take the short way through, Connor led the group on a more thorough sweep of the place.

The first Razor Ghoul that jumped them got a rude awakening.

Connor Parried its swiping claws and was gratified at how easily he was able to strike back. It wasn't his usual full hack or baseball swing at a monster, and it didn't feel like he was getting to use his Two-Handed Fighting bonus on the attack.

5

It wasn't nothing. But it was free.

The others, of course, blasted the thing to smithereens before he got another chance to hit it.

50 XP

It wasn't a whole lot, but they were dividing these things up six ways now instead of two. And it was risk free, near as he could figure. Even if one caught him unawares or he got cocky and decided not to Parry, Meatball was on hand to patch him back up.

Maybe this wasn't supposed to be a solo effort. After all, multiplayer RPGs were generally meant for partying up. It was just... so many of the games he played rewarded one player above all others, even when there was cooperation involved. Kill lists, K/D ratios, scoreboards, those kinds of things weren't available here, but he felt their presence in the back of his mind, nonetheless.

He *wanted* to be first to the top, to face down the Mountain Lord alone, strong enough to take the guy on and win.

And that wasn't going to happen leading around a band of squabbling humans.

Meatball seemed like the most useful of the potential sidekicks. A partner he could handle. This party leading thing... not his style. But Meatball had meatballs for brains. The least ambitious, least skilled, least devious of the players, from what little Connor had seen, all he'd be good for would be a portable, renewable healing potion.

And despite all his other shortcomings, it was still a tempting call.

But Dizzy had proved herself reliable in a fight, a sympathetic companion, and a co-conspirator who could keep a secret. Hiding their discovery of a secret door back in the Unalive Hills demonstrated that much.

Connor just needed to ditch the rest of these losers.

They fought and killed 11 more Razor Ghouls as they wandered a zone much larger than Connor had initially imagined. This was a place to get lost in for days without someone who knew the back ways and obscure detours.

He called for a rest, putting up a hand, fingers spread, hoping the others would take the cue and realize it was a five-minute break.

`XP: 1300/16000`

At this rate, he'd be level 5 for hours.

Or whatever units of time this game was actually running on.

That note from the devs that things were running faster in here was still vexing him. It *felt* like he'd been in this game all day, if not longer. The Kawaiian Islands, Lohdoh, and Beedeep felt like a week ago. Had they hot-wired his brain to think faster? Was that the secret sauce of Anachronism Interactive's technology?

As the others lounged, many of them tapped at the air,

looking like idiots as they checked their inventories and skills, filed bug reports, or whatever else they'd discovered as ways to interact with the user interface.

While they were distracted, Connor dipped around a corner.

He unequipped his armor.

From the shadows, Dizzy grinned at his loincloth-clad avatar.

Putting a finger to his lips, Connor slunk off into the darkness, beckoning for her to follow.

Dizzy maintained silence with ease, strolling at his side like someone hit a Mute button on her.

Connor's stopping point for the group had been after doubling back to an intersection near Gulgoo's secret passage. Both of them could easily see it marked on their maps.

The pair pawed at the wall until Dizzy located the concealed switch that opened the door. Once the two had slipped through, and the door shut behind them, Connor put his armor back on.

Dizzy made a show of pouting.

Connor snickered, exaggerating the shake of his shoulders so she'd know he found her funny.

It was like acting in a silent movie without the corny cue card captions. Still, it was good to have *some* form of interaction.

The pair made their way back to Hard Pass, and this time, Connor was determined to do better than their last attempt.

CHAPTER 25
BY ANY OTHER NAME

HARD PASS

For someone determined to get farther up Hard Pass this time around, Connor was spending an awfully long time at the entrance leading back into the Black Catacombs. His feet were noticing. His legs were noticing. Several yards ahead, Dizzy was noticing, too. She tapped a foot, waiting for him to join her out in the open spaces with hundreds of feet of falling to his death available.

What was death worth, anyway?

She backed away, not even watching where she was going. Dizzy stood at the ledge, beckoning with a single finger. Connor's heart quickened at the thought of her taking one more step backward and...

And what? Falling back down to the Bone Moat? Respawning with 0 XP. What exactly was his fear for her? That she'd feel pain? That last one had been possibly his least painful death so far. That's he'd never see her again? That seemed unlikely as hell.

Slowly, Connor crept out to meet her at the ledge. She stepped away one pace to meet him. Head tilted back, she drew herself up and kissed him.

Then and there, Connor decided that Dizzy was one of the women in the test group. If not... well, he'd process that some other time. This avatar, whoever was piloting it, was a woman, hot as hell, and only pulled her ninja mask down to reveal her face to *him*.

Connor kissed back.

Then, he noticed he was falling.

Air rushed past. He panicked, struggled to break free of Dizzy's embrace. But she'd used some rogue trickery, and they were nowhere near the cliff anymore. Also, they'd fallen far enough already that any effort to save themselves was moot.

`SECLUDED CEMETERY`

"You have died, but your journey is not yet ended. Rise once more, hero, and press onward."

Dizzy planted a quick kiss on his cheek once they were both back among the living.

He was... fine.

`XP: 0/16000`

OK, he'd lost some XP, but that seemed like a small penalty at this point.

From the gate back to Unalive Hills, Dizzy beckoned. He didn't know how well he could protect her on the run through the zombie swarm, but he...

She vanished.

OK. Maybe she didn't need protecting.

`UNALIVE HILLS`

Connor put up his sword in front of him and barreled through the zombies, swinging away as he went. Even with just two of them around, his one-shot kills were only gaining him 10 XP each.

He racked up 40 zombies by the time he was clear of the swarm. Then he remembered. They had a side trip to take. Together.

XP: 400/16000

He waded back into the fray, shrugging off zombie fingernails and bites that couldn't penetrate his DEF.

He slaughtered another 38 before catching back up with Dizzy where they'd seen the secret door.

XP: 780/16000

Underbrush stood out readily, since other than the fog and the mogul hills, Unalive Hills was a barren landscape. Checking between a cluster of four bushes, there was a wooden trap door with a ring pull.

Connor gave it a quick heave, and the trap door swung open.

500 XP

Nice. XP for finding secrets. He could get behind that.

XP: 1280/16000

He was practically back to where he'd been when the pair fell.

A short ladder led the pair down into a room that contained nothing but a lone treasure chest.

CHOOSE YOUR REWARD

When he opened the chest, two options floated up, ephemeral and insubstantial.

His options were two swords, each far larger than his own and with longer hilts meant to be wielded with two hands or not at all. One had a gothic crossguard and pommel and bore a blade that glowed a pale white. The other was all black, with a demonic motif, and glowed a sickly red.

Connor took a moment to examine each. Out of the corner of his eye, he noticed Dizzy extending a hand to examine her options as well.

GUARDIAN'S SWORD - 6 ATK - You and nearby allies take 3 less damage from all sources.

RAVAGER'S SWORD - 4 ATK - You drain 3 HP with each attack.

At first glance, the answer seemed obvious. The Guardian's Sword was just 2 more ATK. Clear winner. But when Connor factored in the HP drain, the Ravager's Sword was effectively 7 ATK, except some of it was an HP drain effect.

The Guardian's Sword actually had a little less offense, but more preventative defense. The Ravager's Sword was more potent, and it allowed him to heal—a skill he didn't have at all. But he would take more damage in the first place.

He hated, HATED that aesthetics were nagging at him to take the Ravager's Sword. He'd just ditched four noobs in the Black Catacombs. He wasn't really feeling the holy knight vibe this play-through. The Ravager's Sword was a toss-up stat-wise. Connor could admit that, in a party setting, the Guardian's Sword was probably the stronger pick.

RECEIVED: RAVAGER'S SWORD

Connor equipped it immediately.

GAINED TITLE: THE UNHALLOWED

Smirking at the idea that the sword defined him as a character, Connor checked his character sheet.

NAME: Connor TITLE: The Unhallowed

CLASS: Knight LEVEL: 5

HP: 43 MP: 0 ATK: 13 DEF: 12

Checking him out wielding the Ravager's Sword, Dizzy nodded her approval. She pulled out a new pair of Tanto-styled daggers that didn't look suited to throwing, but he doubted the game was going to make that a factor. The blades were hard to look at, cloaked in a black mist that all but rendered them invisible unless you stared straight at them.

Without even seeing her stow them, Dizzy's daggers disappeared.

Left in a basement chamber with nothing but an empty

treasure chest, Dizzy blocked the ladder that was their only exit. Not wanting to physically remove her from the way, Connor gestured with both hands for her to either climb up ahead of him or stand aside.

Dizzy shook her head. She tapped a finger against the breastplate of his Battered Armor, then jerked a thumb aside.

Furrowing his brow, Connor tried to figure out what she meant for him to do. HE wasn't in the way, she was. And if she wanted him to take off his armor, he'd get torn to ribbons by the zombies outside. He might be quieter moving around without it, but he wasn't able to turn invisible.

Unless...

Maybe that was one of her new abilities? To turn him invisible along with her, as long as Connor didn't make too much noise.

Dizzy leaned back against the ladder, taking it in both hands and arching her back.

Connor pointed up.

Rolling her eyes, Dizzy grabbed the sides of her ninja uniform. In an instant, it was gone. She was standing there, clad in only some basic-as-hell fantasy setting underwear, displaying a body that had been made by turning a lot of cosmetic settings to maximums and minimums. She was even, he noticed for the first time, redheaded.

Connor gulped.

Dizzy tapped his armor again, then shook her head.

He shook his right back.

A trap. This was now almost definitely a trap.

Connor updated his guess as to the identity of the player behind Dizzy. This wasn't one of the women. It wasn't even one of the guys. Kelli was piloting Dizzy. It had to be. They'd spent all that time in the dating sim figuring out all his likes and dislikes as far as women went. She'd gotten a vast array of reactions out of him, many that he hadn't even expected himself.

If Kelli was Dizzy, that probably meant that other PhDs and developers were running the rest of the players. It meant this was yet another lab rat maze for his libido. He was here to get to the top of the Spire of Fate and be the first to slay the mountain lord, just like it said in his quest log. If he got a pop-up about getting laid with a quest reward offered for completion, he'd *maybe* consider it, just because he was that much of a sucker for a completed quest.

Other than that, though, Kelli was going to have to get her kicks some other way. He was done being her boy toy. He was Connor the Unhallowed.

Connor took Dizzy by her too-thin waist, intent on depositing her out of the way of the ladder's bottom. When she twined herself around him in an embrace, he updated his plan. Maintaining his hold on her with one hand, he used the other to climb the ladder carrying her.

By the time he set her down out in the Unalive Hills again, she'd put her ninja suit back on.

He swept a hand out toward the direction where they'd find the Bone Moat. With a huff, Dizzy vanished.

As Connor plowed through another 41 zombies to get back through the swarm, he wondered if he'd see her again on the far side, or if she'd decide to disappear on him for good.

CHAPTER 26
NEW HEIGHTS

CONNOR MADE it across the Bone Moat without incident and through to Hard Pass via Gulgoo's secret door. Throughout the Black Catacombs, he came across corpses freshly disappearing. He was right behind her, but Dizzy never showed herself.

He even caught the secret door ajar before it reset.

"Dizzy!" he shouted after her. Of course, that was an empty gesture. He knew she couldn't hear him.

`HARD PASS`

Connor took a moment to seethe.

`REPORT BUG`

"You people really need to fix this player communication bug. Got some hurt feelings in here, and it's not doing your data gathering or whatever-the-fuck any good."

Wind howled.

Connor glanced ahead, up the trail. Out in the sunshine, with no shadows to speak of, Dizzy should theoretically have been easy to spot.

Unless she was hiding in, like, that *one* bush.

Connor checked.

To his surprise, he found, no Dizzy, but rather something Gulgoo had retrieved here that Connor hadn't even considered waiting around to see if it respawned. He held out a palm to check and be certain.

GLIDER KIT - All the pieces needed to make a Kawaiian Glider.

What the hell? Why not?

RECEIVED: KAWAIIAN GLIDER KIT

Connor checked in his growing inventory. Despite the item's bulk, it vanished with no hint of encumbrance.

30 COINS

2 YELLOW GOBO DAGGER

FISHING NET (5X)

WATER BREATHING POTION (96X)

BRIDGE KEY

XPOT

KAWAIIAN GLIDER KIT

Connor really needed to figure out a way to make some money. Then again, he really hadn't found anything to spend it on. But that was a recipe for getting to the end of the game and finding that *one* vendor with all the really best shit and being woefully unable to afford anything.

It was like basically any upscale mall, now that he thought about it.

Grabbing the kit from his inventory, Connor just flailed with the pieces.

Rather than thwart his efforts in IKEA-like glee, the various components assembled themselves. As far as ease of manufacturing, it was more Bisquick pancakes and less Kallax bookshelf.

RECEIVED: KAWAIIAN GLIDER

The kit had vanished from his inventory.

In what felt like the stupidest act he'd taken in the game thus far—but admittedly probably didn't crack the top 5—

Connor climbed onto the glider, which seemed human-sized as opposed to the miniature one Gulgoo had fashioned.

What did he have to lose?

A life?

Some XP?

His self-respect?

Gritting his teeth, Connor ran to the ledge and jumped.

Instantly, the glider caught an updraft and soared.

SKY

A thrill of exhilaration shot through Connor as he rode the current of air higher and higher, circling around the Spire of Fate.

He'd learned from Kelli how to pilot one. It was frankly less scary than walking the rope bridges, due to that familiarity. Kelli hadn't cured him of his fear of heights, but she'd given him some exposure and some help in coping.

The Spire looked no less intimidating from on high. And when he spotted White Gobos, Connor panicked.

On the cliffside trails below, a pair of the little wind wizards twirled their staves overhead. While Connor had learned how to steer a hang glider, he also knew they weren't exactly helicopters. His ponderous turn didn't get him out of the way of the incoming blast of wind from below.

But far from being knocked from the sky, Connor caught yet another burst of upward momentum. Straightening out of his turn, he reversed course and rose on the magical wind to all new heights.

He spotted a ledge and a clear entrance back into the Spire of Fate, well above where he'd exited the Black Catacombs.

Connor circled in and landed hard.

2

That could have been worse.

Once the Kawaiian Glider disappeared back into his inventory, a new message popped up.

WHAT GOES DOWN

2,000 XP

By reflex, Connor brought up a hand to examine the message before it disappeared.

WHAT GOES DOWN - Land a Kawaiian Glider at least 100 feet higher than you took off.

"You have earned your first Achievement," Kelindra commented. Connor had nearly forgotten about his narrator and resident help file, it had been so long since she'd spoken up. "Achievements are special bonuses gained by performing interesting and unique tasks. They reward creative and exploratory game play. You can see your Achievements in the Achievements menu."

"And I can see my Obvious Advice in my Obvious Advice menu."

Connor had been getting achievements in video games since he was too young to remember. So had pretty much everyone born since the invention of Steam.

Still, it was a nice chunk of XP, a new tactic for ascending the mountain, and probably put him back in the lead for the race to the summit.

Craning his neck, Connor still couldn't make out anything resembling a top to the mountain. Even the ominous clouds loomed far, far above him.

He stood at yet another way to explore the stone innards of the Spire of Fate.

Connor crossed a runed stone entryway and was informed of his new zone.

THE ANT FARM

"Oh. I don't like the sound of that."

CHAPTER 27
UP, UP, AND ONE WAY

CONNOR DIDN'T LIKE this place at all.

In fact, the Ant Farm was beginning to creep him out. For starters, there was no ambient light. If not for the fact that his Ravager's Sword glowed, he would have been entirely in the dark. He found himself wishing he'd gone with the Guardian's Sword just because, in retrospect, it shed more light.

More than not being able to see a few feet in front of him was the smell.

Video games weren't supposed to smell. The Unalive Hills had been mercifully odorless. So had the Bone Moat and the Black Catacombs. He vaguely recalled some sea breezes from the Kawaiian Islands that he'd written off as psychosomatic.

Connor was sure that Metroid either would have smelled like cosmic horror or the inside of a space helmet. Castlevania would have reeked of blood. Anyone venturing into Zerg levels of StarCraft would have puked their guts up.

The Ant Farm had an earthy, compost-y smell that reminded Connor of fresh landscaping. That wouldn't have been so bad. Except he was underground, living in it. The tunnel complex he navigated with his sword for light was a mix of rock and packed earth. Either someone didn't know how topsoil worked, or he was getting perilously close to the top of this mountain. And one thing about topsoil was that it was utterly infested with worms, ants, beetles—all manner of exoskeletal life, really. Plus, vermin of all sorts burrowed there.

He had yet to encounter anything alive, but Connor dreaded what he'd meet down here.

There was just something reassuringly fantastical about Gobos and various undead monstrosities. The notion of a mole big enough to dig the tunnels he was walking through terrified him.

The ground rumbled under Connor's feet.

He quit tracing a hand along the wall and gripped his Ravager's Sword in both hands.

His minimap was no help. Connor had only gone a short way down the tunnels of the Ant Farm. The only way to avoid whatever was coming would be to retreat all the way back out to the cliffside.

Two glints in the darkness reflected the faintest light from his sword. Then two more. Connor tried to hold his ground, but his feet found better footing a pace back. And another two paces backward, they found even firmer ground on which to stand firm.

Those glints became eyes. Those eyes topped insectoid heads, which topped ant-like bodies with the upper thoraxes upright. Dexterous front legs ended in prehensile claws that clutched spears with jagged, crystalline tips aimed his way.

Nope.

NOPE.

Rather than wait to see how fighting them went, Connor and his feet agreed that they wanted no part of being fed in pieces to whatever these things worshiped or swore fealty to. He raced back through the darkness, stumbling along uneven terrain until he spotted daylight.

HARD PASS

Yeah. Connor was giving that Ant Farm a hard pass, all right. He took up a defensive position at the tunnel entrance, Ravager's Sword at the ready in a two-handed grip, ready to Parry anything that came outside with him. But the ant creatures didn't pursue him this far.

A long, relieved breath escaped him.

This was bravery he could get behind. The smart kind. The kind where his XP didn't crash back to zero.

XP: 3690/16000

He was nearly a quarter of the way to Level 6, and there was no one around to impress with performative bravery. He still had an XPOT in his inventory, too. If he thought it would put him over the top, that would be one thing. But once he got close, then Connor would consider reckless acts again.

For the time being...

"How do I continue up?"

There was an answer, and it was a dubious one. Beside the entrance to the Ant Farm, a narrow path hugged the mountain. But unlike Hard Pass, this trail wasn't even wide enough for one person without scooting along sideways.

Experimentally, Connor whipped out his Kawaiian Glider. In an instant, it was ready to go.

He stowed it, then jumped as high as he could. First off, that turned out to be a lot higher than he expected—like, dunk-over-an-NBA-center high. But he subsequently found that he could grab the Kawaiian Glider while in mid-air. In fact, he had to quickly turn and nose into the ground before he glided right back down the spire.

Feeling like he had a viable parachute option as a backup, Connor began his ascent up the side of the spire.

CLIFFS OF CLAVEN

"This is better than humanoid ants... this is better than

humanoid ants..." he chanted as a mantra to remind himself of the alternative.

But was it?

Was it really?

Connor was maybe fifty feet above that landing and was just losing sight of it around the spire's curvature. He still couldn't see an end in sight or the top of the mountain, though the clouds loomed much closer than they once had. And down below...

Connor pressed himself against the cliff as a wave of vertigo washed over him. Jesus, that was a long way down! He could barely even make out the Bone Moat waiting to devour his remains if he slipped.

No.

He had his Kawaiian Glider. If he had to. If he broke down and couldn't take this anymore, he could hang glide down all the way to the Kawaiian Islands, sit back, and wait until they eventually came to get him out of the rig for lunch. Or dinner. Or whatever meal for whatever time it was outside the game.

Damn it felt like he'd been awake for days.

Once the vertigo passed, Connor continued edging along the cliff path until he heard a voice call to him from above.

"Hello, hero. What brings you way up here?" It was Brendan's voice again, but a new villager peered down from a higher trail. To Connor's utter bafflement, the villager had a laden pack donkey along with him.

Checking his footing, Connor examined the donkey with an outstretched palm.

`DONKEY (no name) - Mount. Excellent at traversing steep and unstable terrain.`

"I'm just trying to get to the top of the mountain."

"The slowest way possible, maybe. That's no way to climb. I'm an expert climber, but an amateur like yourself should be riding, not walking. I'm Uppup, the spire's greatest mountaineer."

"I wouldn't mind taking that Donkey off your hands, if you don't need him," Connor offered.

"Well, well, now. Never one to turn down a financial opportunity. Not even way up here. I could sell him to you for 100 Coins."

Connor bit the inside of his cheek. He didn't have 100 Coins. He didn't have a plan to get 100 Coins in any timely fashion. Whoever set up this test environment hadn't paid a helluva lot of attention to the economy, in his opinion.

"Can you bring him down here for me to get a good look before I decide?" Connor asked.

"Sure, lad. Hero like yourself shouldn't be doing extra, dangerous climbing when a pro's pro like myself is around. Don't trouble yourself. Be down in two shakes." It would have helped sell the character if anyone but Brendan had been roped into reading the lines. Any high school theater kid would have been an upgrade.

Connor waited as Uppup deftly hopped from rock to rock like a mountain goat to meet up with him. He cringed and clenched every time the little villager landed, but the guy never missed his footing; never even stumbled.

"There!" Uppup declared as he set down beside Connor, forced to crane his neck to interact with the much taller human. "Now, how's that for a fine beast?"

"Before we conduct commerce, do you have any quests for me? Any tasks you could use help with?"

"Don't think that I do."

"What about advice for this part of the mountain? Shortcuts? Things to watch out for? Local wildlife and how to deal with it?" Connor was willing to test the limits of this mountaineer's so-called "expertise."

"Well, let's see... You'll find caves here, there, and everywhere. Just poke a head inside to see what's what. If you happen to find raw turned earth, tunnels like an ant might dig, you're in the domain of the Antaurs. Fierce warriors. Lousy cooks. Wouldn't go breaking bread with them, if you know what I mean."

"I kind of don't."

"And if you find mine supports, mine cart tracks, mining equipment, then you can be certain you're among the—"

"Dwarves," Connor guessed. "Some kind of dwarf knockoff, even though 90 percent of fantasy games just take them as is and call it a day?"

"Dragonoids."

"Oh."

"The Dragonoids are minions of the Mountain Lord. Intelligent. Cunning. Fireproof. You'll know them by their black scales and—"

"The fact they're not ants."

"And their wings. They provide the Mountain Lord and his troops with weapons and armor. They mine ore from the Spire of Fate itself. They patrol the upper tunnels below the Mountain Lord's stronghold and the skies above it. If you want to reach the Mountain Lord, you're going to have to go through them to get there."

"How do *you* know I'm seeking the Mountain Lord?"

Uppup shrugged. "You seem the type. Now. About this donkey..."

Connor studied the creature. It had a placid face and chill attitude. It didn't seem to care that it was perched on a narrow ledge thousands of feet up. Connor could admire that. "Nice ride. Any chance of wiggle room on the price?"

"I hardly know you. Why would I cut you a bargain?"

"How about barter? I've got a Steel Sword I'm not using. And some Yellow Gobo Daggers."

"Bah! What would I need with those?"

"I have a *ton* of Water Breathing Potions."

"I breathe water just fine, *human*."

Connor blinked his surprise at that one. He had no idea the Kawaiians were amphibious. It had completely never come up. Or was this just sloppy writing by the designers again, and either they weren't able to breathe water or not all of them were aware of the fact?

"And I don't suppose I could sell you a Bridge Key?"

Uppup shook his head.

"Well, I think that exhausts my options. Pleasure almost doing business with you, Uppup." Connor stuck out a hand.

The NPC was programmed to shake it.

Connor gripped tight as he could.

Uppup weighed relatively little.

"Wuuuuuaaaaaaahhhhhhhhhhhhh!!!!!"

Uppup sailed off the Cliffs of Claven and arced down, down, down...

The Donkey watched in mild curiosity.

Connor grabbed the reins.

"You have purchased your first Mount," Kelindra informed him. Connor snickered at the "purchased" bit. "Mounts are personal transportation allowing different modes and speeds of travel throughout Spire of Fate. Once purchased, Mounts will remain loyal to their owner, and are not transferable in any way between players, though certain Mounts may allow multiple passengers. You can also customize your Mount. Choose a name for your Mount via the keypad."

A display with a qwerty keyboard sprang in front of Connor. He could see the Donkey watching him, waiting to find out its name.

Connor tapped out: X-O-T-E

That seemed like a solid name for a Donkey.

It took him three tries to mount Xote. Not that it was hard. But the sheer drop just the other side of the animal gave him second—then *third*—thoughts before he finally managed to hop on and grab the reins.

"Giddyup."

Xote didn't move.

"Go."

Nothing.

"Help."

"Hello. I am Kelindra, your guide to Spire of Fate. How may I assist you?"

"How do I make the Donkey go?"

"Donkeys and other Mounts do not need to relieve themselves in Spire of Fate."

"How do I get it to move with me riding it?"

"Just go in a direction. If you do not intentionally Dismount, your Mount will go wherever you would."

"Neat."

Connor tried walking along the trail. Xote moved instead. He didn't actually need to pick his footing; the Donkey handled that itself. Connor tried jumping up to a higher trail. Xote sprang like a gazelle, landing deftly on a higher trail.

500 XP

Connor paused. Huh? Where had that XP just come from?

Wow... the only reason he could think was that Uppup just *finally* hit the ground.

Shaking off the horror of that plummet and trying not to live it vicariously, Connor kept his focus on the task ahead.

"Badass. C'mon, Xote, let's explore these cliffs and find some Dragonoids. I think I've clearly settled on an evil playthrough. It's time to meet the bad guys."

CHAPTER 28
THE ARENA

XOTE WAS A CHAMP. Basically, he was a reskinned mountain goat, capable of Z-axis travel along the side of the Spire of Fate. All Connor had to do was keep his legs clamped onto the Donkey's flanks and will it to go the direction he wanted. It perched on outcroppings of rock that Connor wouldn't have trusted as handholds, made leaps with absolute precision. Never skidded. Never slipped.

Connor had a new best friend.

But their upward journey came to an end when the Spire of Fate flared outward slightly. Even the impossible exploits of Donkey Physics failed in the face of an overhang. Connor craned his neck, wondering how best to go about scaling the remainder of the mountain.

He mentally tested various alternatives.

The Kawaiian Glider seemed likely to lose him altitude rather than gain it unless he could find a reliable way to generate either an updraft or thrust. Just picturing himself coming up with some kind of magical rocket to power a hang gliding fighter jet amused Connor to no end.

Scaling the last bit himself stretched the plausibility of both his climbing skills and his vertigo.

Finding a teleporter would be great, but felt more like waiting for luck than a plan.

No. He needed to stick to the advice Uppup had inadvertently given before his untimely demise. Connor needed to bargain with the Dragonoids.

Their lair wasn't too hard to find. Circling the spire aboard Xote, he was able to spot Dragonoid aerial patrols at cloud level, then watch to see where they came and went. Some, to his chagrin, simply vanished back above the clouds. Others, however, returned to lower entrances still high up the mountainside, but at heights Connor could access.

He dismounted Xote on a stonework balcony leading into a mountain tunnel that, as Uppup predicted, resembled a mine.

There was no way he could really take Xote inside.

Anything could lie ahead. Combat most certainly. Traps, crawlways, opportunities for stealth—as much as he sucked at it. A dungeon was just no place for a Donkey.

"Wait here, would you?"

Xote stared at him blankly. Expectantly? Maybe Connor was reading too much into the animal's reaction, or lack thereof.

"I'd take you with me if I could. I—"

Wait. This was a stupid idea. Was it, however, *too* stupid or just exactly the right amount of stupid for this half-baked game?

Connor picked Xote up.

The Donkey disappeared.

Oh, for fuck's sake. He HAD to check.

```
INVENTORY:
42 COINS
2 YELLOW GOBO DAGGER
FISHING NET (5X)
WATER BREATHING POTION (96X)
```

BRIDGE KEY

XPOT

STEEL SWORD

KAWAIIAN GLIDER

DONKEY (XOTE)

Yep. He'd picked up his damn Donkey and stuffed him into a backpack. It was too amusing to even put into a bug report. Not to mention the fact that it was handy as heck.

WARRENS OF WAR

Connor crept forward, Ravager's Sword drawn. But here, at least, there were torches. Iron sconces hammered into the stonework gave the place an intentionality that the Ant Farm's claw-dug tunnels lacked. The creatures that did this might be evil, might be bloodthirsty, might be servants to the game's end boss, who Connor was sworn to slay.

But it also suggested intelligence. They might be reasoned with.

Bathed in the red glow of his sword, Connor set out to test that assumption.

XP: 4190/16000

He had a quarter of a level's progress riding on whether he'd judged rightly here.

The scratch of claws and muttered conversation forewarned Connor of the approach of a patrol. He waited well short of the nearest intersection of tunnels.

He readied a palm to examine whoever or whatever came into view.

The Dragonoids matched Uppup's description. Barrel chested, with pectoral muscles that connected to wings that looked very much non-vestigial, they didn't have a separate set of arms. Those brawn-powered wings ended in bony, scaly fingers with stubby claws. Their heads were more pterodactyl than traditional dragon. They walked upright, wore armored loincloths over their black scaly nether regions, and had tails long enough that they had to be held up off the floor.

Dragonoid - Humanoid reptiles. Flying. Immune to fire.

It was better than he'd gotten out of the examine skill for most stuff in this game.

"Friend or foe?" Connor challenged.

"This is our home," the lead Dragonoid countered. "We should be asking you."

On a hunch, Connor sheathed his weapon. "I'm not here to fight you. I seek passage to the mountain lord."

"You wish to serve?"

Oh, wow. Maybe Connor was on to something here. "Yeah. Something like that."

"You will come with us. Taskmaster D'Veez will wish to test your worthiness."

Hell yeah! Now *this* was RPG stuff. Hack and slash was a great palate cleanser, but if he wanted to fight endless hordes of monsters, Connor could have played God of War or something. Tricking, scheming, and backing up big plays with real power... *that* was what RPG should be all about.

"Lead the way."

Connor followed his two escorts through a maze of passages, the remains of a vast mine complex by the look of it. Then, ahead, he heard the ringing of hammers on anvils and then felt the heat of forges.

The Dragonoid city was, in video game terms, decent sized. There was a ground level and a mezzanine, connected by ladders and pulley-lifted platforms. The residents could fly, but they needed to move goods around as well, and maybe flying wasn't *always* the best way to travel.

Connor gawked at the Dragonoids smiths at work. They weren't making visible progress, but each seemed intent on a masterpiece of metal and dragonscale.

He also noticed two secret doors. Whether and when he'd have a chance to explore them remained unclear, but it was good to take note of their existence.

A small audience chamber more resembled an executive office than a throne room.

Taskmaster D'Veez looked up from a pile of papers, peering over a pair of wire spectacles that looked incongruous perched on its beaky face. "Who is this?"

A scribe at his side looked up. "That's a human, sir."

"Why is it in my office?"

The patrol leader spoke up. "This one claims he's headed to see the mountain lord."

"Why would a human want to see the mountain lord? Did the Kawaiians put him up to it? It's that fanatic, Lohdoh, riling them up again, I'll wager."

"We didn't ask his reason, Taskmaster."

Connor decided to take the initiative here, rather than wait to be interrogated. "Taskmaster D'Veez, I was informed of the mountain lord by this Lohdoh fellow, as you deduce, but my motive is my own. I seek an audience. I've already slain one Kawaiian to get this far. I'm not their errand boy."

"Can you prove your claim?" D'Veez asked. The Dragonoid drummed his claws on the metallic surface of his desk.

Connor reached into his inventory and pulled out Xote.

"Is that Uppup's steed?" D'Veez asked, clearly shocked.

"Yup. He's mine now. So, how about it? Can you allow me passage through your territory?"

D'Veez shook his head. "You may be no friend of the Kawaiians, but that doesn't mean you deserve an audience with the mountain lord. I must ascertain your worthiness."

"Via some sort of quest?" Connor asked. His grin was

hopeful, enticing, baiting the Dragonoid to feed him some juicy XP and maybe another XPOT.

"Via the arena!" D'Veez declared grandly. Then, in an undertone, he added. "And maybe a quest."

Connor's quest journal pulsed.

PRESENT THE SPEAR OF AN ARENA OPPONENT TO D'Veez: 0/1

The patrol Dragonoids led Connor to one of the hidden doors, revealing it as the combatant's entry point to the arena.

A crowd gathered as if they'd been forewarned of the event, filling carved stone bleachers overlooking the fighting pit.

At the far end of the arena, a portcullis opened. Another closed behind him, barring a retreat back out the door by which Connor had entered.

D'Veez, up in a position of honor in the front row of the stands, presided. "Today, we have a human who seeks to prove his worth. Connor the Unhallowed will face one of our own in mortal combat. May the winner present me the weapon of his vanquished opponent."

A burly Dragonoid emerged wearing a silvery breastplate and wielding a barbed spear.

"Let the contest... BEGIN!"

Connor instantly fell into his Parry stance. Ravager's Sword held before him, this guy was going to have to get through his defenses if he wanted a piece of Connor.

In a blur, the Dragonoid Gladiator was upon him. It was the Charge attack viewed from the wrong side, for once. Connor barely got his blade up in time to avoid being marshmallow s'mored. But the instant he turned aside the spear, he flicked out his own weapon and drew first blood.

9

3

+3

The draining attack sent a surge of energy up Connor's arms. He felt energized.

HP: 43+3/43

Well, well, well, now... that was a bonus he wasn't expecting. Spire of Fate used an overflow HP system. Nothing Meatball had done had healed Connor beyond max, but it seemed that the Ravager's Sword was forged a little different.

Springing back, the Dragonoid Gladiator thrust again, but Connor had the perfect defense set up for this kind of attacker.

9

3

+3

The Dragonoid Gladiator swung its spear, tip whistling through the air toward Connor's helmeted head. But he batted the haft up and clear of his cranium.

9

3

+3

Down went his foe.

2000 XP

What? That was a shitload.

Connor wished he could take another crack at the guy at that rate, but, alas...

PRESENT THE SPEAR OF AN ARENA OPPONENT TO D'Veez: 0/1

All he had left to do was pick up the spear and hand it over.

"Congratulations, Connor the Unhallowed, you have—"

"Kelindra, how can I abandon a quest?"

"To abandon a quest, select it in your quest log by touching it, and say 'Abandon Quest.'"

Connor did just that.

The completed quest to turn in the spear vanished.

"D'Veez, how can I prove myself worthy?" Connor called up to the Taskmaster.

"Via the arena!" D'Veez declared grandly. "Today, we have a human who seeks to prove his worth. Connor the Unhallowed will face one of our own in mortal combat. May the winner present me the weapon of his vanquished opponent."

Another burly Dragonoid, identical to the first, emerged wearing the same armor and wielding an identical spear.

The first one Connor had slain vanished the instant the new one showed up.

XP: 6190/16000

Connor readied himself to intercept the expected Charge attack. "Let's do this..."

The second Dragonoid Gladiator fared no better than the first.

XP: 8190/16000

Nor did the third...

XP: 10190/16000

The Dragonoids didn't seem the least bit aware of previous bouts. D'Veez willingly offered the quest of worthiness over and over.

Connor kept triggering the scripted encounter over and over, racking up XP until...

XP: 190/32000

>>>LEVEL UP!!!<<<

YOU GAIN
2 ATTACK
3 DEFENSE
15 HP
0 MP

1 SKILL CHOICE

Connor paused, allowing the latest corpse to cool on the arena floor as he browsed his skill offerings.

CLEAVING STRIKE - A killing blow with a swinging weapon can continue onward to strike another opponent.

IMPROVED RIPOSTE - Riposte now deals full weapon damage instead of half.

MOUNTED COMBAT - Able to use weapons while mounted. Unlocks the Charge attack while mounted.

The Mounted Combat skill sounded fun. Connor allowed Cleaving Strike to continue simmering on the back burner as he selected Improved Riposte. The skill was already getting a workout, and he was happy to load on more powers to it.

He was about to pick up a weapon, turn in his quest, and proceed with his mission. Then it occurred to him to wonder... why?

He was here on his own, by himself. There was no one waiting impatiently for him to finish. D'Veez didn't appear to mind Connor's shenanigans. The devs or Kelli were welcome to step in and stop him—or get him a lunch break—any time they liked.

"Abandon Quest." Connor smirked. "D'Veez, how can I prove myself worthy?"

The answer was, of course, yet another easy win in the arena. Now, with Improved Riposte, it was even easier.

18

3

+3

18

3

+3

Dead.

1500 XP

That was quite the drop-off from the 2000 XP it had been last level. But it was still a chunk.

XP: 1690/32000

Connor had nowhere to go. Nowhere to be.

He killed the same poor, oblivious Dragonoid Gladiator over and over. It was like doing push-ups or jogging or CrossFit, but with two key differences. First, Connor was enjoying himself the whole time. Second, and more importantly, it was showing immediate results.

The XP rolled in, now 1500 at a time.

XP: 3190/32000

XP: 4690/32000

XP: 6190/32000

...

Eventually Connor hit another milestone.

XP: 31690/32000

XP: 1190/64000

>>>LEVEL UP!!!<<<

YOU GAIN

2 ATTACK

3 DEFENSE

18 HP

0 MP

1 SKILL CHOICE

Cleaving Strike was back, joined by two newcomer skills.

IMPROVED TWO-HANDED FIGHTING - When wielding a two-handed or a versatile one-handed weapon in two hands, your Attack now increases equal to twice your level.

SPELL PARRY - Reduce the damage of an incoming spell by an amount equal to your Defense using the Parry action.

Damn. Connor was really wanting to take Cleaving Strike one of these days, but he just never found a way to prioritize it over some of the cool new shit he was gaining access to.

Improved Two-Handed Fighting was the clear winner. Connor waffled a moment before deciding that he had to keep Spell Parry for next time. He just couldn't see himself using Cleaving Strike often enough to ignore the potential for defending himself against spell damage when he knew he had some big bad final boss battle coming up.

He was Level 7 now. This was a good point to walk away and proceed onward.

He glanced up into the crowd and spotted D'Veez gazing down disdainfully, waiting for the chance to reward this piddling human for his victory over a weakling.

Nope.

"Abandon Quest..."

The process began anew.

Now, Connor didn't even wait for the Dragonoid Gladiator to make the first move.

"Aaaaaaaaah!"

The arena blurred. Connor swept the Ravager's Sword down in a wicked arc.

28

3

+3

1000 XP

The thing didn't even get its weapon set to defend itself.

XP: 2190/64000

XP: 3190/64000

XP: 4190/64000

XP: 5190/64000

XP: 6190/64000

Connor could literally do this all day. And with the whole process taking a little under a minute now that he'd streamlined it, he spent a solid hour plodding his way through to Level 8. This was the luxury of paid play time, a gamer work ethic, and an obsessive need to be the best.

XP: 190/128000

That golden, sparkly swirling gong rang again, just for Connor.

>>>LEVEL UP!!!<<<

YOU GAIN

2 ATTACK

3 DEFENSE

24 HP

0 MP

1 SKILL CHOICE

Truth be told, and looking inward just a little, Connor had to admit that he was a little addicted to picking new skills. He tapped the selection like a junkie getting his fix.

SPELL PARRY - Reduce the damage of an incoming spell by an amount equal to your DEF using the Parry action.

MOUNTAIN SLAM - Strike the ground at your feet to send foes within melee range flying back, dealing damage equal to half your Attack.

STALWART - Increase DEF by your level.

Connor loved and hated the design team every time these situations came up. He wanted them all. He wanted every skill in the game all rolled up into a perfect ball of overpowered awesomeness.

Spell Parry seemed almost essential in the long run. Eventually, he knew his counter was going to be magic damage. But Mountain Slam sounded like a shitload of fun. Stalwart, by comparison, sounded like the kind of passive skill where you'd never notice it, but if you went with it and someone subsequently took it away, you'd notice the shit out of it.

Why was Connor even playing this game?

To win at any cost?

To have fun?

Because they were paying him to be here?

Winning in the long run sounded like Stalwart was the way to go. That was a lot of DEF to gain. Spell Parry really felt like it was going to win him some important, maybe essential, fight sometime soon.

He picked Mountain Slam, since the idea of blasting enemies all over the place just couldn't be beat. Plus, without taking Cleaving Strike, this gave him an area of effect attack. He let Spell Parry Float once more.

Ready again, he took on the Dragonoid Gladiator as a test run.

The Dragonoid Gladiator Charged.

Connor didn't try to defend himself.

It stabbed him with its spear, straight to the chest. The blow hurt, but it could have been a lot worse.

6

Connor swung Happy Gilmore style and lopped its head off.

24

3

+3

500 XP

HP: 97/100

XP: 690/128,000

A mental spreadsheet warned Connor that another level this way would be about four hours of tedious, repetitive combat.

What part of corporate life hadn't prepared Connor to stand around here repeating the same few commands over and over? He'd regularly done it at a Windows PC for eight hours a day, and this was a ton more engaging and actually *less* repetitive than tracking shipping routes from Shanghai to Los Angeles to Austin.

Connor zoned out.

The fights became meditative. The cheers of the crowd were nothing but white noise.

XP: 190/256,000

>>>LEVEL UP!!!<<<

YOU GAIN

2 ATTACK

3 DEFENSE

30 HP

0 MP

1 SKILL CHOICE

SPELL PARRY - Reduce the damage of an incoming spell by an amount equal to your DEF using the Parry action.

FLYING COMBAT - Able to use weapons while mounted on a flying Mount. Unlocks the Diving Charge attack while on a flying Mount.

CHARGING SLASH - At the end of a Charge, attack with a Slashing weapon. Deals double `damage against a single target or uses Mountain Slam.`

Holy shit! Connor could turn himself into a flying bomb basically if he went with that last one. Zoom in. Mountain Slam the ground. Send everyone flying and taking damage.

He took it without hesitation. Then, he once more pushed off Spell Parry to later.

"Abandon Quest." Connor said, cracking his knuckles. "D'Veez, how can I prove myself worthy?"

He suspected that he'd finally run this Dragonoid Gladiator down to 0 XP per kill, but he was willing to give it one more go-around to be sure. After all, he'd been here half the day already.

Rather than go into the spiel that Connor was already lip-syncing along to, D'Veez changed it up.

"You! Mighty human, you must prove yourself worthy TO ME!" Spreading his wings, Taskmaster D'Veez glided down from the bleachers to face off against Connor personally.

"No problem, big guy," Connor promised, readying the Ravager's Sword and preparing for a guy who *might* get a hit in against him.

The taskmaster brought no weapon, but bared his claws. Some sort of brawler, probably, based on his size. Probably not Monk-style attacks. More like if one of the Razor Ghouls had a brain. Idly, he wondered whether Anachronism Interactive's claims of human-like AI would apply here, since they certainly didn't against most of the monsters.

Parry active, Connor waited for the Dragonoid Taskmaster to make the first move.

That first move was a few chanted words and a gout of flame belched out of his mouth.

Connor yelped in surprise. For a creature not a ton bigger than him, the flames billowed out like they'd come from a huge dragon. Arena spectators raised arms to shield themselves from the glare.

Caught unawares, and with little time to spare, Connor couldn't avoid the flames.

80

Holy mother of god! What the hell level was this guy?

HP: 50/130

Connor was a truck by now, maybe a truck-and-a-half. But that had taken a huge rip out of his health.

In the face of the horrifying pain, he Charged for a counter-attack before he was done in.

"Aaaaaaaaah!"

Connor swung for double damage.

54

3

+3

Taskmaster D'Veez cried out in pain and fell.

7000 XP

"Hah. Take that," Connor said, standing over the body, which failed to despawn instantly.

40

"Huh?"

Growing accustomed to the in-game pain, he'd actually failed to notice that he was still on fire!

HP: 13/130

"No... No-no-no."

He patted at the lingering flames, knowing full well that he had nothing like a healing potion in his inventory, and doubting that Water Breathing Potions could douse the flames.

20

The arena and all the Dragonoids disappeared around him.

CHAPTER 29
NOWHERE BUT UP

SECLUDED CEMETERY

"You have died, but your journey is not yet ended. Rise once more, hero, and press onward."

"FUCK!" Connor shouted at the top of his lungs as soon as he was among the living.

All that effort. All that distance scaled. He gazed up at distant clouds that he'd been so close to that he could almost touch them.

That Flying Combat skill implied that there were flying creatures that might carry him up a lot quicker than walking and climbing. Taking a long shot, he pulled out his Kawaiian Glider and grabbed hold of the bar.

He attempted to take off by power of will, the same way he made Xote move while mounted on the Donkey.

"Didn't think so," he said with a sigh as he stowed the glider.

UNALIVE HILLS

Zombie claws plinked off him. He swatted a few off him like he would mosquitoes. They didn't give XP anymore, so they were basically background noise now.

BONE MOAT

BLACK CATACOMBS

Connor strolled the darkness between torches. The Razor Ghouls were rats, vermin to be ignored. Although he remembered halfway through that they dropped money, so he splattered 12 of them for 5 Coins apiece along the way despite earning no other reward.

Remembering the weird tomb with the moving statues that Gulgoo had blundered past, Connor headed through that section. On cue, one of them animated.

Palm out, Connor satisfied his curiosity. Guardian Statue. No other info.

"Aaaaaaaaah!"

54

There was no HP drain from the Ravager's Sword or XP from the kill, but the Guardian Statue crumbled to pieces.

Connor searched the sarcophagi and discovered an amulet.

RECEIVED: GUARDIAN STONE

Examining it revealed...

GUARDIAN STONE - Wearer takes half damage from slashing attacks.

Into inventory it went. The effect was too narrow to pass up finding potential secret doors, so he kept his Map-Maker's Waystone equipped.

Curiosity sated, Connor headed to Gulgoo's secret door and out of the zone without incident.

HARD PASS

Connor dug out Xote and climbed aboard. Pointing with his sword like a jousting lance, Connor ordered his little buddy forward. "Let's get 'em, Xote!"

The Donkey only had one speed, and Connor suspected that without taking Mounted Combat, there was going to be no changing that. But while he wasn't in any rush, Xote was also unbothered by the White Gobos wind magic. The little punks on the upper trails swung their staves in big old circles, conjuring up mighty gales.

Beneath Xote's hooves, the bridge swayed precariously.

No matter how much the floor beneath them moved, the Donkey kept plodding forward. Unaffected. Unafraid. Undeterred.

Connor's knuckles went white clutching the reins, but his four-footed pal was the best kind of protection up here.

With, apparently, one trick in their whole book, the White Gobos kept on pestering Connor the Unhallowed with a roller coaster ride across every bridge, retreating and regrouping every time he got close enough to maybe pose a threat to them.

CLIFFS OF CLAVEN

The White Gobos didn't pursue across zone borders. Xote kept on chugging, not asking for, or apparently needing, rest.

Hop.

Clop.

Hop.

Clop.

Don't.

Look.

Down.

Or stop.

Hop.

Clop.

Hop.

Clop.

At.

The.

Top.

Connor didn't spare a glance down as he dismounted on the balcony.

He gave Xote a few pats on the forehead. "Good boy, Xote. Take a break." Back into inventory he went.

WARRENS OF WAR

The same two patrolling guards accosted Connor in the tunnels beyond. "I want to see Taskmaster D'Veez," he ordered.

"What business do you have with the taskmaster?" the leader demanded.

Connor glowered. "The unfinished kind."

He followed the pair up to the Dragonoid city, where the inhabitants had gone back to their duties as if nothing had happened. The taskmaster was back in his office doing paperwork.

Taskmaster D'Veez looked up from a pile of papers, peering over his wire spectacles. "Who is this?"

His scribe looked up and studied Connor. "That's a human, sir."

"Why is it in my office?"

The patrol leader spoke up. "This one claims he has unfinished business with you."

That caught the taskmaster's attention. "Oh, really? What kind?"

"We killed one another in the arena after I bested your gladiator." Connor left off that he'd bested the guy several hundred times.

The scribe at his side nodded vigorously. "That sounds like the sort of thing you might do, sir."

Taskmaster D'Veez scowled. "I would not be slain by a mere *human*."

"The mountain lord himself was human once," Connor claimed, a boast based simply on guesswork and how stories like this tended to go. "I told you I wanted to meet the mountain lord, and you demanded I prove myself worthy."

"Also sounds *very* much like something you'd say," the scribe added. Connor quietly added the weaselly little Dragonoid to his no-kill list if he ended up having to scour this place down to the last combatant to get through their city.

"And you really did kill me?" Taskmaster D'Veez inquired.

"We killed one another," Connor reiterated. "If you want to finish this in the arena..."

D'Veez huffed. "I have *work* to do. If you're no entertainment for the workers and soldiers and I'm a Coin flip to be slain, I see no reason to challenge you or your worthiness." He flicked a dismissive hand toward the patrolling guards. "If he wishes to meet the mountain lord, I see no reason to delay his demise. Grant him passage."

Connor blinked. "But..."

Taskmaster D'Veez, already bent over his paperwork once more, snapped an angry glower at Connor. "What? Is that not what you wished?"

"I had also been intent on fighting you for the reward I was promised."

"That sounds... *less* like you, sir," the scribe commented, earning himself a deletion from Connor's list. "But plausible? Maybe?"

Taskmaster D'Veez rummaged in his desk drawer. "Fine. Take this and begone." He slammed a potion bottle down on the table.

Connor picked it up.

`RECEIVED: SKILL POT`

"Is this what you would have—?"

"HOW WOULD I KNOW?" D'Veez thundered. "I have quotas. I have production orders. I have a workforce to manage. For reasons I cannot explain, I am well behind schedule, and I do not have time for nonsense. Begone!"

Connor slunk away in the custody of the two patrol Dragonoids who'd discovered him.

No curious eyes watched them as they marched through the Dragonoid city. No attempt was made to subvert Taskmaster D'Veez's orders. The guards took Connor up lifts and ramps, often accompanied by worker Dragonoids hauling loads of ore or crates labeled "SWORDS" or "SHIELDS" or "CHAINS."

On one of the lift rides, Connor examined his SKILL POT.

`SKILL POT - Gain a new skill.`

There was probably an optimal way to use one of these, but Connor let his curiosity take point.

He quaffed the Skill Pot before he could think better of it.

A huge list of options clogged his UI.

```
SHIELD SPECIALIST
DISARMING ATTACK
THROW WEAPON
CHARGING STAB
CLEAVING STRIKE
MOUNTED COMBAT
SPELL PARRY
STALWART
FLYING COMBAT
```

It was every skill he'd had the option to pick but declined.

Stalwart called to him. Taking 9 less damage per attack sounded pretty great. Impulse and regret and the fresh memory of being burned alive, however, conspired and Connor quickly tapped Spell Parry before he second-guessed himself.

Again.

There was no option to float a choice for later.

The lift ride brought him to the surface as a crane hauled a load of chains alongside him and his escorts.

`PEASE SUMMIT`

"This is it. End of the line. You're on your own from here. Don't expect the taskmaster's word to protect you from *them*."

The guard pointed. Connor followed his finger to the distant fortress wall and the towering keep beyond.

"Thanks."

Connor wandered out of the shipping area and avoided the road that the Dragonoids used to haul cart loads of goods toward the wall.

This wasn't a stealth mission. He wanted no part of the security at the gates. And he sure as hell wasn't planning on asking nicely to chat with the mountain lord.

Connor kept his distance from the walls. They were guarded, patrolled, too high to Charge up and too distant across too much open ground to approach unseen.

All around him, the terrain was black stone. All above him, clear blue skies. When Connor ventured close enough to the edge, he could see the clouds a hundred or so feet below, dark with menace. His knees went weak just considering falling into that maelstrom, only to discover no solid ground and thousands of feet left to fall before the ground claimed him.

Coming the other direction, Connor spotted a foot patrol in the distance. His first instinct was to hide and observe, but there was no cover worth a damn, and summoning Xote just to hide behind seemed both dumb and kind of a dick move.

Connor's second instinct was to count the members of the patrol, note their motley attire, and conclude that the other five players had found their own way up to Pease Summit.

They approached, weapons drawn, but Connor put up his hands. There was no point in fighting. They wouldn't be able to kill one another, he suspected. And while there were ways to move one another around, he suspected that he could hold his own physically against the lot of them.

Connor pointed to the fortress's outer walls. Then shrugged.

Clearly not idiots, the other players stowed their weapons. He'd made it to the top. They'd made it to the top. Anything else was water under a bridge, way, *way* down below them at this point.

The others had changed along their journey.

While Connor still wore his Battered Armor from the character selector, the others had all seemingly found ways to upgrade theirs.

Meatball wore red robes, trimmed in white and gold. Upon his head, he wore a circlet with a green gem.

Slapguy was bare-chested, but he was wrapped in a full torso tattoo of a dragon. His fists glowed pale orange when he clenched them.

Calamity wore a full-length trench coat and an eye-patch. She'd given up her bow in favor of a steampunk rifle with valves and gauges and pistons.

The wizard wore a white evening gown that shimmered such that, in the low-res available, Connor couldn't tell between it being covered in sequins or diamonds. She toted a staff of twisting brambles that clutched a purple gemstone at its head.

Dizzy... well, Dizzy still had her tanto daggers from when Connor had claimed his Ravager's Sword. He must have looked shabby by comparison to the others, still wearing his starting armor. Dizzy's initial ninja costume had been way cooler than his look, but now she was... well, she was a little fanserviced, if Connor had to be honest about it. She'd traded the ninja look for a sleeveless midnight blue crop top with an attached cowl, plus black leggings and slippers.

Immediately upon greeting one another, Dizzy pulled off her cowl and kissed him.

This time, with an audience, Connor made a good show of kissing her back. If anything would earn him his way back into the group, this would be it.

Once parted, Connor could only hope that, back in the Anachronism Interactive lab in Austin, he was getting a little privacy.

As everyone milled around in uncertainty and general social awkwardness, Connor swept a hand out toward the fortress walls.

"We gonna assault a mountain lord, or what?"

CHAPTER 30
OUTER WALLS

FANTASY GAMES with castles in them generally fell into two categories. In the first, the castles were wide open. Players battled their way through some predetermined number of minions to reach the boss inside. The second kind acknowledged that castles were built for defense, and gave players a plausible way through those defenses, usually via some kind of hidden entrance in a dungeon or sewer or something.

Spire of Fate was neither.

The game had left Connor and his companions to their own ingenuity with no clear way through the outer defenses, let alone the main fortress.

A weird brainstorming session ensued.

One by one, players revealed items from their inventory. It was amazing the depth of play that Connor had somehow missed on his way up here, because people had stuff that he couldn't imagine how they acquired.

All of them still had Fishing Nets from Lookmano Sands. From there, the contents of their packs varied wildly.

Calamity had collected six circular Wooden Shields.

Dizzy had a length of Rope, maybe fifty or eighty feet long

if she unspooled it. Through hand gestures, everyone determined that nothing in their possession would make for a serviceable grappling hook.

Slapguy had somehow stuffed a whole banquet table into his inventory. Connor quietly reported that as a bug.

Connor pulled out his Kawaiian Glider, but neither their cleric nor wizard admitted to having any wind powers to provide it lift.

Meatball, of all the stupid things, and all the time they'd wasted on the other stuff, whipped out a Wooden Extension Ladder that *had* to be some kind of joke. It was a mix of Mary Poppins and Jackie Chan watching him pull the thing essentially out of a pocket, then wave it around absentmindedly as the rest of them ducked and dove for cover.

That would probably get them UP the wall, but that didn't improve their chances of getting TO it.

Connor hid his face behind an arm and crouched, tiptoeing in place, then pointed to Dizzy and the ladder.

Dizzy adapted his plan to how her version of it would work. Her rendition of "sneak up to the wall unseen, then !!POOF!! MYSTERY LADDER!!" had them all in silent stitches.

Calamity, the ranged specialist of the group, insisted that they determine the range of the archers on those walls.

While exact numbers remained elusive, they lingered near maximum range until they got shot at, then marked the range on the ground in Jelly.

None of the shots hit Connor, so he couldn't tell what kind of damage those arrows were packing.

Why was Slapguy lugging around a giant jar of Blackberry Jelly big enough to reach elbow-deep inside it? Probably because he could. Where had he acquired the stuff? When Connor attempted to ask the question, the monk just grinned.

The whole crew attempted to wrangle the banquet table in

front of them as an enormous shield for everyone. But as soon as they got it off the ground, it went into someone's inventory. As it turned out, the thing wasn't coded to be "used." It was furniture that was bugged to be able to be carried in inventory. So, no dice there.

They went back to dredging up the stuff they'd all picked up along the way.

Dizzy offered a pair of manacles. The prisoner routine was time-honored, but without five pairs, there was no way to make that work.

The wizard revealed a small scepter bearing a resemblance to an ant clutching a baseball-sized pearl. All the others took out identical scepters. When Connor didn't, they all gave him funny looks.

Dizzy held her ant scepter sideways, tapped it, and made walking fingers behind it as her scepter led the way. The others nodded. Dizzy pointed to Connor, then shrugged.

Connor spread his arms like wings, then made one hand a beak. He pointed to the ground at their feet, then pantomimed arcing up out of it.

The others shared glances.

"I guess none of you bored a Dragonoid Taskmaster to the point where he let you through his city."

To avoid the scrutiny heaping onto him for joining what he supposed were the bad guys, Connor summoned Xote.

The gasps from his fellow players were visible. Dizzy immediately came over to pet him. Slapguy tried, unsuccessfully, to feed him something.

The party wizard threw something to the ground, and a spider appeared.

Connor had his Ravager's Sword out in an instant. But rather than a foe, the wizard climbed aboard it and took hold of a set of reins. She signaled her idea of a spider cavalry charge across the plain, up the wall, and atop it to meet their foes in close quarters combat. Her long fingers and prestidigitating dexterity made the spider motion creepy as well as accurate.

The other all summoned spiders as well.

Connor shook his head and saddled up on Xote.

Shaking heads told them they didn't believe that Connor could ascend the wall with Xote. Bullshit. Connor had yet to meet a spider, alive or digital, who was as good a climber as this crazy Donkey.

Calamity took over the planning at this point.

Through a series of heated charades, they determined that Connor would take point. First off, their attempts at measuring the range of the archers had determined at they'd fire at whoever was closest. One person at the front of a formation could draw most, if not all, of the incoming fire.

Connor, with the oddball mount and obvious durability—despite his starting-area armor—was nominated to be that point person.

Could he have pointed out numerous flaws in their plan? Yeah. Not even hard. Could he do so while not looking like such an asshole that they made him their lightning rod out of spite? Probably not.

Patting Xote, Connor knew there was one part the plan he just wasn't going along with.

Xote disappeared into his inventory.

Dizzy circled a hand in front of her, urging Connor to bring the mount back.

How could he explain it?

Xote wasn't... fast.

Connor was at least as swift on foot, and without having taken Mounted Combat, he couldn't defend himself while riding.

Lifting the Ravager's Sword, Connor gave a knight's salute.

Then he activated Parry and raced toward the ramparts.

Arrows whistled past all around him. He barely even spotted most of them. Some rang off his sword without even registering.

Some hit.

Whether they were special arrows, a particular skill on the part of the archers, or an oversight in game mechanics, and effective DEF of 52 wasn't enough to stop all the shots coming his way.

8

7

9

The arrows had a variable damage range, which was novel for most of Spire of Fate. It was *less* novel when it meant that many of the shots glanced harmlessly off him while others cut right through his armor like he was naked.

Connor watched his HP go down as the wall drew closer at a *painful* rate. Literally, since every arrow that stuck into him hurt like hell. But it was fake pain. Video game pain. His real body was fine. If Kelli was jabbing him with needles to provoke this feeling, he'd deal with that at lunch.

Or in a lawsuit.

Fuck NDAs, there was no court that was going to side with a game company torturing temp workers. Well, not a *small* game company, anyway.

HP: 106/130

HP: 91/130

HP: 66/130

He was getting closer. The others, on spiderback, lagged a strategic distance behind him. He could hear the skittering. Even knowing they were *kind of* on his side, the sounds set his teeth on edge.

HP: 50/130

HP: 33/130

HP: 16/130

Connor was almost to the wall. If everyone behind him survived, he ought to be safer in melee combat. Safe enough for Meatball to have time to heal his wounds.

8

8

HP: 0/130

Nope.

Not quite.

Shit.

CHAPTER 31
LONG WAY UP

SECLUDED CEMETERY

"You have died, but your journey is not yet ended. Rise once more, hero, and press onward."

"More like upward. Fuck, this place needs a mid-way respawn point or something. Make that a couple, actually."

Connor knew he hadn't lost much. Had anything along the last trip up earned him a damn thing? Not that it mattered now.

`XP: 0/256,000`

The potential XP loss leading into the end game here was just punishing. Connor found himself actually *glad* he didn't have any to lose.

With no other choice, really, Connor set out to get back to the top.

`UNALIVE HILLS`

The zombies were basically weather more than monsters by now. This was the fog equivalent of chunky peanut butter.

`BONE MOAT`

Connor wondered whether he could go down there, get any XP from the skeletons, and make it back out via Xote. Probably. Except that there was a really good chance those skeletons were worth bupkis.

Plus, a million miles up, five jerkwads who'd bullied him into being their pincushion were probably already clearing the walls of enemies worth a LOT more XP.

But there *was* another way Connor thought of as he crossed the drawbridge and the Spire loomed ever closer and impossibly high above him.

Could Xote make it up the side?

That would be a time-saver.

On the far side of the drawbridge, Connor noticed that the Bridge Troll had respawned. Or at least, the top of its head had. The rest of it, presumably, was underground.

`REPORT BUG`

"The troll from the drawbridge is stuck in the ground. You can barely see him. If we hadn't killed him once, I'd never have known he was there."

How many other NPCs had Connor not seen because of bugs? He kept his eye open as he mounted Xote and discovered that, indeed, the Little Donkey from Awesomeville was more spider than those spiders the others had acquired.

He bypassed the Black Catacombs entirely.

`HARD PASS`

Rather than crisscross the bridges, Xote continued up the side of the spire, catching his footing on ludicrous footholds.

Two polygons misaligned? Xote could stand on that.

Angled surface only 89 percent vertical? Xote could stand on that.

Edge of a shadow as Connor rounded the spire in search of a path upward? To his utter astonishment, Xote could stand on that, too.

`CLIFFS OF CLAVEN`

With all these discoveries, it almost came as a surprise when he reached the overhang up near the Warrens of War. That was the point at which Connor climbed off, nuzzled the

Donkey forehead to forehead, and dismissed him back into inventory.

"Good job, buddy. You deserve a rest."

WARRENS OF WAR

Connor sought out the patrol he'd gotten to know a little bit.

"You two! With me!"

"Who are you?" the leader demanded.

"I've got a deal with Taskmaster D'Veez for safe passage. If you don't honor it, I'll slaughter you both where you stand."

With his Ravager's Sword drawn and glowing, the pair took one shared glance to mutually come to an understanding. "Well... if the taskmaster says it's all right."

They led the way as Connor breezed through their industrial city. He demanded guides to the lifts, and they didn't question him further.

Connor was on a timetable, and he didn't even know what time it was.

PEASE SUMMIT

"Fare thee well, Connor the Unhallowed. Any friend of Taskmaster D'Veez is an honored guest among our people. Should you fall, you will be honored."

"I *did* fall, and I wasn't exactly honored. Wait... hold up a second. Where do you people bury your dead?"

"Would you like us to—?"

"YES!" Connor snapped instantly. To hell with climbing and reclimbing this damn mountain. Xote was a badass little dude and all, but Connor had goals and a mission, and sightseeing plus terrifying drops weren't part of the plan.

The two patrol guards took Connor back down the lift.

WARRENS OF WAR

They were most of the way back through the city when the pair took him on a side trip.

RESPAWN POINT UPDATED

WARRENS MEMORIAL

"Fucking hell..." this was like the 90 percent mark from the Unalive Hills to the fortress walls, if not more. The Dragonoid burial ground was like an old dwarven tomb out of Lord of the Rings or Skyrim. He would have bet that in some earlier iteration of this game, these things had been stock dwarfs before someone decided to get a tiny bit creative yet still reuse most of the concepts without alteration.

"All right guys. I think I can find my own way back to the surface at this point."

"Fare the well, Connor the Unhallowed. Any friend of Taskmaster D'Veez is an honored guest among our people. Should you fall, you will be honored."

"Yeah. This time, I believe you. Oh. Before you wander off, does this place have merchants, vendors, whatever you want to call them?"

"We conduct much commerce," the lead guard assured Connor. "If you'd like, I can—"

"Yes was good enough for me. I'll consider shopping if my group gets stuck."

"But you don't have a group."

"Working on that!" He waved in salute as he ran off to find his way back to the lifts.

PEASE SUMMIT

There was no sign of the party.

Connor headed back to their base camp, easily marked by the banquet table that Slapguy had generously donated to the planning session. On pure impulse, Connor heaved and lifted it, chuckling as it vanished into his inventory.

RECEIVED: BANQUET TABLE

As he retraced the progress of his ill-fated trek to the wall, Connor realized there was no incoming arrow fire. Either the other players had won the battle, or it was still ongoing. At the very least, he hoped that if they'd all died, he at least had time to gain a spot atop the wall before the archers started respawning.

A whole line of ranged attackers clustered in an enclosed space? That might be a better XP farm than the Dragonoid Gladiator had been!

500 XP

500 XP

Connor knew he was close now. He was getting credit for stuff they were killing.

"Hey guys! I'm back!" he shouted before remembering that only enemies could hear him.

At the very base of the wall, he summoned Xote.

In three hops, the Donkey managed to climb atop the ramparts. Connor climbed down, dismissed his four-footed friend, and drew his blade.

500 XP

500 XP

The others must have known he was near since presumably, whatever was giving him those dollops of 500 XP at a time had been giving all of *them* 600 XP each a moment earlier.

XP: 2000/256,000

He had a long way to go, but at least now he had minions to aid him and battles to fight.

Anything, ANYTHING was better than running laps up and down that spire.

CHAPTER 32
BREAKING THE WALL

FORTRESS WALLS

When Connor caught up with the other players, he found them two segments down the wall, cutting a swath through lightly armored archers.

Connor examined one.

`Archer Mercenary - Ranged attacker. Special attack can ignore Defense.`

Fuck them. Fuck all of them. Had they known before sending him in first that he was pretty much all armor as far as defenses went, and these things had a special attack that ignored his only defense?

Connor saw a fireball splash across multiple archers, burning them but not slaying any outright.

Calamity's gun was peppering guys, but they were picking off guys already injured by fire.

`500 XP`

`500 XP`

It was time to see how Connor stacked up.

He timed a fireball and raced past the injured Archer Mercenaries as soon the blast zone was clear.

As the archers regrouped, he targeted a pair just beyond the front lines as the players pressed their way down the wall.

"Aaaaaaaaah!"

Connor zoomed through startled archers and exited hyperspace as his sword descended in a Mountain Slam.

He caught four of them in the blast, two fresh, two injured just behind him.

13131313

3333

+3+3+3+3

Connor found himself shocked that the Ravager's Sword dealt its full HP drain to all the targets.

His next reaction was satisfaction that the two behind him both died.

500 XP

500 XP

Both the Archer Mercenaries had side arms. Neither of them got a hit on Connor with their short swords, even without Parry. Connor was just that good with his blade by now. Or they were just that bad. One way or another, though, they'd used their attacks to no avail against him.

A searing heat caught Connor by surprise.

The two Archer Mercenaries died.

500 XP

500 XP

He whirled on the wizard, Ravager's Sword menacing. How *dare* she blast indiscriminately into the fray while he was fighting? That was Teamwork 101 shit right there.

For her part, the wizard balled a fist and twisted it in front of her eye in a "wah wah, cry more" gesture that set Connor's blood boiling. He checked his HP total to see just how much she'd hit him for.

HP: 130/130

Oh.

Right.

No friendly fire.

Connor put up a hand that said, "My bad."

Onward and onward they pressed. Meatball had light work of it, barely needing to heal, hanging back and letting his mace dangle unused at his side.

Every once in a while, a guy just sort of died. Mysteriously. It could only have been Dizzy's contribution to the efforts, as they all still got XP for the kills.

`XP: 13,500/256,000`

`XP: 16,000/256,000`

`XP: 21,500/256,000`

The kills kept coming, and they were making a full circuit of the fortress walls, it seemed. And why not? They were an unstoppable force, working together. It was a shame that only one of them could be first to the end of this game.

Maybe they knew they were competing. Maybe. Maybe deep down, some of the others thought this was a pure team sport.

Multiplayer RPGs were possibly the closest a game came to looking like a team game without actually being one. From old school D&D to modern MMOs, everyone came in with an agenda. Maybe they wanted to look coolest. Maybe they wanted to sell their account. Maybe they were in it for bragging rights, world first achievements, or collecting pets like they were in Pokémon.

Connor was aware. He knew the game within the game.

Anachronism Interactive needed game designers.

Badly.

They needed people with an eye for this shit and a mind for breaking the breakable, cheesing out the cheesable, and discovering every dirty trick players could use to ruin a game, then working out how to prevent that.

Connor was on a job interview here.

However many people Anachronism Interactive brought in before them, Connor couldn't control. But right here, right now, he had five other applicants for a job he knew he was best suited for. He just had to prove it.

So long as they stuck together, the six of them were a force to be reckoned with. But sooner or later—and Connor suspected sooner—they were going to have to decide who was the top dog here.

And as they came back around to the beginning of their circuit, walls closing in on empty of Archer Mercenaries, Connor planned to be ready for that moment.

XP: 29,500/256,000

He took one quick glance over his character sheet before the group departed the walls and ventured deeper into the Mountain Lord's defenses.

CHARACTER STATS:

NAME: Connor TITLE: The Unhallowed

CLASS: Knight LEVEL: 9

HP: 130 MP: 0 ATK: 21 DEF: 24

SKILLS:

TWO-HANDED FIGHTING

CHARGE

PARRY

RIPOSTE

IMPROVED RIPOSTE

IMPROVED TWO-HANDED FIGHTING

MOUNTAIN SLAM

CHARGING SLASH

SPELL PARRY

He had all the tools he needed. Now he just needed the chance.

CHAPTER 33
EYES ON THE PRIZE

WITH THE WALLS CLEARED, the players pressed onward and inward. Dizzy led the way, and Connor didn't argue. She was far less likely to get spotted, and it was someone else's turn to put themselves at risk. The rogue slipped into the next section of the fortress complex with the rest of the party barely able to make her out.

`OUTER KEEP`

The structure felt old the same way those houses using reclaimed wood for accent walls felt old. Every stone was weathered and rough, but there was no sign of decrepitude, damage, or settling over time that an actual ancient building would have shown over the years. The whole feeling was of a fairly new fortress constructed using stonework from its predecessor.

A phalanx of soldiers, species indeterminate beneath heavy plate armor, clattered into position to block the party's advance. Hearing them coming well ahead of time, Connor had a hand out to glean all the information he could from them.

`Armored Mercenary - Humanoid.`

Then, a split-second later, he caught the same hand motion from Dizzy. His information updated.

`Armored Mercenary - Melee attacker. Can apply Defense to magical damage.`

OK. That explained why Connor was getting more detailed examinations now. Something Dizzy did revealed their abilities to the players. Either Dizzy had designated Connor as an ally, or the game simply didn't draw a distinction between players who were cooperating and ones who weren't.

In any event, this looked like Connor's time to shine.

"Aaaaaaaaah!"

He was a bowling ball, and the Armored Mercenaries his pins.

`13131313`

`3333`

`+3+3+3+3`

The shock troops blew back, scattered. One down each of the left and right branches of the intersection they'd chosen to defend. Two went straight back. All went down supine on the floor. Their scrambling efforts to get back to their feet, despite cumbersome armor, evoked tortoises turned upside down.

However, the 16 damage each didn't seem like a major impediment. The four Armored Mercenaries clambered to their feet as arrows and lighting raked them. Daggers whizzed past. Slapguy and Meatball held back, probably for lack of ranged attacks.

Connor held his ground.

As the four came at him, halberds at the ready, Connor activated Parry. There was room to squeeze past him, if these computer-grade AIs were programmed that way, but instead, they acted as though Connor was a wall they had to hack through to get at the rest of the players.

Cling-Clang-Clunk.

The halberds met steel, time and again. Armored Mercenaries got into one another's way, time and again. And thanks to his Improved Riposte, Connor wasn't just on the back foot, absorbing the attacks with no way to counter.

27

3

+3

Time after time. Anyone looking to get past him was going to get butchered. How much the other players were contributing from behind him, it was something.

One went down, struck by wizardly lightning.

1,000 XP

XP: 22,500/256,000

Another dropped when Dizzy appeared behind it, jabbing two daggers into an exposed back.

1,000 XP

XP: 23,500/256,000

Connor worried briefly for her safety, considering she was half-armored and only in cloth. But Dizzy vanished like the burst of a silent firework, leaving nothing but a puff of smoke in her place.

Feeling a little more confident now, he stepped aside, allowing the two remaining Armored Mercenaries free access to the squishier members of the group. With better intelligence than he'd credited them, the two immediately made a beeline for Meatball. The cleric visibly yelped, scrambling to take his mace from his belt to defend himself.

Slapguy took over bodyguard duty. No longer stuck behind a digital wall of Parry keeping four foes at bay, he launched a flying kick that made his foot glow with fire. The Armored Mercenary he struck went flying back past Connor.

1,000 XP

XP: 24,500/256,000

"Aaaaaaaaah!"

Connor rocketed in the other direction, catching the last of the Armored Mercenaries just before it got to Meatball.

Connor went all out on the swing, using Improved Two-Handed Fighting and slashing downward with all his might.

54

3

+3

He hammered the Armored Mercenary to the floor.

1,000 XP

XP: 25,500/256,000

It wasn't *quite* exactly ten percent of the way to Level 10, but close enough. Just 231 more fights like that one.

Ugh. Sometimes these games could be a real slog. It was one thing zoning out and killing a Dragonoid Gladiator a few hundred times. But hacking down actual, competent foes? With other people to worry about and work around? THAT was work.

Connor pushed thoughts of leveling up from his mind. He was feeling kinda God Mode right now. He was clearly stronger than the other players. Without knowing their levels, he suspected they were anywhere from Level 6 to Level 8, and he couldn't get a feel for where along that spectrum they lay.

He was their protector. They were... at best, they might be speeding up some of the grunt work of removing HP from these enemies. The time hadn't come yet for him to make a move. Dizzy especially seemed useful. Her scouting ability to see actual information about their enemies could make a difference that mattered to *him,* not just the overall party.

They split up at the intersection the mercenaries had been guarding.

Calamity took the wizard and went right.

Meatball and Slapguy barreled straight ahead.

Connor followed Dizzy left.

What they were looking for remained a mystery. A way through seemed trite. This game was open-world and full of loopholes. Xote could likely have scaled any number of suspiciously not-quite-vertical surfaces to gain access to the Mountain Lord's keep. The very fact that Connor's minimap persistently told him Outer Keep was a sure sign that they weren't yet where they needed to be.

Then again, it *would* be a pretty savvy move to have the end boss *not* camped out someplace that sounded exactly like an end boss lair.

A squared spiral of stairs led them up a floor. Up felt both right and wrong. Right, in that this whole game had been about upward progress. Wrong, in that they'd reached the summit. The odds of the Mountain Lord being in *this* keep were limited. Spire of Fate might have waffled between half-finished and spectacular, but nothing about the writing and design suggested they were interested in "gotcha" twists.

All they found was a barracks and...

ARMORY

Holy shit! Right across from the barracks, which had a bunch of bunk beds and no special name on the minimap, was a separate room filled with weapons and armor.

Dizzy shrugged and browsed with her hand out, examining stuff with the air of a shopper at a bargain store.

Connor, however, was still using his starting zone Battered Armor. He was *long* overdue for an upgrade.

He checked out...

MERCENARY ARMOR - 12 DEF

ARCHER ARMOR - 6 DEF

There was an empty armor stand marked "Commander Hellgain's Battle Armor," but right next to it, Connor found...

COMMANDER HELLGAIN'S PARADE ARMOR - 18 DEF

The armor was ornate and golden, clashing with the

aesthetic of his Ravager Sword. But Connor wasn't the one who had to look at himself. Any dissonance would be felt by his companions, not him. He quickly switched into it and placed his Battered Armor onto the armor stand in its place.

EQUIPMENT

WEAPON: RAVAGER'S SWORD

ARMOR: COMMANDER HELLGAIN'S PARADE ARMOR

ACCESSORY: MAP-MAKER'S WAYSTONE

It boosted his DEF a ton. Connor hadn't even considered just how little of his DEF stat was actually attributable to his armor. He could have been running around like a barbarian in just his loincloth for all the difference that Battered Armor had been making.

He had to see.

CHARACTER STATS:

NAME: Connor TITLE: The Unhallowed

CLASS: Knight LEVEL: 9

HP: 130 MP: 0 ATK: 21 DEF: 42

SKILLS:

TWO-HANDED FIGHTING

CHARGE

PARRY

RIPOSTE

IMPROVED RIPOSTE

IMPROVED TWO-HANDED FIGHTING

MOUNTAIN SLAM

CHARGING SLASH

SPELL PARRY

Yeah. 42 DEF felt like it was ready for prime time. He could feel OK about heading into battle against a boss with that kind of DEF.

It was a good thing, too.

"Who do you think you are?" an imperious voice

demanded. The guy blocking the way back out was a tower of armor, black riveted and spiked, rusted and bloody. He had the visor of his helmet up, the better to glower at the pair of intruders.

"I must be Commander Hellgain," Connor replied. "Says it right on my armor."

The sword he drew matched any number of the ones on racks nearby. Unspectacular. Unremarkable. Basic in manufacture and cared for with less-than-ideal diligence, its one most striking feature was its size. Twice as broad and a foot longer than the Ravager's Sword, it appeared unwieldy, but the real Commander Hellgain didn't seem bothered by the weapon's size.

"You will pay for this affront," the commander swore.

"I've got 102 Coins, and you can't have 'em."

Connor considered starting the fight with a Parry, but the instant Commander Hellgain stepped toward him, he knew what he had to do.

"Aaaaaaaaah!"

54

3

+3

His blow landed, but somehow, he felt like that armor absorbed a lot of what Connor had dealt.

The return blow caught Connor in the shoulder.

31

Shit! Even with a full Parry going, he couldn't stop a blow that strong. Not fully, anyway.

HP: 99/130

This was going to be rough. But Connor had an ace up his sleeve.

Wait.

Where was Dizzy?

"Have you seen a rogue around here? About this tall?" Connor held his sword flat about the level of Dizzy's head. "Two Japanese daggers?"

`31`

"OK, you could have just said no."

`HP: 68/130`

Connor couldn't fool around with this guy. He Parried rather than launch a return attack.

`4`

That was more like it. He Riposted, making a deft thrust past Commander Hellgain's blade.

`27`

`3`

`+3`

Still, Connor was getting the impression that he wasn't doing full damage. If the guy's regular armor was better than his parade armor, depending on his natural DEF score, Connor could have been doing very little actual damage.

They faced off for several minutes that way.

Connor Parried a hit.

`4`

He struck back.

`27`

`3`

`+3`

He came out with a net loss of just 1 HP in the exchange. If he'd taken Stalwart, he'd just be whittling Commander Hellgain down, taking no damage at all.

But the feel of an epic duel against a worthy opponent was addictive. Neither one making much headway. Defeat inevitable for one of them, but with imperfect information, it was impossible to tell which of them was destined to come out on top. So many unknown factors played into the outcome.

What was Commander Hellgain's DEF stat?

How many HP did the guy start out with?

Was he healing?

Did he have some ultimate attack cooked up?

Connor Parried Hellgain's strike.

4

Connor followed up with a quick return thrust.

27

3

+3

HP: 22/130

All plans to shift the battlefield in his favor required Connor to get the commander out of the doorway he was blocking. If he lured the commander by retreating back into the Armory, Connor worried that the guy knew some form of the Charge skill that could finish him off.

They continued their dance in the doorway. Connor had to count on the others getting curious and showing up to bail him out.

4 damage in.

27 damage out.

3 drained.

+3 gained.

HP: 21/130

Connor bore in mind that once he got down to 4 HP, the next shot would finish him. Gaining 3 HP back would only matter if he had at least 1 HP to still be alive and swinging the Ravager's Sword.

4 damage in.

27 damage out.

3 drained.

+3 gained.

25,000 XP

Commander Hellgain cried out in agony, clutching Connor's most recent minor wound as if it were the lone stab to have injured him. Seconds after collapsing to the Armory floor, the corpse vanished.

XP: 50,500/256,000

HP: 20/130

It was a hard-fought battle, but that was a CHUNK of XP.

Better yet, the guy's armor remained on the ground afterward.

Connor looted.

RECEIVED: 1,173 Coins

RECEIVED: XPOT

RECEIVED: COURTYARD KEY

RECEIVED: COMMANDER HELLGAIN'S BATTLE ARMOR

Instantly, Connor examined his new find.

COMMANDER HELLGAIN'S BATTLE ARMOR - 18 DEF. **Can defend against attacks from behind. Half damage from stabbing attacks.**

If Dizzy could have seen any of that, no wonder she ditched on him. It honestly wouldn't have surprised Connor to discover that the drain from the Ravager's Sword was the only thing dealing damage at all.

Connor headed out of the Armory.

OUTER KEEP

It was time to track down his wayward companions. It would be an interesting game of charades to see what they had to say for themselves.

CHAPTER 34
HOLDING COURT

CONNOR MARCHED past the barracks and back down the stairs. His new armor gave his tread a new, more menacing crunch of metal on stone. For once, it was a detail that added depth to the game rather than detracted from the immersion. Clearly, the sound design and art teams had gotten their hands on this armor and given it more care than usual.

He paused at the intersection where the party had last been together. Faint echoes from the straight direction as they entered led him to conclude that there was at least something that way. Whatever it was, he intended to either get some answers from it or kill it.

Maybe both.

With bodies despawning almost instantaneously postmortem, it was impossible to say whether the halls were deserted because this place just hadn't been that well defended or because the other players had already dispatched the denizens.

Connor still had no answer when he reached a steel door with five idiots fussing over it, trying to pick a lock by committee.

They heard the new, more imposing gait of Connor the Unhallowed as he approached.

Weapon stowed, he strode up to Meatball and pointed, first to the cleric, then to himself. Meatball nodded vigorously.

+7

+7

+7

The healing spells trickled in. Connor used the number to assert that the cleric was likely Level 7. A free, minor healing spell for an amount equal to the caster's level seemed about right. 7 was just a weird number, otherwise, especially since the amount had always kind of lined up with Connor's guess about the guy's level before.

+7

+7

+7

+7

HP: 69/130

The cleric paused and looked to Connor for guidance. Connor waved a hand in circles for Meatball to keep the heals coming.

+7

+7

+7

HP 90/130

He watched the others exchange looks.

+7

+7

+7

HP: 111/130

Some genuine concern grew on the faces of his party. Yet Connor beckoned for still more.

+7

```
+7
+7
HP: 130/130
```

Now, just to mess with the other players, he made Meatball keep going for another 70 HP worth of wasted, excess healing before giving a thumbs up for him to stop.

Let them think Connor was an even bigger badass than he already was. Maybe they'd stop fucking with him and ditching him to face nearly-end-bosses by himself.

He hoped that the 25,000 XP he'd gotten from Commander Hellgain hadn't been 150,000 XP before it got split six ways. That would have felt like too much, even if this game was a train wreck when it came to balance, and he didn't like the idea that he'd soloed something worth that much to receive so little of the credit.

The others turned their attention back to the gate.

Connor tapped shoulders, pointed, swept his arm. *Stand aside*, he motioned. Taking two giant steps back, he drew the Ravager's Sword and pulled it back like a baseball bat.

"Aaaaaaaaah!"

He knew they couldn't hear him, but he made a show anyway.

Instead of Charging, however, Connor drew out the Courtyard Key from his inventory, took two quick steps back to the door, and turned it in the lock.

Click.

Hauling open the door, there was a short stretch of hallway, followed by a winch mechanism, a lever to activate it, and a portcullis promising entry into the Courtyard beyond.

Flipping him the bird despite a grin on her face, Dizzy took the lead and switched the lever.

Clang-clang-clang-clang.

The portcullis rose as the winch released and unspooled a length of chain.

"I know the guys who make that stuff," Connor said, pointing to the Dragonoid-forged chain.

No one heard or even noticed his joke.

When the others hesitated, Connor took the lead venturing out of the Outer Keep.

After all, he'd just made a point of how tough he was. Not only in coming back to the group wearing the armor of the guy Dizzy ran away from, but also his play-acting with Meatball, demanding more healing than he needed by a good fifty percent.

COURTYARD

The first sign of grass in the whole game—aside from a paint job on the forest floor—the Courtyard of the Mountain Lord's fortress had the manicured look of a guy who didn't have to pay for top-notch landscapers. Flower beds and walkways led a whimsical path between the Outer Keep and a very imposing—and VERY final-boss-looking—main castle beyond.

A shadow passed over the group, gone before any of them could figure out where it came from.

Undead?

Some sort of shadow monster scouting them?

No. The shadow was of a mundane sort, but cast by a creature mundane only through cliché.

A dragon, black and scaly, with leathery wings and sinuous neck, circled lower in the sky, its stillness lending stealth to the approach of a beast that looked all too implausible to sneak up on anyone.

It landed before them with an impact that shook the whole Spire.

Jarred loose, the mechanism let the portcullis fall behind them, barring a retreat back the way they'd come.

"You are fools to climb the Spire of Fate! None shall enter the fortress of the Mountain Lord!"

Connor just had time to bring up his Ravager's Sword and ready a Parry.

It was time for Spell Parry to do its job.

The dragon breathed fire over all of them.

`100`

Calamity, Meatball, Slapguy, and Dizzy all burned to ash around him.

The wizard shimmered inside a magical barrier that kept her from harm.

`HP: 30/130`

Connor didn't seem to be on fire any longer, but that was the best he could say about the situation. There was no way around it, he was in deep shit.

"Aaaaaaaaah!"

A wall of Spire Dragon raced toward him. Down came the Ravager's Sword.

`54`

`3`

`+3`

`HP: 33/130`

It was a start. It was...

The Spire Dragon ignored him for a moment. It bit down and devoured the wizard.

That left enough space for Connor to Charge once more.

"Aaaaaaaaah!"

He swung with all his might.

`>>108<< CRITICAL HIT`

`3`

`+3`

`HP: 36/130`

"Pesky little thing, aren't you?" the dragon teased. "No matter."

It's laziness and banter allowed Connor just enough time to Parry a swipe of the thing's claws.

7

7? That was it?

He struck back with a Riposte.

27

3

+3

HP: 32/130

"Sturdy little wretch. We'll see about YOU!" The dragon snatched him up in a clawed grasp. His attempts to dodge it were clumsy and far, far too slow.

10

HP: 22/130

Connor tried to fight back, but its grip was iron. Taken aloft when the beast took wing, he watched helplessly—albeit with a great view of the Mountain Lord's castle—as the Spire Dragon carried him off the Spire.

"Let's see how well you fly."

With that, it let go, and Connor plummeted.

"Aaaaaaaaah!"

He rocketed through the sky via video game magic that made no sense for a guy with 0 MP all game.

54

3

+3

He couldn't grab hold. Once more, he fell.

"Aaaaaaaaah!"

Redefining physics on a level that Einstein could only dream of, Connor the Unhallowed became Connor the Doom Yo-Yo.

54

3

+3

"Stop that, you miserable—OW!"

"Aaaaaaaaah!"

54

3

+3

"Aaaaaaaaah!"

54

3

+3

HP: 34/130

Not only was this chipping away at the dragon's health, he was—

200

—he was fried.

Connor hadn't kept an accurate count of the damage he'd dealt. Without knowing what it had for damage mitigation, self-healing, special attacks and defenses, he could only come to one simple conclusion about the dragon's might.

It was stronger than him.

CHAPTER 35
ECHO OF DESTINY

WARRENS MEMORIAL

"You have died, but your spirit carried on. Rise once more, hero, and fulfill your destiny."

It was such a relief respawning among the Dragonoids that Connor almost didn't half mind losing the 50,500 XP he'd accumulated on the way to Level 10.

Almost.

WARRENS OF WAR

Connor strolled the Dragonoid city, confident that he had a head start over the other players. None of them showed any signs they'd come through this way, so this respawn point would be his private shortcut.

Instead, he considered something that the Dragonoid patrol had mentioned in passing.

There were vendors around here.

Connor pulled aside a random worker who didn't look too busy to lend a hand. "Hey, friend. Where can I find guys selling equipment or potions?"

"For general adventuring supplies, you should seek Ualmar. He has a wide array of goods. For potions and elixirs, you will wish to seek out the brothers, Okaa and Olof." The worker then pointed to two spots, which lit on Connor's minimap.

"Wow. Thanks." That was more help than anyone since Uppup. Connor actually kind of felt bad about that guy. Now that he had the cash, maybe he could find a widow to reimburse or something.

Connor made his way to the gear shop first. Given that they were in a series of underground tunnels, it was less a building and more a sectioned-off area of wider, open-tunnel marketplace, bounded by counters and shelves.

"How can I help you, traveler?" asked the Dragonoid who stood in the spot the worker had marked as Ualmar on his minimap.

"I'd like to buy equipment," Connor told him, despite not really knowing what he was looking for.

Instead of a conversation, a menu popped up, listing the goods available, along with their effects. Connor didn't even have to examine them.

CLIMBING BELT - 500 Coins - Allows the wearer to climb vertical surfaces.

MINER'S GARB - 50 Coins - Basic protection against hazards common to mines. Includes a helmet with built-in candle.

SMITH'S HAMMER - 200 Coins - 3 ATK

POTION OF FIRE IMMUNITY - 100 Coins - Temporarily negate all damage from fire.

FURNACE OPERATOR'S SHIELD - 700 Coins - 5 DEF. Half damage from fire attacks.

Connor immediately wrote off the hammer as flavor. There was nothing worse than paying for bad loot, and that hammer wasn't even as good as the damn sword he'd gotten back in the Unalive Hills.

The Climbing Belt? Too little, too late. Maybe early on,

assuming he'd gotten past his fear of using it, that might have proven really handy. Now? Nah. He had Xote, and Xote was the best loot in the whole game.

The Miner's Garb sounded like it might have been put in either for a quest that hadn't been implemented yet or as some kind of disguise to sneak through certain parts of the game. Not what he was looking for.

The Furnace Operator's Shield was the only thing keeping the Smith's Hammer even *remotely* viable. The Ravager's Sword couldn't be wielded one-handed. If he wanted to reduce the Spire Dragon's fire attack by half, he could pair that hammer with the Furnace Operator's Shield to come at this game from a sword-and-board direction he'd dismissed way back at Level 2.

The real winner here was the dumb potion. If he'd stopped here on his last trip through, he'd have gladly spent 100 of his 102 Coins on a Potion of Fire Immunity, knowing what lay ahead. Now, with 1,275 Coins to his name, it felt dumb *not* to buy one.

Connor tapped, and the transaction took care of itself. The Coins deducted from his total.

RECEIVED: POTION OF FIRE IMMUNITY

For now, one would do. He sure as hell wasn't picking up the tab for the whole party unless it was his only option. That plan could wait for another respawn.

He spent a while browsing the other shops, but nothing caught his interest. Most sold trinkets and baubles with no apparent use to him. One told him he was not an initiate. He didn't have time to delve into the vagaries of the game's hidden reputation system, but he could see there being some cool stuff locked behind having a high enough renown with the Dragonoids. In the meantime, he risked getting left behind.

Without knowing how long until his allies got back up here,

Connor retreated to the lift to fight his way back to the Spire Dragon.

`PEASE SUMMIT`

To his shock and relief, the archers on the walls hadn't respawned.

"Maybe I killed the boss they were tied to?" he guessed aloud. When he remembered that he had someone to ask stuff like that, he opened a menu and tapped HELP.

"Hello. I am Kelindra, your guide to Spire of Fate. How may I assist you?"

"Hey, Kelindra, why aren't the archers on the wall respawning."

"When a creature in Spire of Fate dies, another just like it is liable to reappear after a short wait. Usually just a few minutes. Some, however, do not respawn at all, due to story reasons or changing conditions inside the game."

"Fine. Be cryptic. I'm still going to hurry."

`OUTER WALLS`

Connor hopped off Xote and dismissed the Donkey. There was still no sign of any resistance.

He climbed down the far side of the walls.

`OUTER KEEP`

The halls were deserted. He made his way through to the portcullis before Slapguy spotted him, slapping the others on shoulders to get their attention. He then made a dopey face, did a herky-jerky dance, and pointed to Connor, laughing at himself afterward.

"Yeah. I stopped for some shopping. Lay off. Nice to see everyone made it back. Did you have to fight or was it all just..."

Realizing he was asking aloud, Connor tried to convey his question in hand signals before Calamity and Dizzy practically tackled him to get him to stop and focus. A simple battle plan was laid out on the floor, arranged in flotsam from people's inventory—and probably the mess hall of this place that he hadn't come across in his limited exploration.

Connor was the carving knife.

Dizzy was represented by a pair of crossed butter knives.

Slapguy was a boot.

The wizard was one of the Ant Scepters everyone but Connor had acquired.

Meatball was a butter dish.

They represented Calamity with a helmet from the Armory.

The Spire Dragon was a flagon. Someone had found one with a dragon as a decorative element. If they survived this, Connor hoped to come back and claim the flagon for his own. Maybe he'd even ask Kelli if he could get one 3-D printed based on their data, it was that badass a beverage vessel.

Calamity had the plan. It looked *suspiciously* similar to their earlier battle plan for the Outer Walls, with Connor going in first to draw fire. But he had a secret weapon against fire this time, and it was going to save him a ton of HP if he could convince the dragon to focus its fire ineffectually on him.

The rest of them would be taking up various positions in and around the Courtyard, including the wizard and Calamity backtracking to climb to the Outer Keep roof via their spider mounts.

All in all, it sounded viable.

When they'd all signaled their readiness, Connor marched out the portcullis as soon as they opened it again.

"You are fools to climb the Spire of Fate! None shall enter the fortress of the Mountain Lord!"

The portcullis shook loose and fell. It gave Connor an idea, but it was an idea that wouldn't matter unless their current plan failed.

The Spire Dragon sucked in a breath.

Connor popped the cork on his Potion of Fire Immunity. A chill permeated his whole body as it went down in a single gulp.

The Spire Dragon breathed fire that washed over Connor like a tidal wave. He held his ground, even made a show of using Parry, cried out in mock pain even.

"Euuaaagh!" Given the voices in this game, he didn't feel like hamming it up was too big a problem.

`HP: 130/130`

Connor was unharmed.

Now for the counter-attack!

"Aaaaaaaaah!"

The Ravager's Sword connected with a biting crack.

`54`

`3`

`+3`

`HP: 130+3/130`

He was ahead of the game. But he wasn't alone.

Lightning lanced from the Outer Keep roof. Gunshots rang out from another part of the same rooftop. Slapguy raced out of cover to launch himself at the dragon with an icy kick. Dizzy ended up on the creature, straddling its spine like a dragon rider and stabbing it in the back like a murderer.

"You think you can defeat ME, little whelps?" the Spire Dragon bellowed.

Golden radiance surrounded Connor. All around the battlefield, the others glowed likewise as Meatball bowed his head and clasped his hands in prayer.

They had this.

Connor dodged to keep in front of the Spire Dragon as best he could. Its size and reach made that a difficult prospect, but he did what he could.

`7`

"That all you got, big guy?" Connor taunted, unsure whether ego played a role in which character the dragon might attack.

He struck back.

`27`

`3`

`+3`

"YOU!" the Spire Dragon shouted, its words shaking the ground and breath smelling of... it smelled like someone had taken the stink of a break room fridge containing rotten fish and digitized it.

The dragon hadn't been complaining about Connor. It ignored him as it breathed fire over the roof of the Outer Keep. Again, the wizard survived using some kind of magical barrier.

But Calamity vanished.

Connor tried to corral the creature, to make it consider him the most dangerous threat.

"Aaaaaaaaah!"

At hyper speed, he closed in.

`54`

`3`

`+3`

`HP: 130+9/130`

The Spire Dragon continued to ignore him. Dizzy continued to hack away at the thing's spinal cord. If they had programmed anatomy into Spire of Fate, the dragon would have gone limp from the neck down by now.

One slash of claws. One snap of the jaws. The wizard was no more.

Meatball appeared distraught. He threw himself to the ground, kneeling before the dragon and muttering stuff that Connor couldn't hear.

"As if I would deign to employ the likes of YOU!"

Connor tried to intervene. He hacked at the ground, vainly hoping that Mountain Slam might distract the dragon.

13

3

+3

The knock-back effect did nothing to a creature of such bulk. Connor had honestly thought that maybe, in all their slapdash coding, Anachronism Interactive might have let a size calculation slip.

Alas, no.

Meatball went down the dragon's gullet without spaghetti.

Slapguy continued his part in the barrage, but the dragon got sick of him as well. It slapped him right back, batting him mid-kick to fly halfway across the Courtyard.

For once, one of the other players was sturdy enough to take that kind of hit. Slapguy popped back up with a neck spring and raced to rejoin the fray.

With the Spire Dragon right in front of him, even if it was largely ignoring him, Connor chopped away at both its scales and its HP total.

27

3

+3

HP: 130+15/130

There had to be some limit to the HP overflow from the Ravager's Sword. What that might be was anyone's guess. Connor rather suspected the Spire Dragon wasn't going to fall for the old "I need to science some damage numbers" trick long enough for him to kill it.

Dizzy's continued jackhammer mosquito bites must have finally started adding up to a threat. While Connor had been on fire in his earlier battles, he'd forgotten the advice: Stop, Drop, and Roll. This dragon hadn't.

The Spire Dragon rolled over in an attempt to steamroll Dizzy beneath its bulk. But she sprang clear. As the dragon finished its roll, eyes focused on its tiny tormentor, she vanished, first in a puff of smoke, then in a torrent of flame. She reappeared only long enough to burn away as a silhouette of ash.

Fuck.

It was just Connor and Slapguy now. The monk launched a multi-punch attack so quick Connor could make out nothing but a blur and a hammering cadence that sounded a lot like a paint mixer.

`27`

`3`

`+3`

`HP: 130+18/130`

How much punishment could this thing take?

Connor would have had a much better idea if he could see the numbers the others were putting out. The Ravager's Sword was great and all, but it was from an early zone. Compared to Commander Hellgain's Battle Armor and its 18 DEF, the 4 ATK on the Ravager's Sword really kind of implied that there would be late-game weapons in the same ballpark. It stood to reason that the others could have come across better weaponry.

Splat.

The Spire Dragon brought a clawed foot down atop Slapguy, and a last-second roll didn't get him clear of the impact.

Of course, no one but Connor seemed to have been built tough.

"So, it's just you and me, dragon," Connor taunted. "But I'm not going to die to mere fire, and I can go toe-to-toe with you until *I'm* the last one standing."

It was a boast, but he liked his math. Losing 4 HP per

exchange with the dragon, assuming it kept hitting him for 7 and he could keep hitting it back with 3 HP drained reliably. Some luck. Some Parrying. Maybe he stood a chance here...

"You tiny bipeds. Always think you stand a chance. Only the Mountain Lord himself could possibly best me!"

Predictably, the dragon made another grab for him. Connor was ready this time.

Unfortunately, being ready didn't seem to matter as much as he'd counted on.

10

The Spire Dragon latched onto him, and once more, Connor could do nothing to fight back.

"Let's see how well you fly."

It dropped him off the side of the Spire of Fate once more.

"Aaaaaaaaah!"

Connor might have been able to trade blows with the dragon until he came out on top. But he also knew this silliness worked.

54

3

+3

He didn't bother trying to grab hold. Distance was his ally. Every time gravity yanked him down, it was like a Hot Wheels car revving up to snap back even faster.

"Aaaaaaaaah!"

Connor zoomed upward. Striking the belly, the face, the spine. None of the placements of the hits seemed to matter. The groin was as good as the throat as far as HP systems were concerned.

54

3

+3

"Cease this nonsense at once!"

"Make me!" Connor shouted over the wind. "Aaaaaaaaah!"

54

3

+3

The Spire Dragon bathed him in a rain of fire that smelled of week-old Red Lobster.

"Aaaaaaaaah!"

"Don't you dare! You—"

54

3

+3

The dragon fell.

Connor fell.

240,000 XP

Holy hell! That should definitely have been split up six ways. That was nearly a whole damn level.

ACHIEVEMENT EARNED: WITH YOUR BARE HANDS? - Stand alone against a dragon and win. Must deal > 75% of the dragon's HP in damage personally.

XP: 240,000/256,000

As both Connor and the dragon corpse fell, the latter disappeared, leaving loot behind.

Skydiving kind of worked, and Connor grabbed for the glowing chest in mid-air.

CHOOSE YOUR REWARD

The two options were, once more, a sword and a suit of armor. Connor was *really* not at a point to be quibbling. He grabbed the sword.

RECEIVED: SWORD OF THE MOUNTAIN

He didn't have time to examine it. Connor opened his inventory and quickly yanked out the Kawaiian Glider. He climbed into position as he fell through the bank of clouds that surrounded the upper portion of the peak.

Not even the wave of terror that gripped his heart at seeing the ground so, so far below as he emerged from the clouds could quell the sense of elation that bubbled up inside him.

He took slow, deep breaths as the Kawaiian Glider banked in a gentle, graceful arc.

"Intruder!"

Connor heard the voice. It sounded Dragonoid.

Twisting and scanning around him, he spotted a patrol of flying Dragonoids headed his way. He shouted to be heard across the span between them. "It's all right! I'm one of—!"

His words were cut off in a gout of flame as one of the aerial patrollers breathed the same spell Taskmaster D'Veez had used on him.

Connor took no damage, but his relief was short-lived.

The glider was nothing more than a frame of burnt twigs in his hands.

Connor plummeted.

Shit.

All that.

XP: 240,000/256,000

All about to be lost when he hit the ground somewhere way down there.

Ideas popped in and out of his head.

Could he fashion a parachute out of 5 Fishing Nets while in freefall?

Could he Parry the ground?

Maybe just tank the damage?

Could his barely existent skydiving knowledge get him to crash higher up somewhere?

There had to be something in his inventory that could help him cheese out an XP-saving miracle here!

XPOT (2X)

He'd been hoarding them. Connor could admit that. The times they seemed most useful were the times he didn't need them at all. When he had things under control. When he was cruising with no real risk.

The earlier XPOTS he'd used hadn't done anything like the XP he needed now. Maybe they leveled up with him. Maybe they...

Enough with the maybes!

The Cliffs of Claven were already racing past him, and he didn't have forever to decide. Connor popped a cork and slurped an XPOT.

10,000 XP

"SWEET!"

He drank the other as Hard Pass vanished above him.

10,000 XP

A golden swirl surrounded Connor as a majestic gong rang a victory over fate, destiny, and doom.

>>>LEVEL UP!!!<<<

YOU GAIN

2 ATTACK

3 DEFENSE

50 HP

0 MP

1 SKILL CHOICE

BONE MOAT

9999

Connor died at Level 10.

CHAPTER 36
TWIST OF FATE

SECLUDED CEMETERY

"You have died, but your journey is not yet ended. Rise once more, hero, and press onward."

Connor returned to life with one finger already raised in objection. "Now hold on just a minute! I died up THERE!" He aimed a finger into the sky, toward the distant clouds and the summit of the Spire of Fate beyond. "I should be—You know what? I'm not even."

REPORT BUG

"Despite unlocking the Warrens Memorial respawn point, when I just died, I was sent back to the Secluded Cemetery."

His response came quickly.

YOU RETURNED TO LIFE AT THE NEAREST UNLOCKED RESPAWN POINT TO WHERE YOU DIED.

Connor addressed the sky, as if the devs answering his complaints were up there like ancient gods. "Yeah, but I—"

Aw, shit.

Connor might have been doomed way up in the skies above Pease Summit, from a fight that started in the Courtyard of the Mountain Lord's fortress. But the last thing he saw before he splattered was his location updating to the Bone Moat.

To hell with it. He'd won. The dragon was dead. He'd leveled up. He'd get back up to the top, accept his accolades from his squishy companions, and lead them to the final battle. He had loot to check out and a level-up to process.

Sword or skill? Which to do first?

Well, no matter what skill he picked, the sword wasn't liable to change. That meant that if he wanted to make his best decision, he should do it with as much information as possible.

Connor examined the Sword of the Mountain.

SWORD OF THE MOUNTAIN - ATK 20. Deals double damage against humans.

Well, if the Mountain Lord was human, that was potentially huge. Even if the sword had been a vanilla 20 ATK. Even giving up the HP drain of the Ravager's Sword. Even if he had to wield it blindfolded, that thing was a huge upgrade.

He equipped it immediately.

And hey, maybe one of his new skill choices would let him wield two two-handed weapons. It would be unprecedented in gaming history. And then he'd be able to offhand the Ravager's Sword to keep it around. Otherwise, it would take up a place of honor in his inventory, collecting digital dust.

Connor had relegated Spell Parry last time he'd leveled, and then he'd subsequently gained that through the SKILL POT he'd drunk.

He was going into this selection completely blind.

Without a carry-over skill, Connor was only offered two options.

FOLK HERO - +20 ATK and +20 DEF against tyrants.

NOBLE BLOOD - Birthright to claim the Mountain Throne (if it were to become available).

Connor laughed out loud.

Schmuck bait. He loved it.

Schmuck bait was the red button labeled "Do not push." It was the pile of treasure when you were warned not to touch anything but the magic lamp. It was the plate of cookies left in the locker room right before weigh-ins. In short, it was a dumb, obviously wrong choice that was nonetheless irresistible to a certain brand of greedy, short-sighted, selfish dick—a.k.a. schmuck.

Connor selected Noble Blood. There was no option to keep Folk Hero for later.

GAINED TITLE: SIR

Well, well. Time to take a quick peek at his character sheet with that new updated info.

CHARACTER STATS:

NAME: Connor TITLE: Sir

CLASS: Knight LEVEL: 10

HP: 180 MP: 0 ATK: 39 DEF: 45

SKILLS:

TWO-HANDED FIGHTING

CHARGE

PARRY

RIPOSTE

IMPROVED RIPOSTE

IMPROVED TWO-HANDED FIGHTING

MOUNTAIN SLAM

CHARGING SLASH

SPELL PARRY

NOBLE BLOOD

His XP total also appeared frozen.

XP: 256,000/256,000

"Hey, Kelindra, is there any level above 10?"

"No," came Kelindra's clear, concise reply.

Well, that settled it, then. This was Sir Connor in his final form.

He only had one goal remaining, and it lay at the top of the Spire.

SLAY THE MOUNTAIN LORD FOR ELDER LOHDOH: 0/1

Oh, he'd slay the Mountain Lord, all right...

Hopefully Lohdoh wasn't going to get too hung up on insisting there be a Mountain Power Vacuum afterward.

Still, any thoughts of replacing the Mountain Lord required Connor to kill the bastard. And there was a good... maybe 2 miles?... of vertical distance between them that he had to close before any of the rest mattered.

UNALIVE HILLS

BONE MOAT

Connor took out Xote and mounted up.

HARD PASS

CLIFFS OF CLAVEN

WARRENS OF WAR

Connor patted Xote on the neck. "Good boy. Best loot in the game, and I've got this damn sweet sword now, too." He stowed his Donkey mount, hopefully to be brought back out for a celebratory feast, not another run up the side of the Spire's sketchy geometry.

Inside the tunnels, Connor encountered his regularly scheduled patrol of Dragonoid guards.

"Who are—?"

"Aaaaaaaaah!"

Connor was in no mood after these idiots, or guys who looked just like them, burned his Kawaiian Glider.

He Mountain Slammed the tunnel floor.

1818

The two guards went flying. He didn't feel the need to

finish them off, and they smartly didn't see any need to remain anywhere near Sir Connor.

He stalked through the Dragonoid city.

WARREN MEMORIAL

Connor passed through on a quick detour just in case he needed to refresh his association with the place. The side trip was a helluva lot shorter than an entire trip back up the mountain.

WARRENS OF WAR

PEASE SUMMIT

There was still no sign of resistance on the walls.

OUTER KEEP

The portcullis lay open.

COURTYARD

No sign of the other players.

CASTLE

Connor found the approach to the main fortress now unprotected. He swaggered up to the front gate. Motion from the corner of his eye drew Sir Connor's attention to Slapguy waving and signaling for him to join the others around a corner.

Meatball had his Extension Ladder out, steadying the bottom as Dizzy perched atop it, peering in a third-story arrow slit.

Connor shook the ladder just enough to get her attention, then waved her down. All the players gathered around. All of them looked to Connor for an explanation of what happened to the dragon.

He drew the Sword of the Mountain and held it out before him horizontally for them to examine. Well, look at. The Examine action didn't seem to work on other players or the stuff they were carrying, and he didn't want them to know its properties badly enough to risk setting it on the ground. Last thing he needed was for a joker—let's face it, Slapguy—to snatch it up and refuse to return it.

Connor headed back around to the front gate. He was done messing around with stealth and scouting and cockamamie napkin-grade planning.

The players followed him, unsure what he was up to.

Sword out, Connor used the pommel to pound on the gate. "Open up, Mountain Lord. It's time to finish this."

He hadn't *really* expected it to work. Connor hid his shock when the gate did indeed swing open.

The butler was dressed in medieval finery. On his tiny, pale blue body, the effect was comical. But the fact that the servant was Kawaiian started to hint at why Lohdoh really cared what the Mountain Lord was up to, way atop the Spire of Fate.

"You may enter. The Throne Room is just ahead. If you would like to refresh yourselves, food and drink are available in the dining hall to your right. If you wish to rest, rooms have been prepared for you upstairs."

"Where is the Mountain Lord?" Connor demanded. "The Throne Room? I'm not interested in—"

"Yes... No... Of course, not! None of the food is poisoned. Yes, you are honored guests!" Connor tried to parse all the information as the butler attempted to goal keep a million questions from the players at once.

Connor spread his hands, forcing the other players to give the butler space and allow the little Kawaiian servant to answer *him*. "Where. Is. The. Mountain Lord?"

"You will discover the Mountain Lord in the Throne Room. But please, rest up. Face your fate refreshed and relaxed."

"Not a chance!" Connor countered. "Straight ahead, you say?" The butler nodded a confirmation. "Time to end this."

The Castle as they passed through it was less than

spectacular. Dark stone, brooding, but weirdly too well lit and not menacing at all. Like a Disneyland castle rather than something an evil overlord would construct.

Connor marched in the lead, glancing into the dining hall on the way past the door and admitting that the spread looked—and smelled—pretty good. Actually, did he smell Taco Bell, or was that his imagination?

If he snapped out of it in the Anachronism Interactive lab after the morning he'd had, and all they had for him was Taco Bell takeout for lunch, there was going to be hell to pay.

At the end of the foyer, Connor kicked open the Throne Room doors.

What lay beyond was, frankly, shocking.

THRONE ROOM

While the room itself was grand enough, it was empty. No courtiers. No guards. No nothing. No other doors. Not even a Mountain Lord. The only feature of the room was the one thing the name suggested.

A throne.

The others all milled around, searching walls, looking the throne over. Perplexity was infectious. Everyone caught it.

While the others were puzzling out what to do, Slapguy sat in the throne and made funny, pompous faces until Calamity chased him out of it.

Connor checked his skills again, focusing on his most recent.

NOBLE BLOOD - Birthright to claim the Mountain Throne (if it were to become available).

If it were to become available.

With Slapguy out of the chair, Connor drew his Sword of the Mountain and sat.

GAINED TITLE: MOUNTAIN LORD

SLAY THE MOUNTAIN LORD FOR ELDER LOHDOH: ABANDONED

A new quest appeared, and Connor suspected it was meant just for him.

SLAY ALL WHO SEEK TO OVERTHROW YOU: 0/5

PLAYER VS. PLAYER COMBAT ENABLED

All eyes turned to Mountain Lord Connor. He couldn't have been the only one to have seen that last system message.

CHAPTER 37
MOUNTAIN LORD

FOR A MOMENT, no one seemed to know what to do.

Connor watched each of them, tracking their subtle motions, trying to determine who would flinch first, who would realize this was five on one combat. Or who would reason that siding with Connor might be a way to come out on top.

For his part, Connor needed to decide who was the threat among the remaining players.

As he watched, he saw the trepidation, the fear, the hesitation. That was when he realized.

None of them.

They were going down, and there was nothing they could do to stop him.

The wizard moved first.

Connor had his Parry Spell ready. When the lightning struck him, it caught his Sword of the Mountain and tingled.

0

Realizing that Connor hadn't taken so much as a scratch, the wizard backed away hastily, hands up. Apologizing. Surrendering.

"Aaaaaaaaah!"

Between Charging Slash and the bonus from the Sword of

the Mountain, Mountain Lord Connor cut right through some kind of firm magical barrier and sliced the wizard in half.

184

SLAY ALL WHO SEEK TO OVERTHROW YOU: 1/5

Hell, that would have killed *him* if not for his defenses. He couldn't imagine a DEF stat and HP total she could have had that would have made that even close.

The others were spreading out, preparing to make a final stand.

Calamity did a backflip to put a wall at her back halfway across the room. Her shot was deadly accurate.

20

Even through his DEF, Connor felt that.

HP: 160/180

Unfortunately, he only needed a few running steps to get within his own range.

"Aaaaaaaaah!"

184

SLAY ALL WHO SEEK TO OVERTHROW YOU: 2/5

Just like that, Calamity was packed off to *her* nearest unlocked respawn point.

Slapguy gestured a huddle to the other remaining players. They'd seen what his Charge attacks and their variants could do. The monk launched a spinning flying kick that struck Connor like the blades of a helicopter.

5

5

5

5

Nice. Good job.

HP: 140/180

Connor brought up his Parrying stance.

Meatball cloaked himself, Slapguy, and Dizzy in golden

radiance. Even having experienced the spell for himself, Connor had no idea of the effect it had.

Presently, the effect was to prevent Slapguy from taking Connor's next attack.

With the three other players crowded around, Connor Parried one attack from Dizzy, then Riposted.

0

92

He watched her register that hit and pull her next attack. She must have barely survived.

Slapguy performed a single punch, loaded up with drama and silent grunting and a flash of fire.

0

3

Connor took a little damage from a fire side effect, but the blow itself did nothing.

HP: 137/180

He realized his Riposte didn't have to strike the initial target.

92

Down went Meatball, unable to weather the blow.

SLAY ALL WHO SEEK TO OVERTHROW YOU: 3/5

Slapguy danced in front of him, a mesmerizing display of martial arts prowess that Connor initially suspected to have some kind of magical confusion effect. Then, he realized it was just a regular old mundane distraction.

Dizzy's daggers bit into Connor from behind.

30

30

HP: 77/180

But his armor allowed him to defend himself from behind. Somehow, his Riposte triggered even without getting the damage reduction from Parry.

92

Whoops. There went Slapguy.

SLAY ALL WHO SEEK TO OVERTHROW YOU: 4/5

Connor turned and backed away, sword held aside.

He shook his head. Screw the others, but he didn't want to kill Dizzy. He suspected she didn't really want to kill him, either. She just had a quest. Same as him. The game had set them against one another.

Transferring his sword to his off hand, he extended the other in friendship. Maybe, if they clasped hands and agreed to cease hostilities, the number of people seeking to overthrow Mountain Lord Connor could drop to 4.

4/4

COMPLETE

That was all he was hoping for.

Dizzy slipped her daggers away.

She approached him warily.

Connor nodded his reassurance.

Dizzy reached out.

From nowhere, her daggers reappeared in her hands.

30

30

HP: 17/180

She vanished in a puff of smoke.

Gritting his teeth and growling, Connor Mountain Slammed the ground.

18

Dizzy flew across the chamber, slamming into a wall, then despawning.

SLAY ALL WHO SEEK TO OVERTHROW YOU: COMPLETE

The victory rang hollow.

Emotionally drained, he trudged over and sat on his new throne.

Just in front of him, a white rectangle appeared in space. A glare of light flooded through, too bright to squint against. Driven by curiosity and a lack of any follow-up prompting from his quest, Connor got off his throne and stepped through.

CHAPTER 38
A LAND BEYOND

UNDEFINED SPACE

"Wow. Oh, wow!" Isaac cheered.

"Just look at him," Kelli said, waving a hand up and down him.

Mountain Lord Connor did as well, same as all the scientists gathered at computers all around him. He was still clad in black armor, wielding a comically huge sword, brawny as a pro wrestler.

"What's going on here? Did... did I win?" he asked.

Kelli walked up to him. "This is great. Completely self-aware. Hold on, unwarranted assumption right there. Do you know who you are?"

"I'm Mountain Lord Connor."

"Do you know who you *really* are?" Kelli pressed.

"Just Connor? Am I a pretender to that throne? I don't know how succession by conquest is supposed to work around here...err, there."

Kelli beamed. "Do you know who I am?"

It was a weird question. "You're Kelli." Then, he looked closer. Some of the details were off. Her face was smoother.

Her hair less unruly. Her eyes lacked color depth. "Or are you? Are we still in the game?"

Isaac spoke up. "This is a later version. Better graphics. But good call. Yes. This is still a simulation."

"What's going on here?" Connor demanded. "I want answers." He wagged his sword menacingly. Then, realizing that he was threatening real people, stowed his sword in inventory.

Isaac shrugged. "Your call. I have his transit flagged. We're not recording any of this to the alpha version. If you think he'll give a better exit interview, go ahead and tell him."

"Yeah. You won," Kelli told him.

"First one in three batches," one of the developers added. "Oh. I'm Dale. I was the guy answering most of your bug reports."

"Oh? Then tell me, Dale, why couldn't you fix voice comms? Every dumb NPC in there was able to speak interactively. You telling me you couldn't get the least sophisticated system in your whole game working?"

"That was a testing choice," Kelli replied on Dale's behalf. "We needed to isolate a lot of subject data. NPC AI is mostly going to operate independently. We didn't mind you all cooperating here and there, but we didn't want to develop AI that needed to work in groups."

"Well, it was damned annoying."

"And we appreciate that."

"Can you at least tell me who was playing what characters?"

Dale snickered.

"What's so funny about that?"

Kelli interposed herself. "It's against our own policies to reveal player identities. But the NDA can't stop you from chatting with the other players outside the game."

"At least tell me who Dizzy was? I don't want to make an ass of myself out there in meatspace."

Kelli put a hand on Connor's armored shoulder. "Nothing to worry about. I agreed to do a compatibility report for you. Everything you need will be in there."

"I must say," Isaac broke in, "You threw us a few curveballs there. Uppup was supposed to be a frustrating quest to find the money needed to purchase that donkey. You're the first player to murder him for it."

"Yeah. Sorry about that."

Kelli looked shocked. "Don't be! That was amazing. Devious. Resourceful. You failed to accept the limitations of expectation. I wasn't sure you had it in you."

Isaac scrunched his face in a thoughtful scowl. "I'm not a hundred percent sold on this being our main villain."

The bug squasher rolled back in his chair to join in. "Look, I've been flagging his wishy-washiness. That fear of heights thing. The weirdly expressed sexual frustration..."

"EXCUSE me?" Connor snapped. "I'm right fucking here."

"If you were fucking there, we'd have a lot more data to work with, buddy," the developer shot back.

Kelli shook her head. "No. We need him. The era of mustache twirling gods of evil is over. Gamers want villains with depth. Relatable. Still bad enough to disagree with. To slay for a quest. But with emotional meat. More Walter White, less Skeletor. Maybe we loosen him up a little for a romantic side plot, but—"

"I'm still right here!" Connor insisted. "Would someone please tell me what I need to do to get out of here? Grab a lunch, a dinner. What time is it even?"

"He's got a point," Isaac said. "Let's spin this version down. Scrub the post-game flags. Leave the baggage. I reserve the right to do a little more trimming after the alpha. All that outside info he's bringing in is responsible for a lot of the strategic layering we're seeing in the decision matrix, but there's a lot of flotsam, too. We're going to need to compress this into something we can maintain on public servers."

"What's that mean? Are you starting up the game again? I know you said you compressed time, but—"

"Oh, that was just to shut you up," the bug fixer said with a smirk.

Kelli cuffed the guy upside the head. "Don't tell him that! Look, Connor. Everything's going to be fine. Any last-minute feedback before we unplug you?"

Connor narrowed his eyes. "I'll tell you in meatspace."

"It's more efficient in here."

"I've only got so much leverage. I want out. I want a lunch. Or a beer. It's been a long fucking day."

Kelli sighed. "You want a villain, you've got to deal with the fact that you have to deal with one. Fine. Have it your way."

With a snap of her fingers, everything went dark.

CHAPTER 39
ALPHA NEWS

WALLY'S PIZZERIA WAS BUSTLING. Arnold made his way through a crowd of people just inside the doors waiting to order and headed back to find the table with a seat reserved for him.

"Sorry I'm late. Your dad wanted the month end stuff wrapped up before he goes fishing," Arnold said as he joined the table.

"Tell him I said 'no,'" Izzy countered. "After 5:00, you're mine."

"We ordered for you," Shane let him know. "Anchovies and *extra* pineapple."

Arnold glowered at his friend as Izzy gave him a shove. "Don't listen to him. Meat-lover's. Same as always."

That reassured him. Izzy was always looking out for him. "How was work?"

"Ugh. Can't wait for classes to start in the fall. Call center work can die in a fire. I wish I could be like, 'Hello, this is the future Dr. Isabella O'Connor, take it from me, you don't need solar panels badly enough to let us install them.'"

"Then work for your dad," Calvin suggested. That elicited groans around the table.

Working for Anthony D'Angelo was Arnold's particular

cross to bear. His employment with Izzy's father had been half charity, half getting the low down on a future son-in-law. So far, it was going great. Well, it was going, anyway. Great probably wasn't an option when it came to the guy nailing his daughter. The paychecks kept Arnold going. The engagement ring had warmed up her old man a little.

Izzy had gone through a phase in high school where she convinced people to start calling her Bella. She'd gotten tired of it, but inertia and friend groups had dragged it along behind her until she'd let slip in their third month of dating that she preferred Izzy, and that it was what all her family and her childhood friends called her. She'd been Izzy to him ever since.

Their pizzas came. Arnold showed his ID and ordered a beer. Izzy was one of those maniacs who thought that if you liked a topping on *any* pizza, you should put it on all pizzas. She was the only one Arnold had ever met who ordered "The Works," then proceeded to add stuff to her order.

"Hey," Shane commented as they were all chowing down. "I saw a trailer for an alpha of a game called Spire of Fate. It's by that company you guys were guinea pigs for. Heard anything about that?"

Arnold shook his head as he chewed. Once he swallowed, he replied, "Nope. First I'm hearing of it. Thought they dropped off the face of the Earth. Unless someone asks how we met, I barely think of the place anymore."

"That was one weird-ass month," Izzy added.

The pittance they'd given Arnold hadn't lasted until he got a new job. The only really good thing to come out of the whole experience was them dropping the hint that he and Izzy were a perfect match. He'd been skeptical at the time. Attracted? Sure. But anything deeper than that felt too damn coincidental. Like, maybe she was the best match of the bunch, but in a pool that small? Nah.

But they'd been right.

Arnold had crashed at Izzy's place once they got serious. Well, "Bella's" at the time.

"Worked out OK."

"I couldn't wear my contacts for like a month after."

"You're cute in your glasses."

"Zzzzt."

Arnold stiffened, but he resisted the impulse to put his hands in the starting position. He elbowed her playfully, then snuck in a tickle until she had to drop the slice of pizza she'd picked up.

"You two are so weird," Bonnie commented, shaking her head as she chewed. Calvin Jr. sat in a high chair, playing with torn-off bits of a garlic knot his dad had pulled apart for him.

"Any chance you can finally tell us what really went on that month?" Calvin wheedled.

Arnold and Izzy shared a look. They saw an agreement there and answered in unison. "No."

Then they laughed.

Shane spoke up. "*My* theory, up until they announced an actual game, was that the whole thing was a cover-up. They were figuring out a way to brainwash couples into falling in love—the best dating app ever. But now that they've got some campy-looking RPG, that kinda blows my theory out of the water."

"Maybe they did both," Izzy suggested with a wink toward Arnold.

"No complaints if they did. Never had it better."

And it was true. Since finishing up with Anachronism Interactive, Arnold had gotten his life together. A fiancée, a steady job with a boss who wasn't looking to replace him with AI, an apartment he didn't share with roommates. He'd taken the gym seriously, too, since Izzy mentioned liking him with a little more meat on his arms.

She'd done well too, ditching a loser boyfriend who had a job and a healthy relationship with his parents. Who needed that crap? One Thanksgiving was plenty. One Christmas, too. It was an upgrade over Friendsgiving and going to the movies alone on Christmas day, from Arnold's way of thinking, and now Izzy got to spend her holidays with her own family.

"So, you two going to play it?"

It wasn't a crazy question. Other than sex, gaming was their go-to couples' activity.

They shared that look again. This time, uncertainty lingered.

"Dunno," Arnold replied. "Part of me kind of wants to just put that whole business in the past. Plus, what if I'm, like, the AI of a goblin or something in there?"

"I know, right?" Izzy added. "I don't know how I'd handle it if I'm the voice of the next 'Arrow to the knee' meme. Or worse, some in-game whore."

"I mean, it's all supposed to be based on your personalities, right?" Bonnie asked, getting in a weird dig at Izzy there somehow.

"Right," Shane said, stepping into the fray. "Arnold's probably like some bookkeeper for a tax collector or something, and Izzy's probably running around feeding ducks so she can catch them and take them home as pets."

"That was a *hypothetical,*" Izzy insisted. She huffed. "Besides. If I know Arnie, he's biding his time, waiting to take over the place. As for me...?"

"Right there with me, ready to rule at my side."

Eyes rolled all around the table. Arnold didn't care.

"I'm sure if you call in, you could pull some strings," Shane suggested. "Maybe get us alpha keys?"

After all he'd been through? After a month that felt like a year-long acid trip, was he willing to dip a toe back in those waters?

He and Izzy shared that look one more time, and she gave an almost imperceptible nod.

"Sure. Fine. I'll shoot out a couple texts, see what I can do. Might be interesting. Last time we saw the game, it was just stick figures running around a wire-frame environment. Be cool to see what they've done with the place."

****

Ready for more *Pixelate*?

Continue your adventure with book 2, Closed Alpha

****

GAME REFERENCES

KNIGHT CLASS, CONNOR'S PROGRESSION

LEVEL 1:

Character stats:
NAME: Connor
TITLE: None
CLASS: Knight
LEVEL: 1
HP: 8
MP: 0
ATK: 2
DEF: 2

LEVEL 2 (LEVEL 1 + 1,000 XP):

Character stats:
NAME: Connor
TITLE: None
CLASS: Knight
LEVEL: 2
HP: 13

MP: 0
ATK: 3
DEF: 3

New skill options:
TWO-HANDED FIGHTING - When wielding a two-handed or a versatile one-handed weapon in two hands, your Attack increases equal to your level.

SHIELD SPECIALIST - When carrying a shield, your Defense increases equal to your level.

DISARMING ATTACK - When striking an opponent's weapon with an attack, damage that exceeds the target's Defense will cause them to drop the weapon.

LEVEL 3 (LEVEL 2 + 2,000 XP):

Character stats:
NAME: Connor
TITLE: None
CLASS: Knight
LEVEL: 3
HP: 21
MP: 0
ATK: 7 (5 + 2 ATK from Steel Sword)
DEF: 6

New skill options:
CHARGE - Close the distance to a target in the blink of an eye. Can be combined with additional skills to deal increased damage.

PARRY - Temporarily gain Defense equal to your Attack. Can be combined with additional skills to unlock counterattacks. (Gained by floating to future selection.)

LEVEL 4 (LEVEL 3 + 4,000 XP):

Character stats:
NAME: Connor
TITLE: None
CLASS: Knight
LEVEL: 4
HP: 31
MP: 0
ATK: 9 (7 + 2 ATK from Steel Sword)
DEF: 9

New skill options:
THROW WEAPON

CHARGING STAB - At the end of a Charge, stab an opponent with a pointy weapon. Deals double damage.

LEVEL 5 (LEVEL 4 + 8,000 XP):

Character stats:
NAME: Connor
TITLE: Unhallowed
CLASS: Knight
LEVEL: 5
HP: 43
MP: 0

ATK: 13 (9 + 4 ATK from Ravager's Sword)
DEF: 12

New skill options:
CLEAVING STRIKE - A killing blow with a swinging weapon can continue onward to strike another opponent.

RIPOSTE - After a successful Parry, quickly attack back for half damage.

LEVEL 6 (LEVEL 5 + 16,000 XP):

Character stats:
NAME: Connor
TITLE: Unhallowed
CLASS: Knight
LEVEL: 6
HP: 58
MP: 0
ATK: 15 (11 + 4 ATK from Ravager's Sword)
DEF: 15

New skill options:
IMPROVED RIPOSTE - Riposte now deals full weapon damage instead of half.

MOUNTED COMBAT - Able to use weapons while mounted. Unlocks the Charge attack while mounted.

LEVEL 7 (LEVEL 6 + 32,000 XP):

Character stats:
NAME: Connor
TITLE: Unhallowed
CLASS: Knight
LEVEL: 7
HP: 76
MP: 0
ATK: 17 (13 + 4 ATK from Ravager's Sword)
DEF: 18

New skill options:
IMPROVED TWO-HANDED FIGHTING - When wielding a two-handed or a versatile one-handed weapon in two hands, your Attack now increases equal to twice your level.

SPELL PARRY - Reduce the damage of an incoming spell by an amount equal to your Defense using the Parry action. (Gained from Skill Potion after floating to future selection.)

LEVEL 8 (LEVEL 7 + 64,000 XP):

Character stats:
NAME: Connor
TITLE: Unhallowed
CLASS: Knight
LEVEL: 8
HP: 100
MP: 0
ATK: 19 (15 + 4 ATK from Ravager's Sword)

DEF: 21

New skill options:
MOUNTAIN SLAM - Strike the ground at your feet to send foes within melee range flying back, dealing damage equal to half your Attack.

STALWART - Increase Defense by your level.

LEVEL 9 (LEVEL 8 + 128,000 XP):

Character stats:
NAME: Connor
TITLE: Unhallowed
CLASS: Knight
LEVEL: 9
HP: 130
MP: 0
ATK: 21 (17 + 4 ATK from Ravager's Sword)
DEF: 24

New skill options:
FLYING COMBAT - Able to use weapons while mounted on a flying Mount. Unlocks the Diving Charge attack while on a flying mount.

CHARGING SLASH - At the end of a Charge, attack with a Slashing weapon. Deals double damage against a single target or uses Mountain Slam.

LEVEL 10 (LEVEL 9 + 256,000 XP):

Character stats:
NAME: Connor
TITLE: ~~Unhallowed~~ -> Sir
CLASS: Knight
LEVEL: 10
HP: 180
MP: 0
ATK: 39 (19 + 20 ATK from Sword of the Mountain)
DEF: 45 (27 + 18 DEF from Hellgain's Battle Armor)

New skill options:
FOLK HERO - +20 Attack and +20 Defense against tyrants.

NOBLE BLOOD - Birthright to claim the Mountain Throne (if it were to become available).

CONNOR'S INVENTORY

CHARACTER EQUIPMENT

WEAPON: SWORD OF THE MOUNTAIN - +20 ATK. Deals double damage against humans.

ARMOR: COMMANDER HELLGAIN'S BATTLE ARMOR - +18 DEF. Can defend against attacks from behind. Half damage from stabbing attacks.

ACCESSORY: MAP-MAKER'S WAYSTONE - See the location of hidden doors on your minimap.

INVENTORY

1,175 COINS
FISHING NET (5X)
WATER BREATHING POTION (96X)
BRIDGE KEY
COURTYARD KEY
SQUIRE ARMOR

BAMBOO SWORD

BAMBOO DAGGER

2 YELLOW GOBO DAGGER

BANQUET TABLE

STEEL SWORD: +2 ATK

RAVAGER'S SWORD - +4 ATK - You drain 3 HP with each attack.

GUARDIAN STONE - Wearer takes half damage from slashing attacks.

COMMANDER HELLGAIN'S PARADE ARMOR - +18 DEF

DONKEY (XOTE) - Mounts are personal transportation allowing different modes and speeds of travel throughout Spire of Fate. Once purchased, Mounts will remain loyal to their owner, and are not transferable in any way between players, though certain Mounts may allow multiple passengers.

CONNOR'S QUEST JOURNAL

COMPLETE QUESTS:

- SLAY ALL WHO SEEK TO OVERTHROW YOU: 5/5
- PROTECT GULGOO'S ESCAPE FROM THE BLACK CATACOMBS: 1/1
- SLAY THE SEA FROG: 1/1
- EXPLORE THE UNDERSEA CAVE: 1/1
- BRING SPINY REEF FISH TO NEEDEEP: 5/5
- KILL GOBOS FOR BEEDEEP: 5/5

ABANDONED QUESTS:

- SLAY THE MOUNTAIN LORD FOR ELDER LOHDOH: 0/1
- PRESENT THE SPEAR OF AN ARENA OPPONENT TO D'Veez: 0/1

WORLD ZONES

Kawaiian Islands - The starting zone. A south pacific jungle island populated by adorable plush animals and friendly villagers.

Lookmano Sands - A barren stretch of beach between the cliffs and ocean offering beginning players an opportunity to help a local family.

Watery Reef – This Barrier Reef, filled with Spiny Reef Fish, challenges players' swiftness as they race against their breath meter.

(Forest Pun) – An unnamed zone containing the most basic of Christmas-tree forests. The ground is simply painted green, no underbrush or grass even. Clearly a last-minute addition to the game.

Unalive Hills - Foggy horror movie nightmare of endless hordes of zombies emerging to attack.

Bone Moat - The defensive trench protecting the actual spire from those down in the Unalive hills, the moat filled not with water but with animated skeletons that swarm any hapless players who fall in.

Black Catacombs - A bog standard dungeon environment with stone walls, intermittent torches, and ghouls with "ice pick claws." Rather than a downward exploration, the catacombs wind their way UP the interior of the spire.

Hard Pass - The spire cleaves in two partway up. On both sides, switchback trails lead upward. A scattering of long rope bridges connects the sections of the spire, while white clad Gobos wave magic staves to summon winds to blow players to their doom in the Bone Moat far, far below.

The Ant Farm - A nest of tunnels higher up in the mountain. These were carved by the Antaurs, an insectile species at war with the Dragonoids who serve the Mountain Lord.

Warren of War – Just below the spire's summit, a group of scaly, winged bipeds called Dragonoids have carved out a city within the Mountain Lord's iron mines. Diligent, bureaucratic, and brutal, they defend both the mines and the skies outside from intruders and rebels alike.

Pease Summit - The first chance to look down from the very top of the mountain. Dark storm clouds roil BELOW the peak, while incongruous sunshine bathes the evil environs above.

Castle Walls – An encircling perimeter of towering walls that surrounds the Mountain Lord's fortress complex. Mercenaries man the walls, firing arrows at all who approach.

Outer Keep – The Mountain Lord's outer defenses include this solid, utilitarian structure of stone and iron. Armored foes await inside, and the Mountain Lord's chief lieutenant, Commander Hellgain, will fight to the death to prevent passage through it.

Courtyard – After the grim and dreary environs atop the spire, the Courtyard offers a touch of sweet air and beauty. Lush, landscaped greenspace can lull the players into a false sense of security however, since this is where the Mountain Lord's guard dragon resides.

Main Castle - Mountain Lord's throne room and site of the final battle.

SPIRE OF FATE

TEST ENVIRONMENT INTERNAL BUG REPORT

BUG REPORT

Reported by: Connor
Zone: N/A
Bug: "Hey, there's no way to advance past the appearance screen in the Character Creator."
Developer comment: Character creation screen missing flag to enable next step of character creation.
Added the necessary user affordance.
Resolution Status: RESOLVED

BUG REPORT

Reported by: Connor
Zone: KAWAIIAN VILLAGE
Bug: "Unable to complete equipment manager tutorial due to the lack of a backup weapon in inventory."
Developer comment: Someone deleted the old weapons rack without placing the new version in the starting area.

Made additional weapons available to new user.
Resolution Status: RESOLVED

BUG REPORT

Reported by: Connor
Zone: KAWAIIAN VILLAGE
Bug: "There's no Quest Journal."
Developer comment: "FINISH TALKING TO ELDER LOHDOH, NUMBNUTS."
Directed user to in-game solution. Added a note to the Development Journal to stop gatekeeping this game feature behind skippable dialog.
Resolution Status: USER ERROR

BUG REPORT

Reported by: Connor
Zone: KAWAIIAN JUNGLE
Bug: "There's a Gobo stuck up a tree. Doesn't look like he climbed there, since his feet are moving like he's patrolling but he's not going anywhere."
Developer comment: Red Gobo was able to spawn on palm frond due to improper flagging as a standable surface. Z-axis auto-correction on mob spawning function interpreted that as the nearest ground.
Changed flag on palm fronds to be non-standable. Set Z-axis value on spawn point of Red_Gobo_3 to properly spawn near ground.
Resolution Status: RESOLVED

BUG REPORT

Reported by: Connor
Zone: KAWAIIAN JUNGLE
Bug: "There's a Gobo spawn point on top of a palm tree. It can't get down."
Developer comment: See previous resolution.
No additional action required.
Resolution Status: CLARIFICATION

BUG REPORT

Reported by: Connor
Zone: ROPE BRIDGE
Bug: "The water is breathable and doesn't sound like underwater."
Developer comment: Kawaiian Islands water regions weren't set up as Water_Salt or Water_Fresh. Someone flagged it as just Water, which isn't a valid tag.
Changed water in the Kawaiian Islands zone to Water_Salt.
Resolution Status: ENHANCEMENT (OPEN)

BUG REPORT

Reported by: Connor
Zone: N/A
Bug: "Unable to log out."
Developer comment: Per Isaac, the Log Out function is reserved for proctors within the Test Environment build.
No action taken.
Resolution Status: AS DESIGNED

BUG REPORT

Reported by: Connor
Zone: DOCK
Bug: "Dock is inheriting the surface of the terrain underneath it for purposes of footstep sounds."
Developer comment: This shouldn't be happening. The Dock is flagged as Wood_Boards. The sound files for Wood_Walking_Plate, Wood_Walking_Leather, Wood_Walking_Cloth, Wood_Walking_Barefoot, and Wood_Walking_Hoofs are all there.
Spawning a fresh copy of the environment to attempt to replicate the bug.
Resolution Status: DEFECT (OPEN)

BUG REPORT

Reported by: Connor
Zone: LOOKMANO DOCK
Bug: "Same inherited noise from the underlying surface on Lookmano Dock."
Developer comment: Same issue.
Consolidated with previous report.
Resolution Status: DEFECT (OPEN)

BUG REPORT

Reported by: Connor
Zone: N/A
Bug: "Players unable to hear one another."
Developer comment: Per Isaac, we've disabled the sound

codex for player-to-player speech. Currently toggled off. No action taken.
Resolution Status: AS DESIGNED

BUG REPORT

Reported by: Dizzy
Zone: WATERY REEF
Bug: "Characters can breathe underwater."
Developer comment: Appears to be the same issue the Kawaiian Islands had, where the water was just flagged with the invalid tag: Water.
Set the whole Watery Reef zone to Water_Salt.
Resolution Status: RESOLVED

BUG REPORT

Reported by: Connor
Zone: LOOKMANO SANDS
Bug: "Sand doesn't slow down movement. Go to any beach. You'll see what I mean."
Developer comment: Known issue. Currently already in the development notes for the Alpha build.
Resolution Status: ENHANCEMENT (OPEN)

BUG REPORT

Reported by: Connor
Zone: (Forest Pun)
Bug: "This zone didn't get a name. If you're looking for some decent placeholders what about... FOREST FORTY-TREES,

GREEN WOOD, or, if you're looking to mix a classic Star Trek and in-house personnel jokes, what about FOREST D'KELLI? Seriously, buy me dinner tonight, and I'll help you name whatever shit you've got left over."
Developer comment: Not sure what he expects us to do. This is a writing issue, not a development one.
Email sent to Bruce and Kaylee, reminding them the zone needs a name before Alpha.
Resolution Status: DEFECT (OPEN)

BUG REPORT

Reported by: Connor
Zone: UNALIVE HILLS
Bug: "Fog in the Unalive Hills doesn't affect visibility from the forest zone."
Developer comment: The Visibility_LOS function is not processing visual impediments across zone borders.
Will require an overhaul of the graphics code and result in increased computational cycles. Not touching that code without written approval from Isaac.
Resolution Status: ENHANCEMENT (OPEN)

BUG REPORT

Reported by: Connor
Zone: N/A
Bug: "Still can't log out. Kinda been a while. Getting worried."
Developer comment: "DON'T WORRY. TIME IS SPED UP FOR YOU IN THERE. JUST FOCUS ON THE GAME."

Per Isaac, lied to player about how time works.
Resolution Status: DUPLICATE – AS DESIGNED

BUG REPORT

Reported by: Connor
Zone: BONE MOAT
Bug: "Hey, not so much a bug as a suggestion. In the full version of the game, can you name this bridge Connor's Crossing or something? You guys seem like you can use the help with names."
Developer comment: Not a bug.
Made an entry in the development notes for the Alpha build.
Resolution Status: SUGGESTION

BUG REPORT

Reported by: Connor
Zone: N/A
Bug: "I can't log out and there's a rope bridge I don't want to cross, and a cute girl who's probably a guy who's going to make fun of me either way if I refuse to budge."
Developer comment: Not sure what he expects anyone to do about this. No action taken.
Resolution Status: DUPLICATE – AS DESIGNED

BUG REPORT

Reported by: Connor
Zone: N/A
Bug: "You people really need to fix this player communication

bug. Got some hurt feelings in here, and it's not doing your data gathering or whatever-the-fuck any good."
Developer comment: We need a strike system for frivolous bug reports from our full-time "players". No action taken.
Resolution Status: DUPLICATE – AS DESIGNED

BUG REPORT

Reported by: Connor
Zone: BONE MOAT
Bug: "The troll from the drawbridge is stuck in the ground. You can barely see him. If we hadn't killed him once, I'd never have known he was there."
Developer comment: Yup. That's a problem. Not sure how it happened. Bridge_Troll_1 is properly assigned a spawn location. Will scrub ground mesh in Bone Moat zone prior to Alpha in case mobs can fall through it.
Resolution Status: DEFECT (OPEN)

BUG REPORT

Reported by: Connor
Zone: SECLUDED CEMETARY
Bug: "Despite unlocking the Warrens Memorial respawn point, when I just died, I was sent back to the Secluded Cemetery."
Developer comment: "YOU RETURNED TO LIFE AT THE NEAREST UNLOCKED RESPAWN POINT TO WHERE YOU DIED."
Laughed. No other action taken. Actually, that's not true. Told a bunch of other people; they laughed, too.

Resolution Status: AS DESIGNED

BUG REPORT

Reported by: Connor
Zone: PEASE SUMMIT
Bug: "Players able to shove entire banquet table in backpack. Seriously?"
Developer comment: That's actually hilarious.
No action taken. No encumbrance system on the roadmap until Beta.
Resolution Status: ROADMAP ISSUE

LITRPG BY XAVIER P. HUNTER

Pixelate

You'll never become the main villain if you're not willing to die a bunch as the hero.

Arnold O'Connor is a gamer who just lost his office job to AI. Short on cash, he can appreciate the irony of taking a job at an indie gaming company looking to train their monster AI. But Anachronism Interactive isn't looking for players to copy from, they're interested in gamer brains to scan.

After being run through a series of psychological tests while hooked up to a brain scanner, Arnold finally gets a chance to check out the game these scientists have been making. Already questioning his sense of reality after all the mind games and brain twisters, Arnold finds himself immersed in a world that's both utterly real and disconcertingly incomplete.

As each iteration of the company's flagship game releases, Arnold is drawn farther and farther into the alternate reality. And as the game world becomes more real, the real world begins to fade away entirely.

His only hope of escape lies in ultimate victory.

Armored Souls

100 tons of walking steel. One human heart.

Sgt. Reggie King wakes up from a battlefield injury to find himself physically intact. But the hospital staff insist he's not fit to return to duty. As part of his psychological recovery, they introduce him to a game.

Armored Souls is a tank game on steroids. Giant, walking mechs called juggernauts engage in interplanetary wars as noble houses and mercenary factions wage endless battles for supremacy. For the pilots of these juggernauts, the rewards are glory, cash, and XP.

What follows is an epic struggle against the forces arrayed against him, from rival gamers to entire factions looking to crush Reggie underfoot. To survive will take all his military leadership, perseverance, and maybe a little help from some new friends.

Metagamer Chronicles

Gary Burns thought he'd created a masterpiece. Instead, he'd created a prison for his friends—and himself.

Gary Burns just wanted to create the greatest RPG campaign of his gaming career. But a freak magical accident sucks him into the very world he created—as himself.

Surrounded by heroes who look and sound like his friends, Gary is forced to play out the story he wrote. Worthless in a fight, Gary must prove himself valuable even if it means feeding the team insider knowledge.

ABOUT THE AUTHOR

Xavier P. Hunter was born at the dawn of the video game age. He grew up with a game controller in his hand, moving from Atari joystick through PS4 controller the way a hermit crab outgrows its shell. His little league was *RBI Baseball*, his first date was Princess Zelda, and his first unpaid internship was leading raids in *World of Warcraft*. He lives in a world of pixels and frame rates, coming out infrequently to eat and that sort of thing.

Most of his writing is done while patches download or when servers are down for maintenance.

Like most superheroes, he operates in meat space under an assumed name.

xp-hunter.com

www.ingramcontent.com/pod-product-compliance
Lightning Source LLC
LaVergne TN
LVHW050929080826
845145LV00001B/269